VIRGIN CLUELESS

Scott Becker

Content Warning for: VIRGIN CLUELESS

VIRGIN CLUELESS, Part One: Hero contains Material of Adult Content in Every Respect, including multiple chapters with explicit sex scenes.

www.VirginClueless.com

Cover Design & Book Formatting by Gabrielle Markle

ISBN: 979-8-9900555-1-3

PRAISE FOR SCOTT BECKER'S
VIRGIN CLUELESS

"The most entertaining romance novel of the year! The suspense & sex are spellbinding & delicious!" - Book Envy Reviews

"There are so many wonderful surprises in store for readers of Becker's debut novel. First, he writes so convincingly in the voice of a 32-year-old female. Second, sex so steamy you'll keep glancing at the front cover because it's written by a man. Buckle up, *Virgin Clueless* characters are so compelling that they captivate you from the very beginning with twists and turns to the spellbinding ending. Have tissues handy for tears and secretions." - Erotic Romance Reviews

"An addictive—unputdownable erotic thriller!" - The Busy Book Bee

"*Virgin Clueless* and its compelling—vociferous heroine, Zoey Leary, will take the world by storm. Hitch onto a wild rollercoaster ride of love, pain, and forgiveness. This reader kept rooting for Zoey to overcome her lifelong adversities. Laugh, cry, and cheer with Zoey and her gripping entourage in this suspenseful, fast-paced, fantastic sex, compulsive page-turner!" - The Busy Book Bee

"*Virgin Clueless* is erotic romance at its finest." - Erotic Romance Reviews

"An extraordinary writer, Becker's high-octane page-turner—a hidden gem is easily worth double the asking price—a romance novel for the ages!" - Book Envy Reviews

To Lori,
through **THICK** and thin

Part One

Hero

1

MY PARENTS, GOD REST THEIR SOULS, accidentally met on a sunny Saint Patrick's Day during a courtroom altercation. It was love at first sight, despite the fact that they were both in custody. They belonged to the state of Rhode Island in permanent foster care. Through no fault of their own, the underdogs of society who came from no family, no money, and no safety net, just wanted to be together. A few weeks later, on a snowy Easter Sunday, they were labeled as ward of the state sweethearts.

Mom and Dad's passion, their eros love was so intense that it caused the public employees nonstop turmoil. And when the teenage hellions were separated, they constantly did everything in their limited power to make waves in order to reunite. The victims of the dynamic duo's shenanigans, aka the naysayers, predicted their future looked bleak: they wouldn't amount to much, and before Mom turned nineteen, she would be incarcerated. The state caseworkers that my rebellious parents drove bonkers with their wild hoaxes dubbed them "Misfit Lovebirds." Most people didn't give the naive, outcast couple a fair shake in life. They only had each other (until I arrived) in this universe. In fact, Dad patiently waited over two years until Mom turned eighteen, when the Ocean State set her free.

Shortly afterwards, Dad joined the Navy while Mom raised and homeschooled me in Newport. Mom's side hustle was roller derby where she loved blowing off steam. Besides being the team captain, Mom's teammates unanimously endorsed her with the coveted title of "The Enforcer." Dad, my best friend Emma, and I cheered wildly when Mom hit, hurled, and crushed opponents around the oval track.

Being an only child and a daddy's girl, my dad, a Naval Intelligence Officer taught me everything about computers. From a very young age, I sat on his lap observing him snake his way into secured private networks.

When I was nine, he taught me the holy grail of computer technology: hacking. Dad would time how quickly I could access and overcome an external firewall. His voice still resonated and echoed in my head: "Decide quickly, Zoey! You have only three seconds before you're detected! Infiltrate or abort!"

At will, I could penetrate just about any digital network, and I could easily hack into most types of secured networks: residential, commercial, financial, and government—state and federal. It was elementary to track someone all the time without their knowledge with an exact location via their cell phone. Also, with my advanced hacking skill set, I possessed the lethal carbon monoxide capabilities—invisible and untraceable to view, edit, and create havoc to someone's private information without their consent.

However, my only hacking vice that I was guilty of was snooping. That's my addiction—nosiness, which I constantly indulged in for endless hours, became a major distraction from my career. And for the record, I never once used my hacking abilities to smear or to frame someone, and definitely not for financial gain. I only snooped to gain information to feed my inquisitive appetite. That's where it stopped. But lately, my beast mode hankerings commanded around the clock, untamable amounts of screen time calories.

In spite of having a staggering negative net worth, money bought almost anything, except for good health. Personal information, private business records, and classified government documents that were stored in digital format on a single computer, or hosted on a group of networks, or secured by a third-party cloud provider might be acquired for free. Or be surreptitiously obtained by paying a hacker's asking price.

In a very rare case when I hit a roadblock, and couldn't access what I needed, I simply reached out to a hungry network of sophisticated hackers, and gladly paid their reasonable ransom. And there were an abundance of talented worldwide hackers competing with each other on a variety of unique requests. Besides chomping at each other's fingertips, a hacker's ego craved bragging rights along with the global recognition to be the first one to swiftly deliver the unattainable.

2

THREE DAYS BEFORE my 14th birthday, I witnessed in broad daylight the death of my parents. To this day, I suffered from weekly nightmares, and woke up screaming, soaked in sweat. My nightmares were always the same, and I couldn't escape. Wishing I could jolt awake, I dreamt about Dad's open, dead eyes staring at me blank and lifeless. I hoped that Dad didn't feel any pain because he died instantly, hanging upside down.

Mom's death was extremely gruesome. The way she abruptly exited this earth was flat out cruel. Mom's beautiful face was caved in. Her sculpted body was mangled as blood oozed out of multiple orifices. She was choking on her own blood while I held my fingers on her blood-spitting throat. Tragically, Mom felt the severe physical pain deep in her bones. But worse, she felt the unfathomable pain in her heart with the death of her soulmate when she shook Dad trying to wake him. Mom fought both pains with valor while she was actively dying. She tried to comfort me—mother me one last time as she struggled for every last precious breath of her short-lived life.

Once Mom's eyes closed for the final time, I was drenched in her blood. Mom's blood seeped underneath my manicured (our very first mother-daughter manicure) fingernails. Also, it was caked in my long hair, and smeared all over my face. That's when I snapped and attacked that fucker. Weighing only ninety-five pounds, he had to outweigh me by more than one hundred solid pounds. And I didn't fucking care that he had an object in his hand. In an all-out bloody and blurry rage, I was able to get him to the ground where I kept striking him relentlessly until the police pried my ass off.

A week later, the scumbag charged with my parents' death somehow posted bail, and then to my good fortune was murdered. There was a God because he died a very slow, and extremely painful death. According to the sealed autopsy report from the State Office of Medical Examiners, (I obtained it by hacking into the RI Department of Health's computer system which is responsible for keeping confidential records secured.)

3

that fucker was tortured to the nth degree. I only wished that I killed him with my bare hands while looking deep into his eyes when he took his last fucking breath. And of course, thanking the other person from the bottom of my heart for brutally killing him.

On that dreadful death day when my parents perished, my young, colorful, happy-go-lucky existence turned pitch-black. All of my loving and happy emotions as a child were instantly disintegrated. My feelings for love, hate, happiness, sadness, peace, and anger to decipher at a critical time in my life were all mixing together in a dismal concoction named: Zoey The Zombie. And it was spiked with my new awful-tasting reality: loneliness. And forced daily down my fucking rebellious, teenage throat.

My daily adolescent thoughts and actions consisted of uncontrollable anger and rage. The hopeful outlook of a life filled with love, laughter, and a zest for a happy future laid dormant. It was just a far-fetched dream. The only two things that kept me from slitting my wrists were the fond memories of my parents, and Emma.

3

A YEAR BEFORE Dad was killed, I made a promise to him that I would be an ethical hacker, meaning I wouldn't use my hacking skill set to steal for personal greed. Until this very day, I never stole a dime, or extorted anyone. Although at times, I considered taking the easy way out. But thinking about versus actually doing something illegal were two entirely different issues.

However, it was very difficult not taking a shortcut, especially when I was younger, when my peers were going to prom, having fun, and just being carefree teenagers. Not me, I received a free scholarship to my parents' alma mater from the state of Rhode Island. It took the smallest, cesspool state four weeks to locate my roaming whereabouts. Running for my life—freedom, it took four state workers to corner and subdue my uncooperative urchin ass.

My first stint was two months in the state mental facility located in Cranston. During my first week, I hospitalized two workers during one of my uncontrollable rages. And the harsh outcome from my unruly, violent actions landed me in a small padded room for two weeks. Eventually, after I cooled down, I was fucking forced into foster care. Reluctantly, I did my four-year sentence. In a nanosecond, I would sacrifice another ten years of my life in the time-stood-still Ocean State system in order to have a tranquil, final goodbye with my parents.

Held captive as a white-Irish, fair-skin teenager in the foster care system, I kept pinballing from family to family. Many times, I thought about ending my young, fragile, caged life. But I just couldn't because I promised Emma that I would hang on until released. And then we would escape, and move far out west.

By birth, Emma and I were only six days apart, and I considered her to be my slightly older sister from another mother. Growing up, Emma always had nonstop family turmoil consisting of courtroom drama, and police raids. You name the addiction, and Emma's broken family unit was bound to collectively have it. As a youngster, Emma detested her dysfunctional family dynamics and upbringing. On a regular basis, she was a victim, and woefully witnessed an endless merry-go-round of arrests, execution of warrants, and domestic violence.

Emma once told me, whoever came up with the phrase: "blood is thicker than water," was full of shit. Emma's simple philosophy regarding family: "Since you didn't have a say in your biological family—fuck them. And carefully choose your friends sparingly, and wisely in order to create your own loving, logical family. And the less people in your close-knit inner circle, the better."

Emma was all that I had left in this lonely, cruel world, and she felt the exact same way: us against the world. At eighteen, and between the both of us, we could barely rub two nickels together. In no time, our journey to relocate westward was cut short. Somehow, we coasted over the Connecticut state line where we ran out of gasoline and funds.

Right away, we were forced to hustle since we slept in an old, two-door, dilapidated car with only one, working door. Obtaining jobs pronto, Emma gravitated toward glamour, gainful employment as a server wearing sexy, tight-fitting outfits slinging beer and pub food. And I toiled as a nurse aide in an assisted living facility. My daily routine consisted of helping the elderly with their activities of daily living: feeding, bathing, dressing, grooming, walking, and toileting.

By hook or by crook, combined with our continuous elbow grease, it took us a month to scrounge up enough money. With lady luck on our side, we were able to find a slumlord who didn't care about our young ages, or wasn't too concerned about our nonexistent credit scores, or the need for a security deposit. Because we paid by good old-fashioned cash, our landlady looked the other way. She believed that everyone deserves a chance. Finally, we were reunited with running water in our overpriced, rundown, rodent-infested apartment located in the North End of Hartford. Home sweet home.

4

MY TERRIBLE TEENAGE days faded into my struggling twenties. Every day was about survival. While working full time and moonlighting as an overnight caregiver, I was able to get into law school with Emma's help and connections. After graduating with a law degree, I was in debt (I minored in borrowing money.) with student loans for a whopping grand total of over a quarter of a million dollars. Without further ado, I was thrown into a harsh work world trying to get my foot in the door.

Whether you liked it or not, everyone in the legal profession was judged more so on appearance than ability. The hiring system was biased and rigged. In order to be considered for the job—your legal position, you had to look the part. Did this person look like a judge, or a trial lawyer, or a patent attorney, or a defense attorney? And unfortunately, in my case, based solely on my youthful looks, not one law firm in New England would give me the time of day. Not giving up—Irish stubborn, I continued to bartend during a brutal, unforgiving year and a half of job hunting. Truth be told, I couldn't even land a low paying job in the legal world.

Eventually, I did what every entrepreneur had to do: I went into business for myself. At first, I was a starving lawyer—no work and no clients. Emma, who always had my back, and all of my best interests at heart, introduced me to an older gentleman, Abe Cook, who suffered from multiple health issues, including emphysema. Besides Emma, Abe was the first person who really appreciated my value in the workforce, and hired me to help run his private investigation practice.

And what a shitshow that was. For the most part, it was married men cheating on their wives with younger women. Occasionally, it was the wife having an affair with a coworker. While I lost faith in the male species, my twenties went roaring by.

Abe paid me fair market price for my unique abilities as a hacker to obtain photos, texts, and cell phone pings where an alleged person visited. Abe was fascinated how quickly and efficiently I could compile incriminating evidence for his clients. Completely spellbound by my hacking abilities, it didn't take long before Abe dubbed me his "stealthy sorceress."

Indeed, Abe received—took all of my credit for catching martial cheaters. But I didn't care because as a special bonus, Abe—a natural-born salesman, would refer and promote me as his unbeatable divorce lawyer on staff. It was a true win-win, and that's how I began to grow my legal practice.

The so-called private, secured information I snooped before contract negotiations, or before a dissolution of marriage hearing was how I made my clients thrilled with a monetary victory in their favor. It was like having all the correct answers before a major exam. I stacked the deck in my client's favor, that's what savvy lawyers did *if* they could. And yes, it happened all the time, on both sides of the fence. Notwithstanding, when my clients won, I won. And for the first time in my adult life and struggling career, I began to claw and chisel away at my enormous debt demon.

Knowing what I knew now, fuck the money, you could never make up for lost time, nor could you buy it back. And without thinking twice, I would tumble backwards into poverty with three times the amount of drowning debt in exchange for a husband, and kids. Up to this point in my life, I was dealt this raw hand. In order to survive, I was forced to abandon my adolescence and twenties. Unfortunately, survival came with nasty, negative side-effects: a very lonely, empty, personal existence.

At 32-years-old, my biological clock *is* ticking at warp speed. One of my lifetime goals *is* to have at least one child of my own before departing this earth. I knew this probably sounded cliché, but I didn't care because I really did want to be happily married to the man of my dreams with children.

And here's my fucked-up, third-life crisis. The man of my dreams, I'm in love with, is eighteen. This upcoming September, he will be entering his senior year. And he didn't know that I existed. Not yet. But hopefully, God willing, in the next hour he will.

5

PLEASE GET YOUR mind out of the gutter. I'm not the type of person lurking around at the local high school trying to poach teenage boys for sexual pleasure. Surprisingly, he came into my life, via Emma, who's been with the Connecticut State Police for over a decade.

During a routine traffic stop on Interstate 91 last month, Emma was attacked by three thugs, all of whom possessed lengthy criminal rap sheets. All three scumbags should have been locked up because they all had at least one convicted violent crime under their orange jumpsuits. And all three felons were in violation of their parole with the quantity of drugs and weapons seized. By the grace of God, a Good Samaritan stopped, jumped in, and then saved Emma's life.

God forbid, if he didn't intervene, she would have died, and I would have never recovered. My life would have been severely altered because Emma and her family were all I had left in this lonely world. Besides being my bestie, I'm also the godmother to her two-year-old daughter, Eloise.

The Good Samaritan, Dillon Race, is *our* hero. He's eighteen, and would be entering his senior year. He's tall, fit, gorgeous, and easily looked thirty. Now, here's where it gets very interesting: on that same day, before Dillon saved Emma's life, he collected his lottery winnings.

Seven hours before the dire clash, Dillon, by himself, strolled into the Connecticut Lottery headquarters, and had enough common sense to privatize his copious windfall. And I'm talking millions. During the photoshoot, Dillon cunningly used the alias Blue-Collar Man on the jumbo-sized presentation check, and hid behind it to conceal his identity. Being a serial snoop, I knew actually who he was: my hero, and Connecticut's youngest lottery winner of that size, monetary magnitude. Dillon, a brand-new multi-millionaire, risked his young life with a new, lavish lifestyle on the horizon to help a stranger, nevertheless a state trooper.

From the lottery headquarters, Dillon purchased a brand-new truck. Driving along in his new vehicle, he happened to be at the right place, at

9

the right time witnessing Emma's dire situation unfold on the breakdown lane of the bustling highway. Dillon slammed on his brakes, jumped out of his truck, and then he miraculously improvised against all odds.

As soon as Dillon's feet touched the highway concrete, he was greeted by gunfire. But that didn't stop him from defusing the life and death situation. Heroically, Dillon took a bullet for my bestie, saving her life. Thank God.

Dillon became a statewide hero. When he was presented an award from the governor, and the powers that be from the CT State Police for his heroic act, he gave all the credit to Emma (Her law enforcement career demanded long hours and daily, life and death, stress hazards, which at times, overflowed to her personal life creating relationship tensions with her husband, and on occasion, even with me. Many times, during the last few years, when Emma was off duty, and without realizing it, she couldn't separate her two worlds—work and personal, causing her to be hard-nosed, mule stubborn, and very abrasive with actions and hurtful words.) for doing her duty.

Emma and Dillon shared a very special bond. They talked every day on the phone, and met at least once a week to dine. Emma and I had always shared gossip about everything, and the more she positively elaborated about Dillon, the more discreetly I fell in love. Of course, I couldn't tell Emma about my profound, loving feelings I had for Dillon because it would put a wedge, or worse, she would terminate our lifetime friendship.

6

DURING THE LAST few weeks, I watched the dash cam and body cam videos of the unpremeditated melee countless times. For the first time in my life, I'm in love. I want Dillon Race! Yes, I knew it seemed fucked up. I didn't care. I'm head over heels, obesely in love. Day and night, I snooped on Dillon. I knew his exact location all the time, via his smartphone. I stalked him twenty-four hours a day if video surveillance was available: at work, at the gym, at the grocery store where women gawked at him, and when he entered the foyer, elevator, and hallway in his apartment (not inside his living quarters) building. As each day passed, my love for Dillon grew stronger.

And yes, in case you were wondering, I saw a therapist. Religiously, every week. Twice a week, since Dillon came into my life. She mentioned that I had a severe case of being starstruck, and as time passed, so would my infatuated feelings. However, I believed her professional advice was completely off the mark—hogwash.

To get a second opinion, I visited a psychic. She mentioned that Dillon and I would be meeting very soon, and we were meant to be together. And get this one, she stated very convincingly that we were once married in another lifetime. I really liked her. Nevertheless, being skeptical the psychic might be a charlatan, I consulted with a physiognomist, aka a face reader.

Sitting across from him—the face reader, I placed in no particular order eight different pictures of men on his small, rustic work desk. Seven headshots were men I'd never met and Dillon's photograph. Without me saying a word, and within fifteen seconds, the face reader tapped twice on Dillon's picture. With a smile on his face, he lifted Dillon's photo up in the air, and then to my wildest amazement he concurred in a past life that Dillon and I were once happily married. Also, I really, really liked the face reader. And just to triple check, I was in the process of getting a third opinion from the carnival act.

Regardless of this profound information, and my loving feelings for Dillon, how would I successfully convey this to him? Would he think that I'm fucking insane, and run off to the hills? Plus, there was a fourteen-year age difference. Also, I doubted if I was in his league. With faint face freckles and a pale body complexion, I also sported a slim-thick body. In my opinion, men don't find me that appealing. And he's the epitome of male beauty—an Adonis. Hopefully, by some remote chance, would he even find me somewhat attractive? With a snap of his fingers, Dillon could easily have any woman he fancied.

And even if all the stars were perfectly aligned, how would I break the ice to Emma? She would probably think I went off the deep-end and batshit crazy, and definitely have my love-struck ass committed. Our sacred sisterhood—lifetime friendship would be in jeopardy.

For the first time in a long time, ever since my adolescence days, I wasn't in rational control of my feelings and emotions. These past few weeks seemed surreal because of an unexplainable, around-the-clock adrenaline rush zigzagging throughout my body keeping me up for days on end.

And if you thought I was a hot mess it got worse. Now, for a bizarre, unexplained reason driving me bonkers, a few days after Dillon's lottery winnings, the FBI deposited ten million dollars into his bank account. Followed by a Homeland Security deposit of seven million dollars, for a grand total of seventeen million dollars! Why? The deposits were not a mistake, and Dillon's start-up business was booming. The proof was in his company's daily business deposits. How and why was his wealth traveling into orbit? What was I missing? It kills me not to know! I *must* know since Dillon was my newest, around the clock, black hole time addiction. And unquestionably, he was the most intense craving I'd ever experienced.

Since I needed to know *everything* about my future husband, I reached out to an old classmate from law school, who owed me a favor. She worked in Washington D.C. for the government. She divulged that Dillon had a national-security file that was top secret, and unfortunately, she was not authorized to access his classified folder. How did someone only eighteen possess a confidential file of this type of magnitude?

Was Dillon a government informant? I didn't think so. There was no indication from Dillon's daily routine that he worked for Uncle Sam. There were no texts or emails from any source, foreign or domestic that would suggest otherwise. In my humble snooping and legal opinion, Dillon was one hundred percent squeaky clean.

Regardless, I had to obtain Dillon's classified file at once. After countless, unsuccessful hacking hours of getting nowhere, I broadcasted a global, unprecedented two-thousand-dollar reward for the hacker who delivered the top-secret document. Of course, I was paying by credit card, but more importantly, I was yearning for the results.

7

WHAT WAS SO rare for a person Dillon's age was that he didn't have a social media presence. He didn't subscribe to any dating or hook-up apps, or anything else his peers did at his age. He lived a boring, routine, and predictable lifestyle. In my opinion, for a young lottery winner, he lived like a dull old man which coincided perfectly with my lackluster existence. A match made in heaven!

When I watched the daily live video feeds, Dillon looked depressed. Sometimes, I saw tears in his eyes when he walked into his apartment complex. Emma informed me that he was getting over his ex-girlfriend, Candace who left him for a big time modeling gig in Paris.

Emma introduced me to Candace Faith Ganski, and sometimes I refer to her as Lil Sis, or the Polish Modeling Princess. The two of us shared a very similar, special bond, a life hardship bond, however, Candace's situation was far worse. At twenty years old and seven months pregnant, she was ostracized by her strict, Roman Catholic father because of her misbegotten situation. Her zealot father expected her to raise a baby without any emotional or financial support. During her third trimester, she was forced to drop out of college and became homeless. In order to survive, Candace had to feed herself from random, restaurant dumpsters. Until she secured housing, for three long months, she lived in a crappy car with a colic, asthmatic, newborn son named Lewis Hope.

Candace and I clicked right away, and I'm her attorney and business agent who negotiated her lucrative modeling deal. Candace's likeness was taking off like wildfire. My job as her lawyer and business advisor were to protect her business interests, and to ink her future lucrative deals, which of course, I earned ten percent. What I loved about Candace, who happened to be my favorite client, was eager, smart, humble, and she's just so likable. She regarded me as an older sister and a bestie. And yes, the feeling was mutual, I considered Candace as my younger sister that I always wanted growing up, and unquestionably, she was my other bestie.

When I asked Candace why she left Dillon she revealed it had nothing to do with him. Dillon checked off every box perfectly. Candace confided to me that she always felt like she was meant for greatness. She wasn't meant to be anchored with a family at twenty-one. On her dime, Candace begged Dillon repeatedly to accompany her overseas.

Her first week alone in Paris, Candace was a sobbing basket case. She almost returned to her hometown located in New Britain, Connecticut because of Dillon. As her agent and confidant with a shoulder to cry on, I was consumed nonstop with damage control. Candace actually revealed during one of her meltdowns that Dillon and I would make a great couple. I told her that he was out of my league. She strongly disagreed. Candace genuinely wanted Dillon to be happy and taken care of. She did share one piece of timeless advice the other day that struck a deep chord: "If you don't take care of your man, someone else will." Duly noted Candace Faith.

Here's the part that I'm trying to wrap my brain around. Dillon's young, hot, and rich. Occasionally, he socialized with his only friend Robbie Frominski. Dillon didn't bring girls back to his bachelor pad. He didn't party with the guys. He didn't mismanage his money like the majority of his peers would have. He only splurged on a new truck, jewelry for Candace, and personally loaned a good chunk of his windfall to Race Incorporated.

Dillon's startup company—Race Inc. produced the wild popular and local favorite brand, Sour B!tch Lemonade which was aggressively capturing competitive grocery store shelf space in the Northeast. Twelve percent of Race Inc.'s net profits were dispersed to local grassroots, teenage charities with important causes ranging from homelessness, sexual identity crisis, and suicide prevention. Also, Race Inc. was well-staffed and poised for rapid revenue growth with their new product line—a hard seltzer beverage. The catchy name and logo were scheduled to be revealed this upcoming October. The difference maker with Dillon's hard seltzer libation was more alcohol content per can. Also, waiting in the wings was a state-of-the-art feature on the can itself with a pending, utility patent. Race Inc. should be ready for national distribution by early, next spring.

Dillon *is* a total mystery. A rare anomaly for someone his age. Dillon's only vice I knew of was the underground fight club he belonged to—The Den. For some moronic reason, all the fights were recorded probably because of the cutthroat wagering. If these individuals—fighters were to get caught, there were many, high-profile men: doctors, lawyers, cops, firefighters, business leaders, a local politician, and a judge to boot who would be publicly exposed. Their prestigious, lucrative careers would be in serious jeopardy or worse—terminated.

When Dillon became mine, this fighting nonsense would cease! However, when Dillon fought it was a total aphrodisiac. Not only was he undefeated, but not one skilled, badass fighter, including his father could last more than one, five-minute round before an opponent tapped or got knocked out. Dillon is the reigning king—my king. And hopefully, God willing, by the end of this evening, I *will* be his lifetime queen.

8

THE QUEEN OF tardiness arrived a few minutes early. Trust me, Emma was punctual for Dillon. She parked in the very next spot to my left. Smiling with her hands in waving motion, I killed the engine.

Once I opened the passenger front door of her state police cruiser, I was instantly doused by the overwhelming scent of the expensive, French perfume Candace sent as gifts to the both of us from Paris. Holding my breath, I plopped into the vacant seat. With my free right hand stretched out while we hugged, I discreetly cracked the window open in hopes to shoo away the toilet-water bully.

Glancing at Emma, I laughed inwardly. She dressed sexy for tonight's occasion, wearing a tight-fitting, yellow dress, flaunting her propped up boobs.

"You look fab, Ems," I stated sincerely, and if I didn't know any better, she was going out on a red-hot, third date.

"You too, Zoes!" Ems said with a big smile. "Is that a new outfit?" she asked.

Paying more than six hundred dollars for hair, makeup, and on clearance, a summer beige skirt suit for tonight's special occasion, I admitted, "It sure is," because my first credit card was declined.

After days of self-debate, and countless, mental wardrobe torturous hours, as a crutch, I deliberately sported an established, attorney's attire in an attempt to appear more mature. If I resembled Emma's risqué getup, I would have looked ridiculously young for someone in their early thirties, and definitely felt out of sorts.

"Looking good, Zoes. Hey, I spoke with Candace this morning, and she said Ed and I can stay at her apartment in Paris when she's traveling. Can you please help watch Eloise with Dottie (Ed's mom) on a drop of a . . . dime?" Emma asked—begged with a panicked look.

Without thinking twice, my mouth jumped, "No problem! Love too!" coming to Emma's rescue. Plus, spending quality time with Eloise always made me happy. She was my nonstop mobile bundle of pure, innocent joy.

During the summertime, I loved taking Eloise to the kiddie water park and chasing her around for wet hours of splashing fun. The only downside spending time with my niece was it made the mechanism in my biological clock tick faster.

"Thanks, Zoes, you're a lifesaver," Emma said, relieved while turning her body around, facing the back seat.

From her cooler, she handed me a cold-water bottle. "You're the best, Ems," I said. "You must have read my mind, like you always do because I'm parched."

"No problem," she said warmly. "It's funny, Zoes, the more water I drink, the more I have to pee. And ever since I had Eloise, I have the urge to go all the time."

She raised her water bottle, then tapped mine. We each took a swig.

"Hey, guess what!" Ems said with a high spike of enthusiasm in her voice, wanting desperately to get something earth-shattering off her sunburnt chest.

"What!" I asked, matching her excitement while I took a much-needed, decoy drink with my left hand while my right hand simultaneously cracked the window down a tad more.

"You're not going to believe this one. Last night, Ed gave me a green light, and put Dillon on my freebie list!" she proclaimed with a whale of a smile along with a solid fist bump. "I couldn't fucking believe it!"

From day one, when Dillon came to Emma's lifesaving rescue, multiple times, she confided in me that she wanted to show her bedroom appreciation to him.

"Are you serious! Ed gave you a hall pass? Wait a second, Ems, are you fucking with me . . . is this another one of your jokes?" I asked with great intent.

"This is not a joke, Zoes. And get this, I never even asked Ed," Ems admitted, startled. "And yes, I have the holy grail of hall passes! I was fucking shocked!"

Fuck! This new hall pass revelation would put a damper in my master plans. "Shut the double hall doors!" I announced loudly, knowing Emma always had a healthy, sexual appetite for younger guys (of legal age), and especially for Dillon, her knight in shining armor.

"I'm fucking serious, Zoes!" she confessed, staring intently into my eyes. "Do you know the last time I had an eighteen-year-old dick inside of me?"

Slowly, I shook my head, and coolly replied, "No."

"When I was fucking eighteen!" she retorted in a compelling, strong-voice tonality that sounded like she was jonesing to be fucked by a young stud into the wee hours. She grabbed her water hastily and took a quick sip. "Fucking eighteen, Zoes, a long time ago."

Ems always had been brazenly promiscuous when it came to sex. Regardless of his age, she would point blank ask a guy to bed. Fuck, I was toast!

Debating my next, best move, I asked, "How are you going to ask Dillon?"

"I can't, Zoes. Believe me, I want to," she confessed, "but Dillon's too emotional and clingy. And it would make our friendship tricky."

Phew! And thank God. Clinging would work into my scheme when romantic husband thoughts flooded my wishful mind.

"What about if you were to go over the ground rules with him," I suggested stupidly.

My thoughtless remark must stem from the ill-side effects of the perfume potency fogging my brain.

Snap out of it, Zoes!

"Zoes, I know men, and Dillon can't handle the emotional aspect," Ems replied, itching to be fucked into next week by her hunky hero.

"Are you sure?" I asked stupidly again.

Am I a fucking idiot?! Shut your fucking mouth, Zoes!

"Trust me, Zoes, if I thought he could handle it, *I would be* having this dinner tonight in a hotel room."

I didn't respond as we sat in silence for about thirty seconds nursing our waters. It didn't take long before we were reminiscing and giggling for the next couple of minutes about our Rhode Island summer beach days.

"He's here, Zoes!" she pointed, moving her hand back and forth. From about 50 yards away, Emma's eagle eyes spotted Dillon's truck entering the parking lot.

Talk about being stoked to see her hero, Emma started to move her feet rapidly up and down while she gave me playful shoulder nudges. "He's here, Zoes!" she announced again, enthused. I hadn't seen Emma this excited since her bachelorette party.

When Dillon slowly cruised by us, I gulped. He was either singing or talking hands-free on his mobile when he waved to us. Smiling, we waved back. That was the first time I saw Dillon close-up. Immediately, my heart started to race. For some odd reason, Dillon parked about fifteen yards further away in the row adjacent to the left.

"So, Ems, getting back to what we were talking about before, are you *not* going to take advantage of your hall pass?" I asked again with great curiosity, knowing it had been several years since Emma had a young, stiff cock inside of her all night.

"Fuck! I wish I could use it!" Emma shouted with her hands raised in the air, frustrated.

Fuck! Now, I had to tread carefully because Emma's mood shifted. Gently, touching her upper right shoulder, I said, "Just relax, Ems."

"I'm fine. I'm fine, Zoes. It's funny, one night with me, and I would rock Dillon's world, and he would be hooked! But he wouldn't understand how I'm married and all. And I would feel guilty taking advantage of him, just to hook up. And I never told you about . . . just . . . just forget it!" she paused with enraged eyes. Then she whacked the steering wheel, shaking her head, defeated.

Emma started to confess something paramount, then stopped cold turkey.

My next statement was a gamble. "Go ahead . . ." I said softly, deliberately pausing, staring into her eyes, ". . . and tell me, Ems."

"Fuck it!" she yelled, banging the steering wheel again. "You know, Zoes, I know he would be hooked . . . fuck it, I'm dropping this conversation!"

Or would Dillon rock Emma's sandbox? Would she be hooked to a younger man's penis in its playful prime? Almost half her age. For life. Could she handle the emotional aspect once she got fucked, or swallowed a taste?

Was Emma secretly in love with Dillon? It sure seemed like it, fuck! In their May-December relationship, Ed was twenty-three years her senior, and had difficulty keeping up with Emma's sexual needs. Nevertheless, I made a mental note that Emma was going to say something earth-shattering regarding Dillon, and I had to discover at once, exactly what transpired. Unfortunately, I wanted to know now, it killed me to wait, but I knew not to press the issue because Emma was at her breaking point.

Emma's phone chirped a few times. Rummaging pissed-off through her purse, she struck the steering wheel again. Looking at her mobile, "Dillon texted me, and wants us to meet him inside," she quickly rattled off. "Remember, Zoes, don't bring up his past relationships, and let's keep tonight light and fun. Let's get inside before he does to get a good table!"

My thoughts were racing while we walked on the hot asphalt toward the steakhouse entrance. I knew that Dillon took Emma home from the hospital since I was away on business in Dallas—stuck on the runway in a god-awful two-hour tarmac delay; by car, Ed, Eloise, and Dottie were

12 hours away in Ohio attending a family funeral. And during that time frame, Emma and Ed had already been separated for a few months with the mutual agreement that they could see other people. Coincidentally, the harrowing highway incident reunited them.

Was Dillon and Emma's ride to her house nothing more than just an innocent ride, or did something happen? But the real question lingering deep inside my psyche was, did they sleep together?

For the past thirty years, Ems always told me everything, however, my eerie gut feeling said otherwise. Was Emma concealing a wicked, dark secret?

9

SOME DAYS, DILLON wore a suit without a tie, and other days, he sported business casual. Stepping out of his truck, he buttoned his navy-blue suit jacket. Even from a near distance, Dillon was unbelievably hot! There had to be something intoxicating in the early-evening summer air because he was a lot sexier in person compared to the vast pictures and videos that I had compiled. Make no mistake, Dillon had that very special, rare 'it' factor about him. From head to toe, he radiated charisma.

From about twenty yards away, he looked to be at least six feet, four inches tall exhibiting an incredibly fit, robust physique weighing more than 250 pounds. You could easily see the contour of his muscles through his suit. Walking across the parking lot, his wavy brown hair flowed and shined magnificently. Dillon reached inside his suit jacket for his sunglasses when three women in their forties stopped dead in their tracks, turned around, and gawked while he strutted.

Without thinking twice, I would write a check for a thousand dollars (of course, knowing full well that my check would bounce to Jupiter) if I could fuck him in his truck—this very instant! Correction—two thousand—he swaggered with the utmost conviction.

Reaching into his outer jacket pocket, he grabbed his cell striding toward the front door. Wearing aviator sunglasses while talking on his mobile, Dillon entered. Only a few feet away within an earshot of his heated conversation, he didn't spot us standing inside the quiet lounge.

"You know what, Mafalda, then I should have signed the contract before I left," Dillon said nicely but businesslike with his hand in motion. "And I need for you to please double check the purchase order on my desk because it might cause a temporary cash flow problem. And if it looks good to you, just place the order by the end of day tomorrow. I would appreciate that."

Mafalda Mada, "The Mighty Portuguese Business Princess" was the moniker I gave to Dillon's right hand person and second-in-command at Race Inc. Due to an unfortunate, freak, waterski accident that occurred nine years ago, Mafalda, from the waist down, was paralyzed. As a devoted, non-violent stalker who needed to know everything about my future husband, I left no intricate detail unturned.

Mafalda and Dillon slept together. I knew this because Emma had lunch with Mafalda and bragged how incredible the sex was. In fact, last month, Dillon arranged and had Stephanie, the girl he lost his virginity to in high school, and Candace, meet with Emma individually. That's how I came into contact with Candace.

While Dillon was listening on his cell, I couldn't keep my eyes off of him. Only a few feet away from us, he was so fucking hot! Totally. Fucking. Irresistible!

"That's ridiculous, I'm not a distraction to the women in the office!" he stated, pleading with Mafalda.

Oh, yes, you are a major distraction, Dillon! If I was fortunate to be employed by you, all day long, I couldn't keep a clear thought in my perverted head. From the time I clocked in, until the time I punched out, my panties would be soiled. And if I was so lucky to have you as my hunky piece of sinfully, delicious cheese of a boss, I would proudly display my dirty knees to the company. In lieu of a weekly paycheck, I would accept sex. And I wouldn't care if I had to live in a jalopy again. And once we were married, I would make sure you never stepped foot in the office. As of yesterday, I opened a separate, online, bank account with a measly five bucks to hopefully acquire (within fifteen years) Race Inc. Fuck, Dillon, just throw me over your beefy shoulders right now, and toss me into your truck and do whatever you fucking pleased!

"Please, understand this, Mafalda, we're growing very rapidly, and things don't have to be perfect, your way," Dillon said, then quickly switched his cell to the other ear. "In order for us to keep doubling, good is good enough, and good will have to do for now, since our whole team has been flat out for the last two weeks."

After about twenty seconds of listening, Dillon blurted out sarcastically, "If you feel that way, Mafalda, how about on Friday, I come in shirtless."

Since The Den's surveillance system was probably set up by a twentysomething musclehead, I easily hacked into their joke of a system weeks ago. That's where I had seen Dillon many times shirtless, sporting a hairless, muscular upper body while I masturbated. And from that yummy image, my panties were damp.

When Dillon spotted us, he smiled and waved, immediately ending his call. Emma was standing a few inches in back of me when she bolted out like there was an inferno. Embarrassingly, almost knocking me over, I stumbled forward, colliding into an empty barstool.

Sporting a skin-tight, sun-yellow dress that just barely covered her ass cheeks, Emma darted around two patrons in her 3-inch heels. She embraced Dillon, tightly. Their hug lasted for about five seconds while they patted each other's back. Briefly, they stared at each other smiling and then pecked one another on the cheek.

Stepping back to observe, Dillon cheerfully complimented, "I love your dress, Emma . . . you look stunning tonight!"

Immediately, Emma's face started to blush. Grinning with her fingers running through her medium length, jet-black hair, I wondered what's going on in her freebie state of mind.

"Thank you, Dillon," Emma said, basking and gloating from the sincere compliment, and absolutely loving the attention of feeling desired. "Watch this, you have to see how it flows!" she announced, spinning around carefree twice with her arms extended outwards, flaunting her barely-covered backside.

Oh, my God! I'm surprised Emma didn't stop mid-turn, then bend forward to touch her red pedicured toes while she seductively twerked her hall pass ass in his face!

Dillon's facial expressions spoke volumes. We were both stunned, speechless.

"You're always your dapper, handsome self," Emma chirped flirtatiously with a giggly voice looking upward as she playfully jabbed his arm.

Emma's face continued to blush while she kept running her fingers through her hair. Her right hand rested on her hip as she repositioned her stance toward the center of Dillon's body.

Emma's sexual frustration was so blatantly obvious, you could easily cut it with a butter knife. And I'd never seen her act like a giddy, middle school girl in love before. Would someone please help me tame Emma's puppy love madness!

Dillon chuckled when his cell rang. Fuck! With a genuine smile, he stuck up one finger and softly said gazing in my direction, "This will be quick. It's my mother."

"Hi, Mom," Dillon said to Norah Race. Norah was a former UFC (Ultimate Fighting Championship) champion, and a successful business owner with over twenty-five mixed martial arts locations in Connecticut.

"This has to be quick, Mom, because I'm about to have dinner," he barked.

"Hi, Mom," I said softly under my breath to my hopeful, future mother-in-law.

"No, I'm not moving back with you," Dillon said, then paused for a few seconds. "So, if I move in with you, do I still have to follow all your rules? Let me think about that for a second. No! And I'm not living with Dad either because we'll kill each other! I'm staying at Candace's apartment because it's paid for a full year," Dillon revealed to Norah.

Dillon was probably taking some verbal parenting heat because he raised his hand abruptly in the air with facial expressions to match.

"That's not going to happen, Mom," Dillon replied, hastily lowering his hand down. Pivoting away from us, he blurted out, "Since it's my place now, I make my own rules. And by the way, Mom, I thought about what you said yesterday, and I will be dropping out of high school! Gotta go, love you, bye!"

10

WONDERFUL, NOW MY future brawn husband was going to become
a high school dropout. Removing his sunglasses, Dillon tucked them
inside of his suit jacket pocket along with his phone. We started to
approach one another from a few feet away.

Go for it, Zoes!

Confidently, I extended my hand. Smiling, he met my firm grip. His
grip was ironclad. Without further ado, I wanted his strong hand all over
my lonely bottom.

Snap out of it, Zoes!

With a warm smile, I cheerfully said, "Hi, I'm Zoey."

Smiling, with our hands connected, he said, "Dillon . . . pleased to
meet you, Zoey. And thanks for inviting me out tonight."

Instantly, I'd been love-struck. I was lost for words. Time stood still
while I was so lost in his soft blue eyes. Totally spellbound, I was
blissfully trapped in an infatuated state of mind. All I could do was
slowly nod my head. Thoroughly captivated, I never wanted to let go of
his firm hand.

"Any friend of Emma is a friend of mine," Dillon boasted.

Startling my love-struck thoughts, Dillon gracefully and effortlessly
pulled my five-foot, ten-inch, 177-pound body into his. We embraced!
Briefly, I felt his muscular back—hallelujah! Sporting a huge smile, I felt
like the luckiest girl alive. However, the squinted-rage glance Emma shot
at me was priceless. Talk about Dillon being off-limits, if looks could
kill, I would have been six feet under with her jumping up and down on
the freshly covered dirt pushing my coffin further into the earth.

Mutually, we stepped back.

"Let's go eat, ladies! I'm starving," Dillon ordered.

The hungry alpha dog was a few feet in front of us blazing a trail when
I tapped Emma on the back. Once she spotted my puppy dog, sorry eyes,
I leaned forward and whispered near her ear, "I wasn't expecting a hug."

"No worries," Ems whispered with a devilish smile and matching eyes. Then she quickly poked with enough force my upper left arm making it sting. "Just relax, Zoes, and have some fun."

Talk about mixed signals, was that an off-limit, forbidden prod? The lingering sting in my arm sure felt that way.

Following Dillon to the hostess area, Emma and I were enjoying the backyard view. Emma gave me her—yes this *is* the guy I want to fuck look. Puckering her lips, Emma's misbehaving tongue expanded the outside of her right cheek a couple of quick times. Softly, giggling and loving Emma's slutty imagery, I decided to take her advice and have some fun. I stuck out and flickered my curled tongue a few, rapid times which made Emma softly giggle. Fuck, I would put my tongue anywhere on his sweet-and-muscular body that he desired. Fuck, I just wanted to grab his ass and feel him everywhere. Fuck, his shoulders were so massively broad. If Dillon wanted to, he could easily scoop me up in his massive arms and take me anywhere he desired. Fuck, I couldn't decide what I wanted him to do to me, and vice versa. And I never, ever felt like this before. Why was I thinking like this? How did someone only eighteen who looked my age make me think and feel sexually out of fucking control?

The hostess was leading the way when Dillon stopped to let us walk in front of him. Bummer, the backyard party was over. Quickly, looking over my shoulder at him, I gulped because from the looks of it, he hasn't shaved in two days. And he looked so fucking hot in a suit. In my opinion, he was wearing male lingerie.

We entered a semi-private room with a parking lot view. The hostess seated us in a cozy, mid-size horseshoe booth. Dillon was tucked all the way up in the middle—at the helm; Emma and I were sitting across from one another. In no time, we placed our drink orders.

When our drinks finally arrived, I raised my beer. Dillon and Emma followed suit with theirs.

I rehearsed my speech more than twenty times for tonight's special occasion.

"Dillon, from the bottom of my heart, thank you for coming to my best friend's aid," I said with the utmost sincerity. "Your heroic act saved more than one life. Emma and I are forever in your debt, and you are unequivocally our hero."

We all clinked and drank.

With tears in her brown eyes, Emma extended her hand to mine for a brief moment, and said, "Thank you, Zoes, that was beautiful."

Quickly, Dillon chimed in, "Thank you, Zoey, for a beautiful toast. Emma is lucky to have you as a friend."

"Thank you, Dillon," I replied.

"You know something, Zoey," Dillon said, gazing deep into my eyes, "you look familiar."

I almost spit out my beer during a swig. If only Dillon knew about my obscene obsession. "You look familiar, too," I confessed.

Dillon was about to respond when our server politely interrupted, and then started to recite the evening specials. Perfect timing! Discreetly, I grabbed my cell, and then activated an impending crisis. In less than ten minutes, Emma would be called back to her state police barracks for a bogus emergency.

Each second of small talk felt like an hour. Finally, my decoy plan was in full swing. Emma's smartphone kept chirping while we rattled off our dinner orders. Glancing at Dillon, I was very nervous, since he was way out of my league. Except for my only so-called boyfriend and business-related meals, I haven't been to dinner with a man in over twelve years.

Finally, Emma hugged us and then skedaddled. With butterflies in my stomach, Dillon and I were finally alone.

11

RAISING HIS BEER with a smile, Dillon tilted his bottle my way. Immediately, I followed his lead. "And now, it's just the two of us. Cheers, Zoey!"

"Cheers, Dillon!"

We engaged in small chit-chat while eating our Caesar salads. And I loved when Dillon said my name, it showed respect. His intellectual maturity was on my level, and he could easily hold an interesting conversation.

Okay, Zoes, let's get to know him.

Raising my beer, Dillon quickly followed suit. "Once again, Dillon, a sincere thank you for saving my best friend's life. Words cannot express how grateful I am to you. God forbid, if Emma died," I paused to quickly wipe my eyes with my free hand, "the horrible ripple effects . . . the continuous aftershocks of always remembering her, and in my opinion, would have been far worse than her death because so many people count on her and love her."

"That's very moving, Zoey, and you're welcome, but—"

Not wanting to bask in the moment, I boldly, but very tactfully, interrupted, "You don't understand, I watched the footage from the dash cam and from Emma's body cam multiple times, and you . . . *are* . . . a . . . . true hero. My hero for starters, Emma's, Ed's, and Eloise's as well. You took a bullet to your shoulder . . . and you kept going."

"Technically, the bullet only grazed my shoulder. It felt like getting stung a few times . . . that's all. And according to the EMT and the hospital physician, I was extremely lucky. And during the chaos . . . I just felt like an overwhelming higher power . . . a guardian angel was watching over me."

"Well, call it what you will . . . I'm forever grateful. And I feel that I'm indebted to you for single-handedly saving Emma's life. It's truly an honor to be in your presence."

"Your words deeply move me, Zoey, but you don't owe me anything. Emma is a great person, and God has blessed me with a new friend. And any friend of Emma's is a friend of mine. I consider Emma to be like an older sister."

Okay, Zoes, let's dismiss that fucked-up taboo thought!

If Emma only knew that I would love to have Dillon as a future husband, or worst-case scenario, a fuck buddy, or anything sexual related she would fucking kill me and definitely end our friendship. Especially when she gave me guidelines of what I could talk about tonight.

And now, after the earth-shattering news Emma received, actually, more like the greatest surprise gift of her sex life when Ed gave his green-light consent that she could sleep with Dillon, I knew Emma wouldn't be sexually satisfied until she fucked him. Yesterday afternoon, at Ems's house when we were relaxing on pool floats, drifting aimlessly in the warm water without a care in the world, and after a few frozen, strawberry cocktails, it didn't take long for the blistering sun to escape free from the clouds when she confessed giggling under the steamy-hot summer's influence that Ems coined her new dildo after Dillon: "Dil*n*do." And to boot, she nicknamed her new, multi-speed, rabbit vibrator after his surname: "Mr Race!"

"Thanks, she feels the same way," I confessed, which was a white lie.

After taking a drink, Dillon asked, "So tell me, Zoey, what do you do for fun?"

"Not a lot," I said sounding like a stiff, boring lawyer—oh, fuck! Quickly, I needed to change gears, and try to relax.

"Not a lot, really?" he asked, surprised.

Loosen up, Zoes. Let's have some fun! It's been a very long time.

With excitement in my voice, I said, "Well, actually, I work out most days and powerlift. As for the outdoors, which I thoroughly enjoy, I like to go running and I love rock climbing."

Quickly, I grabbed my smartphone and retrieved aerial photos.

After handing him my cell, I watched his face intently. Immediately, the colors of his cheeks blushed. Very interesting, Dillon feared heights, and I wondered if there was anything else he feared. Quickly, I took off my suit jacket exposing a sleeveless, beige blouse.

Go for it, Zoes!

"Hey, Dillon, check out these guns," I said confidently, briefly displaying my flexed biceps.

To my surprise, Dillon ordered, "Please, do that again."

Dillon did say please, but in reality, I would have done anything he requested. I wished he would forcefully drag me by my long hair into the bathroom and fuck my brains out. Flexing again, and to my delight, he quickly grabbed my left bicep. Firmly, he squeezed once with his massive hand. "Very impressive!"

My smartphone was next to his hand, when I ordered, "Thanks, now it's my turn!" I couldn't believe I blurted out my request without much thought.

Dillon took off his suit jacket exposing a long sleeve, egg shell shirt. OMG, you could see his huge muscles through his wrinkle-free shirt! Gazing directly into my eyes, he extended his right arm out on a slight angle flexing his muscle.

Catlike, I placed my hand on Dillon's bulging bicep. Multiple times, I squeezed around the circumference of his flexed arm. His strength—the Shore hardness of his massive arm resembled solid steel. Instantly, and once again, my underwear was saturated. "Very impressive!" I praised. Now, I wanted him to squeeze my ass and continue around my body in mutual reciprocation.

Dillon's eyes were intently observing Mom and Dad on my right arm. "Thanks, by the way, your tat, it's fantastic. Great art work, who's the couple?"

Softly, I said, "Thanks, my parents, Maureen and Patrick. They died a long time ago."

Gingerly, he replied, "I'm very sorry for your losses."

Somberly, I nodded. I would have loved for Mom and Dad to meet Dillon.

Dillon swiped my mobile. Slowly, he was scrolling through photos. "I would never, ever, attempt to climb that, never!" he declared, turning my phone around. The photo was of me holding onto the side of a mountain with only one hand—hundreds of sky-high feet in the air—waving with the other.

Still trying to shake-off my somber mood, I didn't respond.

"You're much braver than me, Zoey."

"So, you're telling me you would rather risk your life in a deadly altercation than go rock climbing?" I asked in total disbelief.

"Any day of the week and twice on Sunday. You have *your* family, Emma and her family that think the world of you, and in my opinion, that's absolutely crazy. I mean . . . there's no one there to save you if something goes wrong," he admitted nervously.

Emma had voiced the exact same concern over the years.

He was chewing food when I asked, "Has anyone ever saved you?"

Quickly, Dillon swallowed his food. His facial expressions went south. His eyes kept blinking rapidly. With his dinner napkin covering half his face, he tried to mask his erratic breathing to no avail.

Aha, I struck a very sensitive nerve. I knew this because during intense legal negotiations was how I earned a living.

12

"**SO, ZOEY, WHAT** are you and your family going to do with the commission from my ex?" Dillon asked, dodging my question. Stalling to regain his composure, he pried, "Buy a new car or go on vacation?"

No matter how long it takes, no matter what I have to do or say, I will earn his trust in order to discover who saved him.

"I really don't know," I admitted, "because my commission hasn't cleared yet. It's still in escrow overseas for another week or so."

"I understand."

Clearly, he didn't understand, and I had to spell this out. "Hey, Dillon!" I said louder than normal, making his eyes blink and head jerk. Bravely, I revealed with the utmost conviction, "I have *no* husband, and I have *no* kids. And I *do not* have a boyfriend! It's just me."

It seemed like Dillon was surprised by my last comment. His eyes widened and his head shifted awkwardly to the right. "Are you kidding me, a beautiful woman like yourself has no one?" he asked with enthusiasm, but also with some skepticism, probably because he spotted Mom's platinum diamond and emerald wedding band on my left ring finger.

Mom wasn't wearing any jewelry when she was killed. And strangely, her diamond engagement ring that I cherished, and was supposed to inherit was nowhere to be found in our home during the bank foreclosure.

Yes, Dillon was attracted to me! But, I *must* find out what sensitive nerve I just struck. My hunch screamed it was paramount. I *must* know everything about him. I knew what I had to truthfully say, even if I risked embarrassment.

It's now or never, Zoes, just fucking say it!

Gazing into his soft blue eyes while he chewed his food, I boldly announced, "Hey, Dillon, if you're surprised that I'm single, then you'll be really surprised to know that I never had sex. And I also never had time for a serious relationship because I struggled for such a long time just to stay afloat."

33

He continued to eat his salad.

Now, really put a stamp on it, Zoes, and really fucking sell it!

"So, Dillon, you're having dinner tonight with a 32-year-old virgin," I said confidently.

Our eyes were locked as he kept chewing.

"And in case you're wondering," be bold, Zoes! "I do watch porn."

His eyes widened.

Now, quickly, Zoes, put the ball back in his court.

Staring into his eyes with great curiosity, I asked, "Do you watch porn?"

He put his fork down, then wiped around his mouth. Now, I truly had Dillon's full attention. Confidently, he said, "I'm jealous of you. And I wish I could have changed my past, and waited like you. Your first time should be special . . . something you always will remember. And yes, Zoey, I do watch porn being eighteen and recently single. If you invest in the stock market, I would strongly advise you to buy stocks in companies that produce tissues."

Immediately, I burst out laughing, uncontrollably for a solid ten seconds. Fuck me, talk about not being bashful, I would love to be a fly on the wall and watch him masturbate. By far, that was the funniest remark anyone has ever conveyed to me. But why did Dillon wish he could change his past?

Lowering the linen napkin from my giggling mouth, I said, laughing, "Classic, Dillon!"

Smiling, he dipped his bread in extra virgin olive oil.

"So, tell me, Dillon," I paused nervously. Grow a set, Zoes. Just fucking ask it! "What's your go to . . . porn poison?"

13

LICKETY-SPLIT, DILLON DIVULGED, "It's a toss-up between doggy style and licking pussy."

Fuck me, and silent as a mouse, I sat frozen. My lustful thoughts were racing with sexual fantasies: being on all fours—his handsome face buried in my crotch.

"And how about you, Zoey, what's your go to porn poison?"

Dillon was clever putting the ball back in my court. Fuck, now I really needed a new set of panties.

Now, match him, Zoes!

"Depending on the time of the month, my go to is blowjobs," I paused purposely. Nervous no more, while batting my eyes, I also revealed, "And reverse cowgirl."

Let's stop right there, Zoes.

Raising his beer with a slight tilt my way, Dillon replied, "Touché."

Waiting for the moment of truth to surface, I asked, "So tell me, Dillon, if I met you tonight without Emma, what would be your first impression of me?"

Casually, he confessed, "Since you have a youthful appearance, and you're dressed professionally, I would think you were in high school in an entrepreneurial class looking for a loan on your project."

Almost spitting out my beer, I said, "Good one, Dillon," giggling as the beer bubbles tickled the inside of my nose. "So, what do you do for fun?"

"I enjoy drawing, cooking, and painting, but overall my life is uneventful. I do force myself to work out four times a week, and I run on my rest days. The only good thing about a workout is it kills time, plus you feel good afterwards. Emma advised me to stay active, and try to get out of the apartment."

"That's it? No going out with the guys to get girls, or going out partying," I replied, already knowing the answer and realizing he could have just about any woman.

"That's never been my style, and I don't do drugs, and I don't drink in excess," Dillon said a little agitated. "Sometimes, my friend Robbie comes over and we watch sports. And Emma strongly advised me that I needed a solid month off from relationships."

"Always listen to my bestie. She always has your back," I said smiling, and inwardly laughing, knowing Emma would love to be on her back with Dillon on top with her legs spread a mile wide, getting her rocks off. "She considers you like a younger brother."

Zoes, stop harping on these taboo thoughts!

"Thanks, she always speaks positively about you. Emma was a godsend when Candace left," he said looking a little depressed. "I was down for the count for a couple of days, and she was very helpful getting me through that tuff time, until I hit my reset button."

Emma was a day away from contacting his mother since he was so depressed. Keep digging, Zoes. "So, in your ideal world, what type of woman would you want?" I asked with great curiosity.

Without any hesitation, Dillon admitted, "I would love another person, just like Candace."

And Candace had told me numerous times she wished there was a way to clone Dillon. She cried on my phone shoulder from Paris for days on end. It was my job to keep her on the straight and narrow until we inked her lucrative, modeling contract.

"That's a very nice thing to say," I replied.

After wiping around his mouth, Dillon revealed, "The day she hit me with the Paris, modeling news, I already started house hunting, and I was going to ask her if she would want another child. You know, Zoey, I never told anyone this so please don't—"

Stopping Dillon mid-sentence because now, he had my full, undivided attention with children, I said, "This conversation tonight stays just between us, okay?"

"Okay," he murmured.

"Really, you wanted a child with her?" I asked, sort of in disbelief.

Who wouldn't? Candace was an absolute knockout. And I would love to have a baby as of yesterday in order to keep the age gap as close as possible to Eloise.

"I did because Candace gave me stability. My childhood growing up was dysfunctional. My mother was seldom around because of her training and traveling, and with her business. And my dad who technically raised me, really didn't. I was on my own at a young age fending for myself while he was out chasing women. And him and I always had our differences," Dillon said, finishing his beer. "For the first time in my life, I really enjoyed a peaceful homelife with Candace and Lewis. And I don't like being alone."

I knew the feeling of a great homelife until my parents were killed. At least, I had many happy, stable years. To put it mildly, the differences between Dillon and his dad were unfortunately monumental. Emma mentioned to me numerous times that at any moment they could violently explode and physically harm one another.

After I swallowed a quick leafy bite, I said, "You're far more mature than your current age, Dillon, and that's very rare in today's day and age. Trust me, with your charm and style you won't have any problems finding someone special."

Hey, Dillon, my love, look no further, I'm right here in front of you.

While dipping his bread in olive oil, he replied, "Thanks, and I appreciate your kind words, and that's what Emma said as well."

"You're welcome."

After swallowing his food, Dillon asked, "So, how come you never been in a committed relationship?"

14

AND NOW, FOR the truthful, embarrassing explanation, I admitted, "Because I always put my career first. And also, nobody has ever measured up to the standards of my dad. He was the kindest and most generous person I'd ever known. And also, I didn't want to be distracted from my personal and financial goals. I always came first."

Oh, shit, I now realized how stupidly I placed my foot in my mouth a few seconds ago.

Am I fucking idiot? I always came first—really, Zoes?!

"I understand," Dillon replied genuinely. "And I give you a lot of credit for staying the course without any distractions for such a long time."

Phew, I dodged that fucked-up statement.

Chuckling, he teased, "So, you *always* came first?"

And just when I thought I was off the hook, Dillon reeled me back in. He was smooth to acknowledge Dad and my career first with empathy before he decided to playfully tease me.

Undoubtedly, I collected additional, embarrassing ammunition that made me look super foolish. Wondering how many times he could make me come, I admitted, giggling, "Yup, guilty, Dillon, I always came first. Talk about putting my foot in my mouth."

Laughing, he said, "I just couldn't resist, Zoey."

With no response back except for a quick smile, our sizzling steaks arrived.

###

FORTY MINUTES LATER, Robbie stopped by and dropped-off a large-sized, manila envelope. Dillon and Robbie spoke Polish for about a minute which I didn't comprehend. Candace taught Dillon how to speak Polish in less than a week. It sounded like Dillon wanted Robbie to do something important because Dillon handed him a platinum credit card. Oddly, Robbie requested us to get closer. Using his smartphone, he snapped a few pictures, then left.

As we were winding down our enjoyable dinner, my impatient, curious mind needed to know the scoop. Go for it, Zoes!

Believing I'd earned his trust, ever so softly with a sweet, calm voice, I said, "Hey, Dillon, I asked you a little while ago, has anyone ever saved you. And . . . I want you to know, it's okay, and safe for you to tell me."

Dillon's sensitive nerve was struck again because his eyes blinked rapidly a few times. Placing his utensils down, he wiped around his mouth. "Two people saved me," he admitted, pausing for a quick sip of water. "One is dead. And the other person who is alive, I never told. And what I'm about to tell you stays between us. And just to let you know, I've never told a soul before, not even my best friend Robbie. Can you promise me, Zoey, that my secret is safe with you?" he asked nervously while looking around the restaurant paranoid.

"I swear, I promise, Dillon, your secret is one hundred percent safe with me," I assured in an honest, gentle voice. I was dying to know his innermost deepest secret. And he never told Emma which made me feel truly honored.

Dillon's demeanor started to change. His face turned ghostly pale. His blue eyes filled with tears. His mouth opened, but he was lost for words. His broad shoulders slumped—deflated, resembling a large-sized, 'get-well' floating balloon which lost a good portion of its helium.

Without eye contact, in a trembled, choppy, unconfident voice, he said, "Um, I can't believe um, I'm going to tell you this. Um, um, three days, um, before my, my . . . 11th birthday—"

Dillon stopped dead in his tracks. With a warm smile, I extended my hand. Immediately, he grasped my hand for dear life as if it was the very last life jacket on a sinking ship.

Gently squeezing his hand, I softly said, "It's okay, Dillon, you're safe."

Speaking slowly, he revealed, "I was um . . . sexually assaulted by my friend's older sister and her three girl . . . friends. I was supposed to play video games with him at his house. And when I arrived, they cornered . . . they um . . . trapped me. Once they bolted the basement door shut, they showed me their bodies, and they made me drink alcohol and they got me drunk. And aroused. And at times, I was blindfolded," Dillon said, pausing for a drink. "They *did* fucked-up stuff to me and they made me do fucked-up stuff. They told me if I said anything . . . I um . . . would embarrass my family, and nobody would believe my story."

Unfortunately, from the look in his distressed eyes, I knew there was more. He reached for his iced water, then took a shaky swig. Dillon closed his eyes for a couple of seconds, and when they opened, he admitted, "When um . . . it was Stephanie and my time, it was awful because she asked me if it was my first time, and I lied to her, and I hate lying. It fucked with my head for the longest time. When Stephanie ended our relationship, I had a failed suicide attempt. Shortly afterwards, I met Candace unexpectedly in her apartment foyer, and we were getting along just fine. And out of nowhere, the lie I was holding in, flooded my mind causing a hyperventilating feeling, so I walked away. And at that very moment, I decided when I returned home, I was going straight to the bathtub to blow my brains out. While I was walking away," he paused with tears streaming down his face. "She stopped me. Candace saved my life!" he screeched. "And the rest is, you know—" Dillon bawled—sobbing with his hands covering his face.

My hero was probably feeling exposed, vulnerable, and stripped to his core. In my eyes, he was stronger than ever. Much braver than me. With tears in my eyes, I scooted over and embraced Dillon tightly.

Holding Dillon in a secure, comforting hug, I said in a soft, assuring whisper, "I'm very sorry that happened to you. It's not your fault. What you just told me is true courage. You are now free."

Instantly, Dillon embraced me tighter. And I loved the way he squeezed. My body felt calmness—pure love when I felt his teardrops on the back of my neck and shoulder. My grand wish was for his salty teardrops—his DNA to dissolve into my skin—into my entire being. God willing, his DNA would enter my bloodstream and merge—coincide perfectly with mine, and ultimately, become my new inner strength.

Slowly, I whispered, "You are now free, Dillon."

Those fucking cunts raped my future husband. What made my blood boil was that Dillon was only ten-fucking-years-old! And he was in puberty. His voice was changing as I recalled the videos from hacking into his mother's social media accounts.

Trust me, Dillon, they're all going to pay. No matter how long it takes, I will seek justice for you. And I will do it in the ugliest, fucking manner.

Quickly, I had to recompose, and take away my violent emotions. I wasn't ready for that mindfuck. I'm deeply honored and also disturbed at the same time. Dillon emotionally exposed himself in less than two hours. Wow, he trusted me with his innermost, darkest secret. We were meant for each other, and I definitely wanted him to be my everything.

Emma mentioned that Dillon has a genuine, gentle soul. My mind wandered how I would break the news to her. Could Emma ever forgive me, or understand how I felt? Or would she end our lifetime friendship?

Dropping his hands from his sad face, Dillon was trying to locate his dinner napkin. After he wiped around his bloodshot eyes, he said, "But the icing on the cake on that fucked-up day was before I returned home. Before they kicked me out, they forced me to drink more booze until I puked. And one of them gave me a beating . . . I really thought she was going to kill me. She rubbed my face in my own vomit. And when I finally made it home, my dad smelled alcohol on my breath. And um, he beat the shit out of me so bad . . . I went unconscious. He put me in the hospital. And since I'm coming one hundred percent clean, when I stopped to help Emma, I knew there was a good chance I would die. And I was at peace with it. Sometimes, if I'm lucky, I find peace and answers in chaos. But by no means was it a suicide attempt. My goal was to help her anyway I could." He took a quick swig of water. "I mean, I just won the lottery and came into a lot of money, and at that time, I felt like I didn't deserve any of it. The money felt like a sham because all I did was buy ten dollars' worth of tickets like I've been doing every week since I turned eighteen. And all of a sudden, I skyrocketed into this new world where I could buy just about anything. And before that…for many years, I worked on ladders and roofs for my dad's handyman side business while listening to his rants and bullshit stories, working for peanuts and always being broke. And all of a sudden, I'm rich, and I get a bright idea, and I walked into a car dealership, and flat out bought a fully loaded truck with every option, and with all the bells and whistles for over a hundred grand . . . it just . . . it just felt like I was in a dream driving along the highway when I saw Emma in distress. And I just didn't know how to process it all. In my opinion, that's chaotic."

"Dillon, in my opinion, you handled the situation perfectly. You're a true hero."

"Thank you, I'll be back in five minutes," Dillon said, reaching inside his suit pocket for his cell. He slid out of the booth, then walked away.

Quickly, I compartmentalized the last part of Dillon's gut-wrenching hospital story with a couple of deep breaths which cut off the raw-sad emotion. And just like that, I was recomposed. Scrolling through my smartphone—inbox, I now possessed Dillon's top-secret file of national security. Also, included were two bonus files: Brett Race Junior and Brett Race Senior.

Taking in a deep breath, I opened Dillon's file first.

Oh, my God!

15

DILLON'S CURRENT PICTURE was centered on top of my mobile screen. Underneath and to the left, were a laundry list of his stellar accomplishments:

National Hero
United States number one asset
Protect at all costs
Responsible for saving the life of the president of the United States
Stopped the explosion of the Golden Gate Bridge, and the nuclear explosion of the financial district in San Francisco
Stopped the nuclear explosion in Milwaukee
Estimate total lives saved over one and a half million
Founder and owner of Race, Inc.
Genius IQ
Fluent in Polish, Portuguese, and Spanish
Great out of the box thinker
Protected by a special joint task force: Secret Service, FBI, and Homeland Security
Strong possibility Brett Race Senior wants subject dead
Warning: when engaging the subject, he can be temperamental

What the monkey fuck was going on? Growing up, I wished I had a grandparent, or a cousin, or any kind of relative would have sufficed. Why would a grandfather want to kill his grandson? This had to be a joke, and I was being played. Dillon walked into the restaurant alone and unguarded. Baffled, I abruptly stood up, then walked around the restaurant. After a quick, random room inspection, I didn't spot any people that remotely resemble federal bodyguards. Not even people in normal clothes trying to be disguised as undercover. The only peculiar patrons were a conspicuous couple: an attractive woman in her mid-twenties dressed in colorful, skin-tight workout clothes conversing with a gentleman dressed to the nines. He appeared to be at least twenty-five years older. They were flirting at a cozy candlelit table for two with olives in their martinis. Typical clientele for a fine steakhouse where successful, older men blow one's own trumpet with their young eye-candy. Definitely not feds.

And who wouldn't boast about saving the president's life? Strike one!

Once I returned to the table, I took a quick bite of mashed potatoes. Next, I opened Brett Race Junior's file with his photo (A very handsome man for someone in his late forties.) centered on top. Underneath and to the left, it read:

Honorable discharge from The United State Marine Corps
Employed by the New Britain Police Department
Special consultant to the FBI
Responsible for the death of Senator Spanski
Warning: when engaging the subject, he can be unreasonable, he does not follow direct orders, he acts bizarre, and behaves erratically

What the fuck?

Last, but not least, I opened Brett Race Senior's file which was extensive. Centered on top, was his mugshot. Brett Race Senior's list of achievements were lengthy—pages long, so, for now, I only focused on the first page:

United States Navy, World War II Veteran
Medical doctor
Nuclear scientist
Technology expert
Fluent in nine different languages, followed by a slew of other important accomplishments
Warning: when engaging the subject, he quickly kills his target without any remorse

What jumped out was his age and his appearance, they didn't match his current photo. There was no way someone ninety-nine looked sixty-something. Strike two! But what startled me the most was something extremely disturbing. Directly underneath his mugshot, it declared: number one world terrorist, aka "Isosceles."

After using two different search engines, Isosceles was nowhere to be found.

Strike three!

My first piece of bogus intel from a trusted source that I used in the past. Quickly, I checked my credit card app. For the first time in my life, I was swindled by a hacker.

<h1 style="text-align:center">16</h1>

WALKING BACK TO the booth, Dillon was on his phone, and from his facial expressions, I sensed that he was involved in a heated argument. Dillon was pivoting and looking all around the restaurant for someone.

"I don't see you anywhere in the restaurant!" Dillon said, pissed-off from about a foot away from our booth, looking around aimlessly.

Who in the hell was he talking to?

"I'm so tired of hearing about your fucked-up advice," Dillon said angrily. "If you didn't purposely hold me back, I would have graduated by now. Like I told Mom, I will be dropping out of high school!"

Dillon muted his phone while his dad was ranting. "Sorry about this. I will be off soon."

"No problem," I said with a friendly smile.

Dillon smiled back with a thumbs up.

"Oh, so you're now in the parking lot! Where?!" he asked loudly, unbuttoning his dress shirt. "I'm warning you, Dad . . . *do not* interrupt my dinner!" Dillon said hastily, tossing the cotton garment in the rounded-corner of the booth.

What an unbelievable body! Correction, it was the best body that I'd ever seen—bar none! Dillon's chest, shoulders, and arms were massively muscular. Also, you could see the veins in his huge forearms. His flat abs were unfortunately covered and looked to be chiseled as well. If I didn't know any better, his jacked body looked like he was a step away from being on steroids. Nevertheless, I desperately wanted to jump Dillon's rockin' bod this very fucking second!

Tucking in his white tank top while his phone was glued to his ear, Dillon calmly walked over to the large, wall size window about ten feet away from our booth. I gulped in fear because I didn't want any family quarrel to ruin our dinner.

"Oh, so you're not actually here. I'm warning you, Dad, if you show up, I'll put you in the hospital!"

Dillon was listening for a brief moment.

From an earshot away, he boldly said, "You know how sure I am, Dad. I could fuck all night, wake up, and jerk off a few times, then drink a six-pack, and enter The Den, and *easily* kick your fucking ass!"

I wanted to jump up out of the booth with my hands raised to the sky and scream at the top of my virgin lungs: "I volunteer to be your bitch all night!"

And trust me, Dillon, you won't be jerking off in the morning. Nope! I just won't allow it. Not on my watch! My sex-crazed mind was spinning out of control.

Seeing this side of Dillon was exhilarating, but also very nerve racking.

Dillon blurted out, "Stephanie climbed three balconies, and entered my place last night because of your warped advice. She won't leave me the fuck alone! I keep telling her we're over."

Tell you what, Dillon, let's up the ante. If you were in a high rise over a hundred floors up, I would eagerly climb to you wearing only a silky bathrobe.

With his hand raised in the air, Dillon broadcasted, "I'm not going to thank you. Your branding advice backfired!"

There was a brief pause.

Dillon barked, "Oh, so you forgot to tell me about the negative consequences! You know something, Dad, I should have known better! You know what, fuck this! I'm in the middle of dinner . . . I'm hanging up!"

Dillon branded her? What did that mean? Would Dillon brand me?

From a short distance away, I observed Dillon with his eyes closed taking some deep breaths. A few seconds later, he calmly walked back to the table, then gracefully plopped into the booth. But there was something different about him. He recomposed himself swiftly, but how? He looked so fucking irresistible in his tight-fitting tank top. Please don't put your dress shirt back on! I should have tipped him for the view. Fuck, I just wanted to jump all over him.

What the fuck is wrong with me, Zoes?

"Hey, Zoey," Dillon said, startling my one-track mind—wishing he would fuck me in this booth. "Sorry about that call. My dad sometimes gets underneath my skin."

Only comprehending bits and pieces of what he was verbalizing, the cat most definitely had my tongue-tied. I remained totally entranced, gawking at Dillon, completely lovestruck.

What the fuck, Zoes! Just say something for God's sake.

Like a complete mute of an idiot, I just kept nodding, hypnotized.

"I have never opened up to someone that quickly before. By telling you my darkest secret was truly a relief," Dillon admitted, taking a quick drink. "It feels like a huge weight has been lifted from my chest, and I feel much better now, and I'm thinking more clearly. And I owe you a big thank you for getting it out of me. Also, I want you to know that I'm a lot stronger mentally now than I was when Candace left me. And I don't have any suicidal thoughts any more. Emma was uh . . . a big help when it all went down last month."

Dillon attacked the few pieces of rare steak he had remaining with enthusiasm. And the way Dillon ate was sexy.

Snap out of it, Zoes!

"Glad to hear it. And yes, Emma thinks the world of you, too," I said, still tranced, and probably sounding stupid.

"Thanks, that means a lot, Zoey. And Emma's big message to me was . . . no woman, or person should hold you mentally captive."

Still, trying to snap out of whatever it was he had over me, it felt like being willingly trapped under his masculine influence as I continued to nibble.

Cutting into the midsize section of my ribeye steak, I placed the lion's share on Dillon's plate. "Thank you," he said.

"You're welcome, and I agree with her. And you should never feel like someone has control over your actions or thoughts."

Pouncing on his new found red meat, Dillon nodded in agreement.

Something so compelling was coming over me at this very moment, I didn't know what internally hit me. This nostalgic feeling reminded me of being a child when Mom and Dad would kiss and tuck me in for the night. My body felt relaxed with pure, calming love running through my veins. This unexplainable nostalgic love that was racing throughout my body felt blissfully tingly. My very being was resonating with blissful, feel-good tingles. Add in the purest form of unconditional love into the equation and it produced: Lingles—love tingles. And lingles equaled: Linnacles—love's pinnacle. Lingles and linnacles. Wishing I could buy magical lingles in a pill format, and the way Dillon made me feel at this moment, I knew it was most definitely him. I had to ask Dillon to be my first, and God willing, my last.

My inner, hibernating, sexual desires, my comatose feelings for commitment, and my dormant emotions to love, all at once had finally emerged to a fierce boil.

It's now or never, Zoes. I *must* risk the status quo for the uncomfortable. Even if my heart gets broken.

"Dillon," I said louder than normal. My heart started to race when I asked, "What I'm about to tell you, stays just between us, alright?"

17

EAGERLY, I GRASPED Dillon's welcoming hand. My body terrifically lingled as my relaxing hand swam in his mitt. And once again, I was hopelessly lost in his intoxicating blue eyes.

Wholeheartedly, he said, "Your secret is one hundred percent safe with me, Zoey."

Unquestionably, Zoes, it's him!

"I asked Emma to arrange tonight's dinner to give my sincere appreciation to the person who saved my best friend's life, and that's one hundred percent true. The other reason which I didn't tell her was to get to know you personally. Emma doesn't know that I'm responsible for her leaving," I admitted, taking a quick sip. "What I'm about to tell you is very uncharacteristic of me. I've always been emotionally and logically in control of my life until I've watched the dash cam and body cam videos of the clash. I watched it countless times, and I'm starstruck over you. And I feel like I've known you for a very long time. So, I'm just going to ask, Dillon, I would be honored if you would be my first."

Dillon's face was beaming. "Your kind words touch me, and I want you to know that no woman has ever been so bold and direct with me before, and it's truly refreshing. You're an amazing woman and braver than me. I wanted to tell you first that I somehow knew you, but you beat me to it. Thank you for going out on a limb, and yes, Zoey, I would be honored," he boasted with a gentle hand squeeze. "You deserve to have a very special memory, and I will take you anywhere in the world. Just name the place, and I will handle everything."

How would he have known me? It didn't matter. Dillon in the most romantic way, convincingly said yes!

"Thank you, Dillon, that's the nicest gesture anyone has ever offered me."

"You're welcome."

"Let me think about it," I stated knowing the bathroom would have sufficed. I should have removed my saturated panties and forked them over as a good-faith deposit.

"Sure, take as much time as you need. And I know this is going to be a delicate situation. And I don't want us to be at odds with Emma. So, I'll take the blame if she finds out," Dillon suggested, coddling my forbidden solicitation.

Remarkably, Dillon at a young age understood the delicate friendship dynamics. However, my Achilles heel, self-doubt bitch kicked in at high speed. My thoughts raced. Was Dillon one hundred percent into me, or just doing me a one-time favor? Would my first time be only once with the man of my dreams, or would Dillon break my heart if it's only a one-time fling? More importantly, did I have the thirty-two-year-old goodies to make Dillon fall in love with me? Because competing with Candace's twenty-one-year-old repertoire of modeling goods, set the goody bar into orbit. Regardless of the outcome, I was grateful for the opportunity.

"Thanks, Dillon, but I have to. No matter how you present it to Emma, I will get blamed, and rightfully so. Trust me, you can do no wrong in her eyes," I confessed, knowing full well that it was my brainstorming idea to begin with, along with my guilty head on the chopping block.

Dillon understood and agreed with my point of view. We engaged in small chit chat while we finished our carnivore and Irish bites. Catching me off guard, Dillon placed his hands in mine. Instantly, my entire body was flooded with lingles. We did not speak, only gazed at one another. Blissfully, I was lost in his mesmerizing blue eyes for eight, very long seconds. I'd been frozen. But my heart was racing. Without any warning, or permission, Dillon gracefully pulled me forward—into him.

Yes! Our very first kiss! Now, I was officially bedazzled under his spell! The feeling of his soft lips and tongue were undeniably welcomed. It was the most amazing kiss ever! As our tongues got acquainted, we were lost in a moist, gentle-soft, turtle's pace, canyon-deep kiss. His testosterone ricocheted lightning fast throughout my veins. And for the first time in my life, the man of my dreams—Dillon, had me jubilantly awake and alive *everywhere* in my body!

Red! Hot! Alert! I wanted Dillon now! I could no longer control my sleeping, sexual urges.

Breaking off our thirty second French kiss, I strongly suggested gazing into his eyes, "Let's get out of here now!"

18

"I KNOW, ZOEY, we both want this," Dillon replied with his soft, large hands caressing my cheeks. "But we must wait. I'm not going anywhere. Let's get to know one another. How about we spend the day together tomorrow and do something fun?"

Without thinking twice, my mouth jumped, "I would love that!" Dillon was a true gentleman, and in all fairness to him, I didn't exist in his world until this evening. However, he consumed me for weeks. Tirelessly, I snooped on him everywhere around the clock, and lived bi-curiously through Emma of what he was thinking and feeling. "I'm all yours!"

"Thanks, Zoey," Dillon replied, then quickly kissed me again. "And I'm all yours, too."

Mutually, we lunged at each other. In no time, we were passionately kissing. However, my body couldn't go on any more rollercoaster hormone rides. I overheard our server collecting dishes, and after a fake, loud cough, announced that our dinner was comped. With our tongues now gently tumbling, I decided to break off our kiss. My head was in a whirlwind when my loose-cannon mouth blurted out, "So, Dillon, is there anything I need to know about you?"

"Yes, Zoey, there is," Dillon confessed, dead serious, staring nervously into my eyes. "There's something important I must tell you. I believe that I'm being followed."

"And why do you feel that way?" I asked, trying to tame my sexual urges.

Reaching into his wallet, Dillon pulled out five, one hundred-dollar bills. "I have more money if you need it, just let me know. Can I please hire you as my lawyer?" he asked nervously, handing me the retainer.

Instantly, I handed Dillon back four hundred. "This is fine," I said, placing the lonely franklin into my purse.

We exchanged contact information, even though I already knew his by heart. With his thick finger on my smartphone surface, he signed my standard client confidentiality contract agreement.

Gazing into my new client's eyes, I said, "Anything you tell me now, Dillon, and going forward, is attorney-client privilege and one hundred percent confidential."

"Perfect! That's good to know, and that's a huge relief," Dillon stated, sounding confident and looking more relaxed in his facial expressions.

I'm all yours baby, forever.

Businesslike, I asked, "As your attorney, Dillon, how can I help you?"

Dillon leaned in and we resumed kissing, and very quickly, my sexual urges spiked.

Stop it, Zoes!

Feeling that Dillon was about to divulge something paramount, I had to try my best to remain level-headed.

Breaking off our French kiss, I said, "Mmm," all hot and bothered about an inch away from his luscious lips. "I really love the way you kiss, and mmm, I could kiss you all night," I admitted. After another brief potent smooch, I asked, "But mmm, Dillon, I need to know why you feel like you're being followed?"

With my hand in his mitt and our eyes locked, he admitted, "Last month, the FBI and Homeland Security ambushed me at the hotel where I had Candace's birthday party. They needed my help decoding a threat of national security my grandfather wrote. Right away, I knew the answer, but I didn't tell them because I was livid being taxed 17 million dollars from my lottery winnings," Dillon declared as he took a quick swig of water. "I demanded it back, which they agreed to. Just to let you know, Zoey, if they would have said no, I would have told them because I couldn't live with the guilt of innocent people dying. And lately, I have a strong feeling that I'm being followed, and I think they want to talk to me again."

Oh, my God! It's true, Dillon *is* a national hero!

19

LUNGING AT HIS mouth, we were once again engaged in a fierce, passionate kiss. That was so fucking hot—taking the feds for a staggering 17 million! And I thought I was good at negotiations; Dillon could teach me a thing or two. We were meant to be together!

Stop this right now, Zoes! Because my shooting star panties couldn't take any more abuse!

Breaking off our kiss didn't slow down my body's floodgates. My thoughts were in a vortex. If Dillon really was a national hero and the country's number one asset, why wouldn't he divulge that? But more importantly, did his grandfather want him dead? And if Dillon's life was in imminent danger, where were his much-needed bodyguards?

My head was still off kilter from our last kiss, and I wasn't thinking clearly when my opened blender, spinning mouth, spewed out, "Did you save the life, um, of the president of the United States?"

Oh, shit, Zoes! Now, the cat was officially out of the bag. Fuck me! My jig is up.

Suspiciously, Dillon raised his eyebrows, then said, "No, but I do believe that I stopped the explosion of the Golden Gate Bridge, but I can't prove it."

Phew! Don't give anything else away. "Do you think—"

Abruptly, my words were cut-off.

"No son of mine is dropping out of high school! Let's see *who* puts who in the hospital! Let's go, you, motherfucker!" Dillon's dad—Brett Race Jr. threatened in the most challenging voice I'd ever heard.

Three feet away from our booth, Brett was dressed in his New Britain Police uniform. Brett appeared younger than his age, and was more than six feet, two inches tall—well-built, weighing at least 230 pounds. He provoked Dillon with hand-waving signals. Oh, fuck! Here we go!

Quickly, and forcefully, I placed my hand on Dillon's arm trying to hold him down to no avail. Instantly, Dillon dashed out of the booth like a cannonball.

53

Charging at his father, Dillon tackled Brett. Awkwardly, they both forcefully landed, skidding on the floor—colliding into—sending an empty table with silverware, plates, condiments, and two chairs smashing against the wall.

In a split-second, Dillon was on his feet with his muscular back facing me. He was only wearing brown dress shoes, navy-colored suit pants, a brown leather belt, and a white, wife-beater tank top.

"Get the fuck up, Dad!" Dillon ordered as he stepped back toward the wall window.

Immediately, workers came scrambling out from the kitchen to observe the ruckus. Nosy patrons from the adjacent room stood up to watch. Well, now, tonight's dinner came with a free show: a family fight night.

Oh, my God, I couldn't believe what I was witnessing! I would never think twice about striking my parents. The one stupid time that I challenged and snapped at Mom, she sent me backwards on my butt—almost into Portsmouth.

Once Brett was on his feet, he instantly charged his son with rage in his eyes. Dillon moved to his left causing Brett to hastily collide face-first into the wall window. When Brett turned around, he was instantly met with a kick to his midsection, sending him backwards, slightly airborne.

The force of the inside glass window shattering sent Brett violently through the posh, air-conditioned restaurant, falling a few feet onto the outside parking lot.

Leaning forward with my hands on the table, my tush sprung off the comfy banquette seat. Brett laid motionless on his back. His entire body was covered in jagged pieces of shard glass. From the unforgiving pavement, I saw his eyes were blinking, looking up at the full moon.

Do something, Zoes!

My butter fingers were fumbling inside my purse searching for my phone to call for help. Fuck it, scooting out of the booth in high heels, I screamed, "Dillon!"

Charging full throttle, I was just a few feet away from wrapping my arms around him when I stumbled forward.

Snatching me out of my nosedive—out of thin air, Dillon in one swift motion, raised me above his head. Remarkably, his body balance was planted like an oak tree and didn't move an inch from my forward force. Airborne and relaxed, I extended my arms out resembling a flying motion.

Flying back to the booth above Dillon's head felt exhilarating. Gracefully, he planted my feet on the floor. Gingerly, he placed me into the booth. Bending forward, he took a strand of my natural strawberry blonde hair away from my face.

"Stay here, Zoey, you're safe," he ordered, then quickly kissed my lips.

But it was no ordinary brisk smooch. It was a high-potency, testosterone-kiss, paralyzing every muscle. From head to toe, I was frozen.

Out of nowhere, and screeching loudly, a fleet of unmarked, federal vehicles and vans pulled up creating a perimeter surrounding Brett. Slowly, rising to his feet, Brett was vigorously shaking off shards of glass.

Walking out of the side door toward Brett, Dillon clinched his fists.

Jumping out of vehicles and vans, many armed agents stood only a few feet away from Brett. However, they weren't protecting him. Every armed agent—more than twenty of them, had their weapons pointed at him. What the fuck!

Dillon really was guarded and protected at all costs. He really was the country's number one asset. And Dillon really did save the life of the president.

<h1 style="text-align:center">20</h1>

QUICKLY, I WALKED to the side door, and then descended carefully down the concrete stairs onto the parking lot. With my head purposely looking downward while pretending to be talking on my phone, I was weaving in and out of scurrying agents charging in my direction. I was trying not to get detained.

Federal agents—more than ten of them, ran up the stairs. They were keeping the restaurant patrons at bay by physically securing the broken glass window, and the side door with their ballistic shields.

With his gun slowly rising from his duty belt, Brett shouted, "If it wasn't for me, you would have never been born! I brought you into this world, and now, I'm going to take you the fuck out!"

"Once again, you're wrong, Dad!" Dillon barked provokingly while walking fearlessly toward his demise. "Mom brought me into this fucked-up world! And *you* fucked me up beyond repair!"

Brett's pistol was now suspended at his midsection.

"Go ahead and shoot me!" Dillon challenged boldly. Was this another suicide attempt? "You don't have the fucking guts to pull the trigger!"

The temperamental part in Dillon's file should have come with a much stronger warning.

Suddenly, there was a loud commotion, and all the ballistic shields unfolded causing everyone's heads to swivel toward the restaurant.

"Drop your gun, Brett!" blared the trumpet man walking down the concrete stairs. "Do it now! Or we will kill you!" ordered the cradle robber I saw schmoozing in the restaurant with the much younger, eye candy, fitness woman.

Thank God, Brett lowered his gun. Swiftly, and methodically, five men in dark FBI SWAT tactical gear approached Brett with assault rifles. After they confiscated his gun, Brett was detained upright against an unmarked van.

"Hey, Sullivan . . . you, FBI prick!" Brett yelled wildly looking over his shoulder in the direction of the trumpet man who ordered him to drop his gun.

The largest SWAT man forcefully frisked Brett while two men restrained his stretched-out arms. "Look at me, Sullivan! Look at me!" Brett screamed as he tried to shake free. "Let us fight, you . . . Irish prick!"

Was Brett insane, or did he possibly have a rare case of human rabies? Because he sounded and acted like a full-moon lunatic. First, he had no chance of beating his son. Dillon was decades younger, faster, stronger, and never beat him at The Den. Come on, Brett, why won't you just give up? Second, the feds won't allow anything to happen to Dillon—protect at all costs. Game. Set. Match.

Dillon approached Sullivan. From about fifteen feet away they seemed to be having a quiet, but heated conversation. What on earth were they talking about?

"You got my word, Sullivan!" Dillon said with a handshake. "It's a deal!"

What kind of deal did Dillon just make?

"Drop your weapons!" Sullivan ordered. "Let them fight!"

Were you fucking kidding me! I couldn't believe the FBI sanctioned this totally unnecessary fight.

Before I could utter a word to stop this senseless nonsense, out of nowhere, I was jostled when two big men grabbed me underneath each armpit. Instantly, they dragged me out of harm's way.

Slowly, with a smirk, Brett took out from his duty belt an expandable baton. Unbelievable, he didn't fight fair. Like clockwork, twenty plus guns were back on Brett about to pump him full of lead. Fearlessly, Dillon hand signaled for the firearms to be lowered.

Immediately, every armed agent looked at Sullivan for the final approval. With a concerned and hesitant look on his face, Sullivan ordered, "Lower your weapons! Let them fight!"

Slowly, all the armed federal agents lowered their widow-makers.

Father verse son, oh boy, here we fucking go!

21

FLIPPANTLY, DILLON ASKED, "So, tell me, Dad, which hospital do you want to visit this evening. Do you have a preference?"

Outraged, Brett charged his son with a swinging motion of his baton. Dillon's left hand stopped it coming from a downward motion while his right hand hit Brett squarely in the face sending him backwards onto the merciless payment. Once again, Brett was on his back twitching, but this time, he sported a bloody mouth.

The baton was only a few feet away from Brett's hand. Slowly, he rolled over trying to secure it. Dillon beat him to the punch and picked up the baton, then to my wildest amazement, he placed the weapon back in his dad's hand.

Was Dillon also insane? Was their relationship so fucked up it came to this? It must have stemmed from this branding ordeal, and whatever that entailed. More importantly, could I actually be with someone who had a totally different personality? I felt that Dillon would never physically harm me, but what I was witnessing appeared barbaric.

"Hey, Dad, I warned you, if you came here tonight, I would put you in the hospital," Dillon said in a calm-neutral tone. "You can walk away now and shake this off, and I'll eat my words. There's no shame if you walk away."

In all fairness, Dillon was giving his dad a very respectful way out. Please, Brett, just shut the fuck up and skedaddle.

Looking upward from the pavement, Brett announced, "You're the one going to the hospital, you motherfucker!"

Slowly, Brett rose from the concrete with the baton in hand. Swaying on his feet, Brett looked dazed. He had a snowball's chance in hell beating his son as he projected blood through his mouth onto the charcoal payment. Pissed off, Brett threw the baton up and away into the glowing moonlight. Removing his police shirt and bullet proof vest, Brett snarled at Dillon.

"So, you're thirsty for more, Dad. Hmm, tell you what, for all the times you put me in the hospital, I'm going to touch up your tattoos, for free," Dillon chastised in a flippant tone. "Hope your favorite color is bright red."

Brett was no slouch. He was a very fit, fourth degree black belt, and the second-best fighter at The Den.

In a blood-stained T-shirt with angry eyes, Brett charged Dillon with his hands in striking motion. Catlike, Dillon juked left, sending his father off balance to the right. Swiftly, Dillon was behind him.

Lunging at Brett from behind like a lion about to kill his prey, Dillon pulled him into his upper body. Instantly, Brett was in an unforgiving chokehold. Dillon's right arm deepened, bulging underneath Brett's chin. Dillon's left hand was locked on the back of Brett's head. Frantically, Brett tried to free himself to no avail. His arms erratically moved above his head while his lower body twitched—jerked out of control.

Sullivan had a very concerned look on his face while his fingers kept rubbing around his mouth and chin. And I wondered how long it would take before he would put a stop to this utter nonsense.

"Go ahead, Dad, and tap," Dillon demanded, deepening his chokehold grip.

Brett's eyes kept rapidly blinking until they rolled back into his head. Stubbornly, he refused to tap. A few seconds later, his head dropped. He was unconscious.

However, Brett's problems were far worse, he couldn't breathe.

22

THERE WAS NO way my future father-in-law was going to die on my watch.

It's now or never, Zoes!

"My name is Zoey Leary!" I yelled, wiggling free from the two men who were intently watching tonight's family fiasco. "And I'm Dillon Race's attorney! And I want this fucking stopped now!"

There was no action, only silence.

"Please, Dillon!" I screamed at the top of my lungs running in his direction. "Let him fucking go!"

Looking at me from a few feet away, I never witnessed someone's eyes as enraged as his. Hastily, turning away, Dillon dragged his dad several feet, hurling Brett over his hip. Unfortunately, Brett landed dead center on top of an unmarked federal vehicle windshield.

Whoosh, small spider veins started to emerge, crackle, spread, and slowly increase in length, zigzagging across the windshield.

Head first, Brett slithered lifeless, and very slowly down the hood of the car. His final descent to the unforgiving payment was loudly interrupted when the windshield shattered. Luckily for Brett, two quick-thinking moving agents in the nick of time caught his head near the headlight.

Was Brett dead?

Slowly, Dillon walked toward Brett, and to my wildest amazement, I saw him clenched his fists. Oh, my God! Dillon wasn't done with him! Would he kill his own dad?

"Please fucking stop, Dillon!" I shouted and begged with tears streaming. "Please . . . Dillon!"

A woman in her fifties came sprinting out toward Dillon. Immediately, she placed her hands on his upper body, looked up, and then conveyed something for about fifteen seconds. Dillon's demeanor quickly changed. Thank God, I saw people kneeling on the ground attending to Brett.

Sullivan shouted into his smartphone, "Send in the ambulance!"

Dillon glanced my way, and I saw tears in his eyes. Sheepishly, he turned away walking toward Brett on the ground. What did this woman say to make Dillon stop and tear? What the fuck was going on here? How could someone have this level of rage one moment, then quickly stop cold turkey, and then turn empathetic?

Come on, Zoes, let's be honest, that was me at his age minus the empathy.

From a near moonlit distance, it looked like Dillon was helping his dad. But why? Dillon took the end of the stretcher helping the medics lift Brett onto the ambulance. To my surprise, Dillon hopped in the back. It seemed like they were having a few words when they shook hands. Why? Dillon bent forward for a quick embrace. What the fuck?

Catching me off guard, I felt a forceful tap on the back of my shoulder. As I turned around, the woman who de-escalated Dillon's rage, already had her hand extended.

"Hi, Attorney Leary. It's a pleasure to meet you," she said warmly and confidently. "I'm Jill Forte with Homeland Security."

23

SHAKING HER FIRM grip, Forte looked vaguely familiar. "Thank you, Ms. Forte for stopping this fracas."

"You're welcome, so, Ms. Leary, what do you—"

Interrupting, "Please, call me, Zoey."

Forte asked, "Okay, Zoey, what do you know about your client?"

She was testing me probably because of my youthful appearance. Regardless, as Dillon's lawyer, I must sound convincing, but more importantly, act the part, perfectly.

"Dillon tells me everything," I replied confidently, staring into her eyes. "We can't prove it, but Dillon and I feel he stopped the explosion of the Golden Gate Bridge. And I'm aware of the money *your* department, and the FBI awarded him."

"Please, join us, Zoey, when we talk to Dillon," Forte requested.

Instantly, I liked her. "Dillon insists I be with him when speaking with you. By the way, Ms. Forte, what did you say to Dillon to calm him down?"

"It's confidential. You'll have to ask Dillon yourself," Forte replied. "And thank you, Zoey, for breaking up the boy's fun."

Walking toward the ambulance, Forte abruptly stopped, turned around, and then asked, "Zoey, by any chance was your dad in the Navy, stationed in Newport?"

Walking closer to her, I replied, "Yes."

From about a foot away, she asked, "Were your parents Patrick and Maureen?"

Dumbfounded, I said, "Yes."

Catching me by surprise, Forte stepped forward for an embrace. Stepping back with her arm on my shoulder, she proudly boasted, "Your dad was the greatest. He was my commanding officer, and saved my military career, and also John Sullivan's . . . and a few others. It's an honor to meet you. Please walk with me, Zoey."

We walked to her unmarked, federal vehicle in silence. Growing up, I had no idea exactly what Dad did for the Navy, except that he was a

Naval Intelligence Officer, and whatever that entailed. One time, Mom explained that Dad was always working on something very important that protected our daily freedom. And on Dad's days off, Admiral Smith would sometimes call for Dad's input on how to handle certain types of cyberattacks. Mom always bragged and claimed that Dad was the naval station's linchpin, and Admiral Smith's good-luck charm and right-hand man.

Once we were seated inside her car, Forte admitted, "Last month when my Homeland Security team and my counterpart's John Sullivan's FBI special unit intercepted Dillon, we brought him back to our hotel suite. And I never seen someone as young as him quickly take charge. There must have been twenty of us feds, and just him. He commanded our room, and the flow of the conversation with a very rare charisma. When Dillon left our room seventeen million dollars richer, I asked John who Dillon reminded him of. We both, hands down agreed, Dillon reminded us of your dad."

Forte made me smile while I was lost in many happy Dad memories.

She asked, "You don't remember me, do you?"

Looking at her, I replied, "You do look sort of familiar, but I can't place it."

Forte touched my left knee and said, "I patched you up, remember me now?"

To my memory, I was five or six. "That was you!" I said, taken aback.

"It sure was," Forte replied, smiling. "Before I was transferred to your dad's special unit and command, I was a Navy ER nurse. Your dad was teaching you how to ride a bike when you fell off and cut open your knee. So, he rushed you over to my place so I could help you. And I remember your little friend was with you holding your hand as I stitched you up. Your dad was so worried that your mom would flip out, that's why he avoided taking you to the hospital."

I started to giggle because it was true, Mom would have killed him if I went to the hospital while she was at the gym. After I was stitched up, Dad took Emma and I out for an ice cream bribe in order to get our stories straight.

"You mentioned my mother's name, did you know her?"

Forte started to laugh.

"What's so funny?" I asked.

"Would you like to see a video of her?"

"Yes!" I hollered in excitement. "Are you kidding me?!"

"Zoey, I'm too tired to kid around at this hour. I considered your mom a good friend. Now, before I show you this video, your dad knew about this. Actually, he approved this. And when I played the video for him the next day, he got the biggest kick out of it. He couldn't stop laughing."

"Knew about what? What did Dad approve of? What was so funny?" I rattled off in great anticipation.

"At the very last second, one of my friends backed out of the all-male review in town because she had the flu. And I was stuck with the cost of an extra ticket. When your dad called me into his office, he noticed I wasn't myself and asked what was wrong. After I told him . . . he called your mom in front of me, and told her that she was going. He paid me on the spot for your mother's ticket."

Quickly, I fired back in total disbelief, "Get the fuck out of here! Dad let Mom go see male strippers!"

"He sure did. Your dad trusted your mom one hundred percent. And they loved each other deeply. Just give me a second to find the video, it's been a long time since I've seen it."

I sat in silence thinking about Mom and Dad while Forte searched.

"Oh, here it is!" she said with enthusiasm after a solid minute of searching for the archived video. "I'm glad it wasn't deleted. It's almost two minutes long."

When Forte pressed play, I was blown away because Mom looked drop-dead gorgeous that evening. Her long strawberry-blonde hair flowed perfectly. Mom was dressed sexy in shiny leather, knee-cap boots, skin-tight blue jeans, and she rocked a snug, black square neck sleeveless top. God damn, her upper body was buffed. That was the first time I'd viewed Mom as a strong sexual person. And Mom wasn't shy with the male dancers. Actually, she was the rowdy ring leader, having a blast. And yes, she was making it rain! To my surprise, Mom actually did a tequila shot off one of the dancer's ripped abs. Way to go, Mom!

Just to see her young, beautiful face—angel face—the way I remembered it—vibrant. And to hear Mom's soothing voice again, the sprinkler system in my eyes burst. I screeched, "She died when she was my age!"

Immediately, Forte embraced me. And I latched on for dear life. It felt like forever since I'd been lovingly held.

"I know she did," Forte whispered. "I know it sucks, and I'm sorry it still hurts."

Wailing in Forte's arms, snug into her upper body, my thoughts and emotions were racing. I miss you so much, Mom. I miss your smile. I miss your boldness. I'm sorry if I ever caused you any heartache. I'm sorry that I made you mad at times. I should have told you, "I love you" more often. I ache for your touch—your smile—your scent. I yearn for your loving hugs, and for you to squeeze me again. I miss feeling safe in your strong arms. I miss brushing your hair—I miss the smell of it. And I miss you brushing mine. What I would eagerly sacrifice for you, Mom, just to see you again—even if it was for a brief moment. Endlessly, I tried to negotiate with God. But He doesn't negotiate. I wish He did because I would eagerly kneel on rice before Him, and beg at the top of my lungs for you to hold me again. Thank you for everything you did for Emma and me. And from the bottom of my heart, thank you for making me feel special. Kiss and tell Daddy, "I love him more."

"Thank you so much for showing me that," I said, sobbing in her arms.

Forte broke our embrace. "You're welcome," she said with tears in her eyes.

Reaching into a fast food bag, she handed me a couple of clean napkins. "It's funny, Zoey," she laughed, startling me. "Your dad thanked me, too, when he came in two hours late the next morning, exhausted."

Immediately, I burst out laughing with tears streaming down my face.

You rock Mom and Dad!

24

TRAVELING ON THE back roads of Bloomfield, there were three federal cars in front and three sandwiched in back of Dillon's truck and my car when we veered onto a deserted, unpaved side road.

Steering down the whirling, dusty, dirt road, it was very difficult to see a few feet in front when my thoughts drifted. What a fucking crazy and wild night so far. Our dinner was great up until the fight. And I'd seen a lot of fucked-up shit in my lifetime, but this by far, took the cake. Am I now having second thoughts if Dillon would be my first? Yeah, right, Zoes, who was I fooling, that was me at his age. And the rage I saw in his eyes, I once possessed until I had intense anger management treatment.

Finally, we all parked at an open, mammoth moonlit field. Front and center about forty yards away, were two large-size tour buses. Also, to the left of the jumbo buses were small spotlights shining bright upon an ambulance and two helicopters. The front doors of the buses were ajar, and guarded with many armed federal agents around the perimeter of each bus.

Once everyone stepped out of their vehicles, I quickly approached Forte and informed her that I needed a few minutes with my client. She obliged and communicated when we were done with our chat to head toward the buses for further instructions.

Sensing that Dillon's truck was bugged, I directed him to my car. Once we were seated with the doors closed, I firmly said, "Give me one good fucking reason why I shouldn't fire you as a client!"

"You should fire me, and you shouldn't waste your time on me. You're pure and innocent, and I'm damaged beyond repair. And I'm all alone in this fucked-up world," Dillon admitted, choked-up, pausing for a few seconds. "I'm sorry for ruining your evening, and I'm sorry, Zoey, you witnessed that side of me. I wish . . . I could take it all back, and take a beating. Again, my deepest apologies," he said, opening the door to exit.

Dillon thought I was pure and innocent, yeah right, but I knew he was sincere, protective, and also scared. Unfortunately, I had to be very hard on him. "Shut the fucking door!" I ordered while yanking on his left arm with all my might, trying my best to restrain him from leaving.

Dillon closed the door, but was hesitant with eye contact. He was breathing on the passenger side window, fogging it up. Why did he wish to take it all back, and take a beating? What did that mean? I could never let Dillon, being only eighteen, talk to the feds alone. Emma would fucking kill me.

Firmly, I ordered, "Tell me the deal you made with Sullivan!"

"The deal was, um, if we could fight," Dillon confessed, sounding nervous while avoiding eye contact, "I would, um, talk to them afterwards."

Are you fucking kidding me! What kind of shitty deal was that? Who in their right mind would make such an awful deal? Did Dillon have a lobotomy that I'm not aware of? A jackass could have made a better deal with the feds.

Don't forget, Zoes, he's only eighteen.

"Look at me, Dillon," I requested.

Dillon turned sheepishly toward me, avoiding direct eye contact.

"Fucking, look at me!" I demanded. "As your attorney, who has your best legal interests at heart, no more deals with the feds until you cleared it with me, got it!"

Staring at me, he softly said, "Got it."

"What did Forte say to you?" I asked with great curiosity.

Dillon placed his hands in his face, bent forward and then started to gently weep.

Reaching underneath the steering wheel, I pushed the trunk button, then stepped out in the dark grass-dirt field to fetch a roll of paper towels.

After plopping into my seat, I tore off a sheet. "Take this!" I ordered.

"Thanks," he murmured, wiping his eyes.

Not backing down, I demanded to know, "Well, I'm still waiting for your fucking answer! What did Forte say to you?"

25

IT TOOK DILLON a few seconds to recompose himself. "Forte informed me that my father has a brain tumor," he admitted with genuine empathy in his voice. "And it needs to be operated on because it's affecting his fine motor skills."

Remaining silent on purpose, my left hand was gently tapping the driver's side window.

"I would have never fought him if I knew," Dillon admitted somberly. "I feel horrible and like a total piece of shit."

No words exited my mouth. At least, Dillon stopped right away once he heard the upsetting news.

"And you know something, Zoey . . . you shouldn't waste your time on me," he said, opening the door. "And I shouldn't drag you into my family's fucked-up mess."

At least, Dillon had a family. And dealing with Emma's family anarchy in the past, I was used to crazy flesh and blood bedlam.

"Again, Zoey, I'm very sorry for ruining your night," Dillon said genuinely apologetic. "Take care."

With two hands and all my might, I couldn't restrain him from exiting—slamming the car door. For a few seconds, I watched Dillon all alone in his fucked-up world, walk directly toward the bus, fearless with his fists clenched—ready for battle. And guess what, also, I was all alone for the longest time, in my timid, fucked-up world. However, I was constantly battling my own demons. Plagued by my self-doubting demons, and my false evidence appearing real demons, aka "the what-ifs", that never came to fruition in my secluded, chosen existence. Pathetic!

It's now or never, I had to escape from my decade-long, lonely rut. Lay it on the line, Zoes!

Jumping out of the car with teared eyes, I almost lost my footing in the uneven ground because of these fucking heels. Unbalanced, I scurried ahead of Dillon turning around into his muscular chest. Copying Forte's pose, I placed my hands on his upper body. With finesse, I pushed him backwards a couple feet, knowing full well that he could have easily hurled me back to the Ocean State.

"Look at me!" I ordered. "Fucking look at me, Dillon!"

It took him five seconds before he made eye contact with me. "You . . . are not a waste of time, Dillon, and I forgive you!"

Instantly, Dillon embraced me tightly. "Thank you, Zoey. Your words mean the world to me, and I owe you one."

Desperately, I wanted to kiss him, however, I had to remain level-headed before I headed into the most important meeting in my life. "Do not answer any questions without my consent first, got it!"

"Got it."

Forcefully, I ordered, "When you ended your call in the restaurant with your dad, you took some deep breaths and recomposed yourself. Do it now!"

26

WE STEPPED ONTO the luxurious government bus—govbus which was a front. It really was a government, mobile command center for one very special person, the one and only, Dillon Nitrogen Race. Surveillance cameras and live color monitors were strategically stationed everywhere along the ceiling and walls. Several color mugshots of Dillon in various places: sitting at his work desk, exercising at the gym, eating inside a diner, running outside, walking through the park with Candace and Lewis, pumping gas into his truck, and taking out his trash were placed along the length of both sides of the walls. What the fuck was going on here?

Ms. Forte rose from her chair, and warmly greeted us. However, we experienced some unpleasantries with one of her subordinates. Unfortunately, Dillon and I were forced to surrender our smartphones, and then we were subjected to a quick wand-down for weapons, and probably for any recording devices. Now, I felt naked (I hate it when my cell is not in my possession!) and violated.

We followed Forte to the middle part of the govbus where she tapped in her clearance code, followed by a fingerprint and eye scan. Once Forte was granted access, we walked through the secured back area. Immediately, we were seated at a slim rectangle table for six. Already seated across from us, Sullivan was softly talking on his mobile. Cordially, he acknowledged us with a hand wave.

After exchanging business cards, we were each handed a bottle of water. So many thoughts flooded my hyperactive brain at once. Regardless, I had to remember that Dillon and the feds were not aware that I had three top-secret files. My number one concern that I feared most was Dillon's safety. Did his grandfather want him dead? Finally, Sullivan's call ended.

In order to prove my credibility, that my client shared everything, I broke the silence by confidently announcing, "Dillon made me aware of Brett's brain tumor. Which hospital is he at?"

Forte and Sullivan shared a silent, two second glance. Forte, who was seated next to him, replied, "Saint Francis."

"Thank you, and how can my client help you?" I asked warmly, glancing at Forte and Sullivan.

"We'll get to that in one moment," Forte said, grabbing the slim, remote control next to Sullivan's laptop. She pointed for us to look up in the far-right corner at the flat screen. After she pressed play, Forte reached into her suit jacket, then took out her smartphone. Immediately, her fingers were actively in motion.

It was the president of the United States thanking Dillon for saving his life. The president was supposed to be on the Golden Gate Bridge during the explosion that never happened, thanks to Dillon. My hero and future husband received the Presidential Medal of Freedom award. And the funny thing was, Dillon could have cared less.

"Dillon, on behalf of the president of the United States, the FBI, and Homeland Security, you will be receiving a wire transfer of ten million dollars," Forte stated with her mobile in her hand. "This is a well-deserved tax-free gift for leading us to your grandfather's website, and for your direct involvement with stopping the nuclear explosion in Milwaukee. We all sincerely thank you."

Of all cities to detonate—blow to smithereens, why would Isosceles choose Milwaukee? The math didn't add up. Was Milwaukee a decoy? And the feds just don't giveaway ten million dollars, tax fucking free. Knowing better, there had to be a catch. Something extremely horrible had to be lurking on the horizon, and the feds really needed Dillon's help.

Dillon leaned over, cupped his hand, and then firmly whispered with the utmost conviction in my ear, "Do *not* contradict what I'm about to say!"

That's the Dillon I knew because the proof was in my damp panties. But what on earth was so important that he's going to convey without consulting me? Or worse, was Dillon going to make another awful mistake, a sweetheart deal that favored the feds?

Leaning into his ear, I conveyed louder than a whisper, "Do *not* make any deals without my consent first!"

Nailing his hand into my ear, Dillon firmly reiterated, "This deal, Zoey, I'm about to make is one hundred percent nonnegotiable, or you're fired!"

QUICKLY GLANCING AT Forte and Sullivan, Dillon said, "You're welcome. Please, deposit nine million into my account, and one million into Attorney Leary's account," he directed with the utmost authority. "She gets ten percent of my likeness."

Oh, my God! I just became an instant millionaire! And I never had earned so much money, so effortlessly. By far, Dillon was the most generous person I'd ever met. He was one hundred percent forgiven for his prior actions. Fuck, I would donate twenty-five thousand dollars of my million to a trouble-teen charity of Dillon's choice right now, if we could kick everyone off the govbus, so we could christen it.

"No problem," Sullivan said.

Leaning into my ear with a cupped hand, Dillon whispered, "Do you think Forte and Sullivan are sleeping together?"

Loving Dillon's humor, and trying not to laugh out loud, I quickly glanced at them. Leaning into his ear, I seductively said, "Most definitely." My body ached for him, and I wanted another kiss to remind me what I felt a couple hours ago. "And thanks for the million. Now, I owe you."

Quickly, Dillon whispered in my ear, "Thank you for having my back. It means the world to me. You're a great lawyer, and a very special person, Zoey."

Instantly, my heart melted. Dillon really valued me as a true professional, and didn't judge me because of my youthful appearance. And with his heartfelt vote of confidence based on my acquired abilities, I would always have his back.

We probably resembled a young couple in love, because Forte faked a loud cough, then interjected, "The reason for this unscheduled meeting is because we believe your grandfather *will do* something horrible of mass destruction, just like he did last month in Tokyo. And we need your help again, Dillon."

Giving Dillon a reassuring nod to answer, he asked, "How can I help you?"

"What I'm about to tell you is confidential," said Forte, "and at the highest level of national security. The United States and a few of its key allies have classified and deemed your grandfather to be the number one terrorist in the world. He's harvesting nuclear energy in a manner never done before."

"How's he harvesting it?" Dillon asked.

"That's classified information, and the only thing that I'm allowed to say . . . it's a game changer, and *not* in a good way," Forte admitted, extremely concerned. "And only a few intelligent agencies in the world know about this. With that being said, he only gave us one clue this time around. Actually, just one word," Forte said, pausing for emphasis, "it's."

Immediately, Dillon repeated in total disbelief, "It's?"

Intently, Sullivan said, "Yes, that's correct, it's. And that's all we have. Do you have any idea what it means, or refers to, or any idea of your grandfather's next target?"

"No, I don't," Dillon replied, very concerned. After he took a shaky sip of water, he said, "I wish I did know because I would tell you right away."

Startling us, the secured door opened. Forte waved her hand, and to my wildest amazement, the gorgeous woman from the restaurant entered. She sported bright-pink spandex shorts exposing a colossal cameltoe, and a white crop top revealing her tight abs and sculpted arms. And how could you not miss her tight ass and perky fucking tits. This bombshell was an absolute knockout, a couple of pay grades above me. And she knew how to flaunt it.

Cameltoe was almost on Candace's level. She was tall with long blonde hair, a pretty face and a killer body. And probably not older than twenty-five. Regardless of her age, any straight man would be stoked to fuck her. Did Dillon sleep with her? And how did I not know about this?

Leaning into my ear, Dillon whispered, "I recognize her when I go running. She hit on me, twice."

Leaning into Dillon's ear, I asked, "And what did you do?"

Dillon whispered in my ear, "I ran off both times."

Wholeheartedly, I believed him.

"Oh, my apologies," Sullivan said as he typed something on his laptop. "This is special agent Lovely with the Secret Service."

"Hi, Dillon," Lovely said flirtatiously in a Southern accent. Her red glossy lips pouted perfectly. "Remember me, sugar?"

Dillon glanced at her, then looked away remaining silent. If I could, I wanted to get up, and punch this fucking fit, Secret Service sugar bitch in her plump collagen lips.

Sullivan swiveled his laptop so it faced us, then played a video showing Lovely stopping Dillon running. Brazenly, she asked Dillon up to her place—paid for by Uncle Sam with no strings attached. And this was how our government was spending our hard-earned tax dollars, with a high-end call girl, nestled in a plush cathouse apartment. Secret Service my ass! It was more like a public service booty call. I so wanted to kiss Dillon for rejecting her farce, government-handout ass.

"I wish you said yes, Dillon," Lovely confessed, sounding slutty while batting her phony eyelashes. "I had a big green light to keep you . . . *very happy.*"

28

INSTANTLY, DILLON PLACED his hand firmly on my thigh, pressing down. I wanted to stand up and punch her fucking lights out. Dillon pressed down on my thigh again as I was trying my best to remain cool, calm, and collective in my wobbly chair.

Pissed off, I asked, "What's the purpose of Agent Lovely?"

"Three days after Dillon stopped the nuclear explosion in Milwaukee, we decided to conjure a woman that resembled his current girlfriend in case things went south," Sullivan confessed. "We tried to entice Dillon with agent Lovely during his relationship, and after the breakup. However, our plan failed."

"I don't understand, and please help me connect the dots. Let's say Dillon did take the fake bait from this government tramp, how could he be of any help?" I asked snarky, but deep down I was extremely proud of Dillon for not taking the fraudulent bait.

"We have subliminal ways to unlock the unconscious mind during the day, and at night during sleep to find answers," Sullivan admitted. "I can't give specific details in the process because it would be a breach of national classified information. Agent Lovely's sole function would have been to simply tire him out. But that's not the case anymore. So, Dillon, would you be willing to undergo some safe treatments during the day, or at night? And Zoey is welcome to observe. We would pay you both very handsomely for your time and cooperation. Will you please help us, Dillon?"

In a concerned tone, Dillon asked, "Is there any other alternative?"

Sullivan and Forte stared at each other briefly. Sullivan gave her a slight go-head nod.

"Yes, there is Dillon," Forte said. "Would you be willing to play football for the Navy?"

######

INTERRUPTING THEIR HEATED conversation, the young woman hands Jill K. Forte, director of the Cybersecurity and Infrastructure Security Agency (CISA) which is a key component of the Department of Homeland Security (DHS) the newest top-secret file that was reviewed and sent from the president of the United States.

"Thank you, Stacey, and good work today," Jill Forte warmly says to the young woman. "That's all for tonight, see you first thing tomorrow."

Once Stacey A. Lovely exits the bus, Jill drops the bulky file on the small table. "This is fucked up, John, so you're telling me you never heard of Zoey Leary?"

"That's right, Jill. I'm telling you my intel team didn't drop the ball with Dillon's involvement with Zoey. We didn't know she existed until this evening!" replies John T. Sullivan, head of the FBI's Cyber Action Teams (CATS). "So, I go back to what I said five minutes ago, this Zoey . . . lawyer development is all new to us. And are you sure that's not Patrick's granddaughter because she looks like she could be one of my granddaughter's friends in high school?"

"You know, John, that's why I have to put your leftovers front and center in the refrigerator because you would never find it! Do I have to put your name in big bold letters on it too?" Jill says sarcastically. "Of course, that's Patrick's daughter! She's a spitting-image of a younger Maureen. I'm surprised you can't see it!"

"Okay, Jill, I know we are all exhausted at this hour. I promise to investigate this matter thoroughly. Your team will have everything on Zoey by the end of day, tomorrow."

"Thanks, John, and I don't mean to snap at you. I just need a drink to process all of these thoughts flying around in my head. I . . . I still can't believe Zoey is Patrick's daughter. And you and I both know he was the best commanding officer ever. All of my risky mistakes, and all of your crazy fuck-ups . . . that man always took the heat for us."

"Patrick always did, but Jill," he says laughing, "didn't you fuck-up more than me?"

"Patrick once told me a drunken alien would have made less mistakes than you, and if you were not on the field with him, he would have shipped you off to Guantanamo Bay."

"He really said that?"

"Hmm, also, Patrick told me he had to *slowly* explain . . . multiple times to you what a safety was."

Angrily, John fires back, "I know what a safety is! We were both on defense!"

"Would you happen to have any three-dollar bills in your wallet?" Jill snorts. "God John, you *are* so gullible!"

John starts to laugh as a sigh of relief to his vulnerable ego. "Good one, Jill, you got me. Do you want to tackle this file now, or go back to the hotel and do it there?"

"We will review it now," Jill says, "but all kidding aside Patrick loved you. After all, you were his best man when Maureen and Patrick eloped."

"Yeah, I loved him too, still do. And I remember, it was just Pam and I," John says, doing the sign of the cross in remembrance of his deceased wife, and Patrick. "And Maureen's cuckoo-crazy twin sister from Providence. She was a total wackadoo."

"You know how I feel, John, when you use those hurtful words about people who have a traumatic past. I'll tell you this, Maureen should have been a lot worse off than her sister, I forgot her name."

"You're right, I'm sorry, Jill. I should have said, deeply disturbed. But come on, right after the court wedding during the luncheonette, Maeve, that's her name, was so off-the-wall blotto drunk. And I shit you not, she crawled behind the bar and swiped a bottle of Irish whiskey, and chugged it on the way back. And get this, when she popped up, she kissed Pam on the lips with a mouthful of whiskey."

"That's hilarious!" Jill says laughing. "To my memory, Pam was a prissy person. Maybe she liked it."

"Jill!" John screeches, throwing his right hand in the air.

"I'm very sorry, John, my deepest apology," says Jill, feeling horrible. "You have every right to be mad, and I shouldn't have talked negatively about Pam, especially when she's dead, and it won't ever happen again."

"Apology accepted. I need a drink now."

"Me too, where's the bourbon stashed at?" asks Jill.

"You read my mind, dear," John says. "It's on the other bus. I'll be back in a moment."

"Are you going to crawl to go get it, dear?" asks Jill, giggling.

"Yes, in fact I am," John says laughing. "I'm going to chug it all."

John travels to the other bus to fetch two glasses and the bottle of bourbon while Jill starts to comb through Isosceles's top-secret file.

Stepping back onto the bus fifteen minutes later, John says, "Sorry it took so long, I had to take an important call. Anything interesting in the file?"

"Oh, yes, and all of this is mind boggling. Take a seat," Jill orders. "I don't know why they separated Isosceles's records to different areas in the country to begin with. This very old file we have here is from the secured underground storage facility from Valmeyer. And it says here that Isosceles was part of the original atomic bomb group. And he was dismissed from the group because his peers felt he belittled them. But get this, when the group was stuck on developing the bomb, a special team went to Bristol, Rhode Island where he lived to show him the blueprints. And get this, he knew where their errors were in less than three hours. And John, I'm talking about over sixty huge pages of complex mathematical equations."

"Wait, are you saying that Isosceles knew more than the entire group of scientists?"

"It sure seems that way, and get this," Jill says, sliding a paper toward John, then she takes a big guzzle. "Look at this page, it says that Isosceles was the youngest scientist in the group."

John states in disbelief, "And they labeled him a super genius?"

"Yes, they did, and not only that, Isosceles was held prisoner in Japan during World War II, and somehow, he successfully escaped. And getting back to the bomb blueprints, he would only tell them where *their* errors were in exchange for his demands. And his demands were very odd."

"What do you mean by very odd?" John asks.

Jill says, "For instance, he wanted the position as police chief in Bristol."

"Wait a second. That makes no sense," says John in a puzzling voice. "With Isosceles's superior level of intelligence, he could have any high paying job in the world. And he wanted *that* job?"

"I agree with you, John, it doesn't make any sense . . . it's very strange. And get this, when you were gone I did a quick search on your laptop, and it mentioned that he was chief of police for forty-six years with the lowest crime rate in the country for all forty-six consecutive years. And it also said in the article, that Isosceles ruled the small town with an iron fist."

"Very interesting, but not to change the subject, what was your takeaway on Zoey and Dillon?"

"They're in love."

"Are you sure? Because he looks to be ten years older, and he could easily pass as her older brother," John says, then takes a drink. "You really think they're in love?"

"Come on, John! Do I have to match your socks for you, too? From the way they carried on, they were having a blast. I sense they're in love. Plus, no one just randomly gives away a million dollars. Zoey was beside herself. She was relishing everything tonight."

"Okay, so for argument's sake, Jill, let's say tonight was the first time they met, is your answer still the same?"

"Yes, dear, my answer is still the same. They were having fun, until I purposely had Stacey crash our party," Jill confesses, then takes a sip. "And the look on Zoey's face . . . she wanted to kill her, and Dillon had to hold her down. It was the exact same look Zoey had when I went to go see her at the mental hospital. She didn't recognize me because I went incognito. And I saw a young Maureen freak the fuck out, I thought Zoey was going to beat one of the staff members to death. It was horrifying to watch. It took staff members from two hospitals, and a bunch of mattresses scattered on the floor, and a few brave workers to climb and go get her near the top of the ceiling to subdue her. It reminded me when Patrick had to stop Maureen from drowning her twin sister. And I hate to admit this, but Zoey possesses a killer rage inside of her just like her mother. And that's when I knew I could never adopt her. She would have been the straw to break my weak marriage. For years, I felt horrible that I let Patrick down."

"It's not your fault," John says, "and I feel you made the right decision."

"I still feel horrible about it," Jill says, slowly nodding her head. "Patrick always went to bat for us. He saved our careers, and pensions before the Joint Chiefs of Staff dismantled us."

"Oh, trust me, I'll never forget what he did for us. Patrick was the best."

Jill's cell chirps. "Look at what my CISA surveillance team just sent me," she boasts, turning her smartphone around. "Does this convince you now, Johnny Boy?"

"Holy shit!" John shouts. "They are making out like a couple of teenagers in the car! I just can't believe if tonight was their first-time meeting, she knows so much about what happened to him. And they quickly . . . fell in love?"

"I told you, John. Call it women's intuition. I can spot young love a mile away."

"So, getting back to the file," John says, "what else strikes you?"

"This right here, John!" Jill announces sliding a page with a picture on it. "Look at that marvel invention."

Bewildered, John asks, "Is that some kind of computer . . . radio device?"

"It sure looks like it. And it says here that Isosceles invented it in 1937, and the device is considered beyond genius for the time period because of the limited resources, and raw materials available. From my understanding, his device intercepted radio signals from warships, aircraft, and submarines. And his device could dissolve a message entirely, or alter the content. And are you ready for the kicker? Drumroll, please, his doohickey device ran on . . . sunlight.”

"Great," John sighs, "we are dealing with a genius renegade.”

"No shit! Check your cell, it just dinged.”

Startled, John says, "I didn't hear anything.”

"By the way, when do you get fitted for your hearing aids?”

Glancing at his cell, John says, "First thing tomorrow, and get this, Maeve is alive, and still lives in Providence.”

"Why would you check into that?" asks Jill, baffled.

"No particular reason, I just wanted to know.”

"Well, I'm glad you checked," Jill replies, "because under no circumstance do we tell Zoey that she has an aunt.”

Confused, John asks, "Are you sure Zoey doesn't already know?”

"I'm positive Zoey doesn't know because Maureen told me a long time ago, she cut all ties with her sister after their wild ocean brawl when Zoey was a toddler," Jill states firmly. "I know certain things about Maeve, and unfortunately, she's mentally unstable.”

"I'll delete her file right now for you, dear.”

"Thanks," Jill sighs. "Who was the other woman at dinner with them, the one that left early . . . where's the footage?”

"Oh, that's Emma Evans, you know, the state cop Dillon helped out on the highway. And there's no footage of their dinner because we inexplicably got bumped from the restaurant's server.”

"Come on, John," Jill scoffs, "that's child's play hacking!”

"My team only has the footage when they enter the restaurant. It's edited and around three minutes long. Do you want to take a look?”

"Of course, I do! Duh!" Jill says irritable. "This will let us know if they knew each other. And bartender, another refill please, and go heavy on the hand.”

John kills the bourbon bottle. With a drink in each of their hands, he says, "Cheers, my dear.”

"Cheers!”

The two directors were sipping bourbon while watching the three-minute, edited version on John's smartphone. When the video ends, Jill states, "Unbelievable! You don't need women's intuition here. So yes, this was the first time Dillon and Zoey met, but the more disturbing thing is—”

Interrupting, John replies, "Emma is crazy about Dillon! Flirting and twirling around in a skimpy dress like that! And did you see the look on

Emma's face when Zoey hugged Dillon? If Emma had her firearm around her waist, she would have shot Zoey. Who knows, maybe Emma is in love with Dillon."

"Exactly, John! And I bet you, Emma wasn't wearing any undies!" Jill snaps. "And I also bet you she was wearing a tiny red bow underneath her dress. Talk about throwing yourself at somebody . . . she came in first place in this razzmatazz contest! You know something, John, do you have a file on Emma because she looks familiar?"

"Of course, I do, it's on the other bus," John says. "Like I said before, and I was right, my team didn't drop the ball on Zoey. I'll be back in a moment."

"Stop!" Jill shouts. "Don't bother, I just figured it out."

John stops walking, then turns around.

"Don't shoot the messenger," Jill says, "but this situation is going to get a lot more complicated because Emma is Zoey's childhood friend."

######

29

ANOTHER DEAFENING HELICOPTER flew over my property. The Hartford hospitals must be hectic tonight because this was the third very loud helicopter I heard since arriving home. Quickly, I changed into shorts and a T-shirt. And since I had a lot of snooping to accomplish, I grabbed two water bottles, and then headed full steam ahead toward my office, aka the command center.

My mobile chimed, and I knew it was Dillon time! Only a step away from the command center, I lunged forward plowing through the unlocked door.

Immediately, I turned on all seven color monitors with surround sound stationed on my makeshift desk consisting of three eight-foot folding tables shaped like an upside-down square U. Plopping into my cozy leather swivel desk chair where the main computer was stationed—front and center, I was eager for tonight's entertainment.

Dillon appeared frozen standing next to the elevator door. He stood still for about twenty seconds. Startling him, the elevator door opened, it was empty. He walked a few feet away, then sat on the foyer carpeted floor with his back up against the wall. Gracefully, Dillon placed his head down between his knees. It killed me to see him like this. Why did he look so depressed? When we left the govbus, we were both excited to spend tomorrow together. We sealed our deal in my car with a very long passionate, goodnight French kiss initiating my hormones to gleefully ricochet everywhere in my body.

The foyer door opened, and here she came strolling in for the kill. Without further ado, I cranked the volume to hear the audio. Secret Service Agent Lovely, the government cameltoe tramp wearing an oversized white cover-up T-shirt took it upon herself, and slithered down the wall. Sitting next to Dillon, she pulled out an earbud placing it near his left ear. Startled, Dillon jolted his head up from his knees, looked to his left and then quickly lowered his head.

82

"Don't be sad, Dillon. Tell ya what, sugar, all you need sweetie is a hot shower, and a cold beer," Lovely suggested brazenly in her southern belle accent. "Let's go back to my place, and chill."

Slowly, and loudly, Dillon said, "Please! Go! Away!"

He just earned brownie points.

"Let me take special care of you tonight, sweetie. Promise ya, we'll have a good time," guaranteed the sugar whore, assertively. "I have some special CIA weed, potent as fuck that will go perfect with a cold beer. It will relax ya, sugar."

Quickly getting to his feet, Dillon ran toward the staircase. I watched the footage of him entering his apartment. Good night, my love. You passed the test with flying colors!

Two minutes later, my cell chimed again. Glancing at my monitor, Dillon was abruptly leaving his apartment backwards in distress.

Stephanie bitch-slapped Dillon hard in the face. Dang! Forcefully using both hands, she pushed him backwards causing his back and head to slam against the corridor wall. Ouch! Dillon did not defend himself nor retaliate.

Stephanie had broken into his place again, what the fuck! She was dressed in black capri yoga pants, a ribbed-knit pink crop top exposing her flat abs, and defined upper body. Also, she sported bright-pink fuck-me pumps. Her long, blonde hair and makeup were picture-perfect. She was solely there for an unannounced booty call.

In the middle of the public hallway, Stephanie kept forcefully poking Dillon in the chest. "Please stop!" Dillon begged with his back nailed against the wall.

After another humiliating bitch-slap, Stephanie, at the top of her teenage lungs, demanded to know, "Why won't you sleep with me anymore!"

30

"I TOLD YOU last night we're over!" Dillon yelled with a stern face. "We *are* over, Stephanie!"

"Okay, I will say it. I'll say it, Dillon! It's yours," she said sarcastically. "Are you happy now?"

"Go . . . home . . . Stephanie!"

"Please Dillon," Stephanie begged in a soft voice. To my surprise she dropped to her knees. Looking upward, she admitted, "It will always be yours. I love you."

"I only said that in the heat of the moment. I didn't mean it! You should know that. Now, leave me alone so I can clean up the broken glass!"

"I'm sorry. I'll help you clean it, and I," she said nervously, ". . . will pay to get it fixed."

"I'm good, I'm all set. I don't need your money. Good night, Stephanie."

Springing up catlike, Stephanie snapped back in his face, "I decide when *we* are over!"

"Go home, Stephanie!"

"You know, I leave for Cali in a few days," she snarled with her finger poking Dillon's left shoulder where he heroically endured Emma's death bullet. "C'mon, Dillon, please—"

Quickly taking a few steps away from the wall, Dillon ordered, "Go home, Stephanie, and don't come back. We are over! Next time, I will call the police!"

"Fuck me like you did a week ago, that was the best ever!" Stephanie confessed distraught, spiraling out of control in the long narrow hallway. "Did you fuck Candace like that? Don't you answer that! You know what, I don't care if you did! Oh…oh, I know what it is! And I should have seen it! Stupid me! Kudos, Dillon, you really duped me this time, and I feel like an idiot. I bet . . . I bet you are fucking that . . . MILF state trooper. What's her name *you made me* have lunch with? Oh right . . . Emma. Didn't you? I bet you did—you pig!"

"I had enough of your fucking bullshit!" Dillon yelled. "If you don't leave right now, I'll call the cops!"

"C'mon and fuck me one more time before I leave for college! Please, Dillon!" Stephanie beseeched.

"You leave me no choice!" Dillon yelled as he reached inside the outer pocket of his suit jacket for his mobile.

Quickly, bending down, Stephanie removed her vibrant pink spike heels.

Dillon started to dial.

Stephanie, a second-degree black belt, who was trained by the one and only, Norah Race, started to scream profanities. The anger projected on Stephanie's face was pure anger—rage. Quickly, summoning her violent emotions, she effortlessly managed to gracefully spin around kicking Dillon's cell out of his hand.

Dillon shook his stingy hand in distress. Zero retaliation. Dillon won't hit a woman.

"C'mon, Dillon! I leave for Cali soon!" Stephanie screamed. "What the fuck!"

The next-door tenant abruptly came out in her bathrobe with one hand on her hip, and the other in her hair. Immediately, I started to laugh because one of her hair rollers fell out of her busy head onto the hallway floor.

Before the old woman could utter a word, Stephanie snarled with her pointed finger and barked, "Mind your own fucking business!"

Quickly, retrieving her runaway roller, the frumpy old woman stormed back into her apartment slamming her door. Thump!

Stephanie's eyes started to tear. She walked closer to Dillon with her arms open for a hug. Stepping backwards, he retrieved his cell, and then dashed down the hallway with Stephanie hot on his trail. Dillon passed another trust test.

Dillon, an innocent free man, turned down two, very attractive women. Both willingly threw themselves at him with their ankles-to-ears. Did he reject them because of me? Or did he not want casual sex? But what did Stephanie mean when she said, "It will always be yours." If I had to pick a question to be answered, it would be, did Emma sleep with Dillon?

I did feel bad for Stephanie. I knew her anger all too well, but not from a lover's standpoint. She lost her virginity to him, broke up with him, and once Dillon was with someone else, it drove her mad.

Twenty-five minutes later, my cell chimed again. Looking at my monitor, it was Dillon leaving his apartment with a large-sized, black duffle bag over his right shoulder. How did he get into his place? Oh, my

God, he climbed three stories, probably because he wanted to avoid Stephanie!

But where on earth was he gallivanting too, since it was almost midnight?

31

I RETRIEVED THE video footage when Candace and Dillon first met in the apartment foyer. In spite of the fact that I watched it multiple times, I missed something very important. Dillon recomposed himself with Candace identical to the way he did with me tonight. How did he instantly recompose himself?

Since I knew Paris was six hours ahead, I pressed Li'l Sis.

"Hey, Zoey!" Candace said upbeat. "You're working late."

"Hey, Candace!" I said, matching her cheerful tonality. "Yeah, I'm burning the midnight oil. And I know you're getting ready for work, so I'll be quick," I said knowing she was probably getting ready for today's photo shoot.

"No problem, Zoey," Candace said welcomingly. "I always have time for my big sis and favorite agent. Go ahead and spill."

"I had dinner with Emma, and Dillon tonight," I announced, letting Candace know for the first time Dillon and I met. "And I have a question for you?"

"You guys would make a great couple," Candace said genuinely with enthusiasm. "Go for it, Zoey!"

"Thanks, but I think he's out of my league," I sighed, not knowing if my first time was going to be my last.

"Not true, girlfriend," Candace assured, ignoring my lack of confidence. "I know Dillon, and trust me you're his type. And every day I pray that you two get together."

"Really?" I asked in bewilderment.

"Absolutely!" Candace said confidently.

"Out of curiosity, how come?"

Normally, Candace would quickly respond back witty, but not this time. After a few seconds, Candace admitted, "I broke Dillon's heart, and I never forgave myself. He did everything perfectly for Lewis and I. He gave us love and kindness, and generously laid the world in front of us for the taking. And I left him to pursue my dreams," Candace said, blowing her nose. "My last image of him, and his last words still haunt

87

me to this day. I had to forcefully rip the covers off the bed to say goodbye. And he wouldn't even look at me."

"Wow, really, he wouldn't look at you?"

"It's true, Zoey, and get this, Dillon told me while he was bawling his eyes out face down in the pillow that he would never contact me, and he never wanted to see or hear from me again. I ran out of the apartment crying hysterically," Candace stated, choking up. "The next day, when I was on my way to the airport, I must have called him a minimum of ten times, and he wouldn't answer. And that's when I called Emma because I was concerned for his well-being."

Candace's melancholic voice tone resembled the death of a loved-one. She blew her nose a couple of times, and I knew there had to be more. Desperately, I needed to know why.

Very softly I asked, "But why do you want us to be together?"

"You told me a few weeks ago the reason you have never been involved with someone was because no one could measure up to you father. And I'm willing to bet you that Dillon would measure up, and then some. And also, Zoey, I mean no disrespect to you, but in many ways, you and Dillon are both loners, just like me. And knowing your past and his . . . I just think you guys would make a great couple."

Lost for speech, and in deep thought while Candace's words dissolved into my bloodstream, she was one hundred percent accurate. Like Candace, Dillon and I were loners.

"That means a lot to me," I said, breaking the silence.

"And Zoey, it still kills me that I broke his heart," Candace admitted. "Life is too short, and you both deserve to be happy."

"Thank you, Candace, that means the world to me."

Candace remained silent. In the background, I heard the sound of hangers in motion since she was probably choosing her outfit.

Breaking the silence, I asked, "Dillon told me how you guys met. He mentioned that he was walking away, and you stopped him. Can you please tell me why you stopped him?"

Once again, Candace was lost for words. In the background, I heard her softly weeping.

"What I'm about to tell you is extremely upsetting. Dillon had a disturbing . . . a distressed look on his face. Unfortunately, it was a look I had seen before, and I did nothing. A friend of mine had the exact same upsetting look, and he committed suicide. And I stopped Dillon as he was walking away because I . . . thought—" Candace admitted, sobbing.

Thank you, Candace. You are my second hero for saving Dillon's life. Softly, I said, "It's okay, Candace, and I'm very sorry for your loss."

With tears in my eyes, I waited for about ten seconds. With great curiosity, I asked, "What happened when he walked back to you?"

"And that's the biggest mystery of all. And till this day, I can't figure it out. Dillon just had this incredible—this masculine, oozing sex appeal. I can't explain it . . . I just couldn't resist him," Candace replied, a little bit more upbeat. "He stopped me dead in my tracks, and no one has ever done that to me before."

And it was true, Candace, a supermodel was fidgeting with her long, blonde hair looking downward. And she probably felt like me that Dillon was out of my league. What the fuck did he do to me? He totally spellbound me. But how? What's his secret sauce?

"Hey, Zoey, it's Dillon calling! I'll call you back later on today or tomorrow, love you, bye!"

From the overwhelming spike of enthusiasm in Candace's voice, I knew she still loved Dillon, deeply. And Candace would probably never get over him. So how do I even compete with a 21-year-old supermodel who also has a kind heart, a great personality, and brains? Candace was the all-around, complete and total package. And that's why Dillon mentioned during dinner that he would love to have another Candace. Fuck me!

And why was Dillon calling her so late? Candace just mentioned that he would never contact her. Did Dillon suddenly have a change of heart? Was Dillon still in love with Candace? Did Dillon change his mind because of our dinner? Or did Dillon finally break down, and want to be with Candace, and move to Paris? But more importantly, was my virginity request still alive, or on life support?

And who was I kidding with my husband fantasies of Dillon becoming my lifetime partner. My gut said that if he didn't back out of my pop the cherry request, Dillon and I would be a one-time fling, which I was more than willing to accept. Beggars can't be choosers.

32

######

WITH A HUGE smile, Candace F. Ganski enthusiastically says, "Hi, Dillon!"

"Hi, Candace," Dillon N. Race replies in a monotone voice, "sorry to call you so early."

Candace is startled by Dillon's tone that he's not too overly happy to talk with her since it's been a few weeks of any type of communication.

Upbeat, Candace replies, "No worries, I just hung up the phone with Zoey, and heard you guys had dinner."

"Yeah, Emma was there too," Dillon says in a neutral tone, "but she left early."

"Hey," Candace says, still upbeat, "you and Zoey would make a great couple."

"Thanks, Candace. That means a lot. But the reason for my call is because I wanted to thank you for saving my life. If you didn't stop me when we met in the foyer, I was going to end it," Dillon admits, sounding choked-up. "You are my hero Candace, and I'm forever in your debt."

Candace is lost for words. She tries to mask her teary weeps. Dillon is also sad and feels Candace's pain. He waits for Candace to calm down.

This is Dillon's final goodbye to set Candace free. Doing his best to disguise a sorrowful voice, he says, "And Candace, I want you to know that I'm very happy for you. I really am, for your success, and I should have told you sooner, to tell you how proud I am of you for chasing your dream, and making it come true. But I was selfish and stubborn and I failed you . . ." Dillon pauses with tears streaming down his face, ". . . you deserved better. And I just wanted you to know that I'm truly sorry."

They both remain silent.

Dillon couldn't mask the pain in his voice anymore. "Hey, Candace . . . I" he murmurs, ". . . I only want the best for you. Make us all proud back here in New Britain . . . gotta go now."

Instantly, Candace knows this is the end. Frantically, she blurts out, "Hey, Dillon, for what it's worth, you're the kindest person on earth. And I only wish you came with me. *I miss us. I really do.* But an opportunity like this only comes once in a lifetime, and I had to do this. I didn't want to be sitting on my rocking chair sixty years from now saying to myself, 'what if.' And I'm sorry my decision hurt you. And I never told you this, Dillon, you saved Lewis and me, but in a different way. Thank you for everything. You're our hero and always will be, and we're forever in your debt. Just promise me something, Dillon," Candace begs as her mascara runs down her face.

"What's that?" he asks confusedly, wiping his tears. Deep down, Dillon knows he owes his life to her, and loves her for that.

Candace understands she's at the time-mercy of love's changing seasons. Her new reward, gratification of fame and fortune, unfortunately, comes with sacrifices. The outcome of 'was it worth it' can only be determined at the end of her shelf life modeling career.

"Fifteen years from now," Candace says, planting her hopeful love seed in the windy, cold ground, "if you and I are both single, we get married."

Dillon is speechless.

"Just promise me that you'll think about it," Candace suggests as her last Hail Mary. "I'm late for work. You take care, Dillon, love you."

######

33

MY PHONE RANG. "Hey, Dillon, miss me already?" I asked, smiling, and hopefully he's calling for a more than welcoming—deserving booty call.

Wondering if Dillon would divulge the conversation that he had with the model goddess herself, he said, "I want you to know, Zoey, I spoke with Candace a few minutes ago," Dillon admitted nonchalantly. "And thanked her for saving my life."

Dillon's honesty was refreshing. "Okay, that's great you told her," I said. "And I also spoke with Candace."

"Yeah, she mentioned that as well," Dillon replied, "but I have a question for you. During our dinner, you asked if I saved the president's life, and I had no idea. How did you know?"

Fuck! I had to come clean with my snooping addiction. "It would be easier for you, Dillon, if you could stop by, so I can explain everything."

Dillon asked, "If it's not too late for you, can I swing by later on?"

"No problem, I'm a night owl."

Chuckling at my last comment, he said, "Great, and since it's late, and if you have the space, can I stay over because my balcony sliding door is smashed-in and there's glass everywhere . . . and it's very humid inside my apartment."

Yes, I'm finally going to have a man sleep over—I literally jumped in the air! The man of my dreams would be sleeping over! I wanted to scream at the top of my lungs: "You can stay for the rest of your natural life!"

Be cool, Zoes.

"Yeah, no problem," I said coolly with my fist raised in the air.

"Awesome, thanks, Zoey," Dillon said, relieved. "Do you need anything at the twenty-four-hour grocery store—anything you can think of like food or tissues?"

I let out a loud laugh. Dillon's humor was witty, totally refreshing. But the mere thought of Dillon possibly being poached in public where lonely women roam in the middle of the night didn't gel with me. I just wanted him in my home this very fucking second—imagining him comfortably tied to my bedpost while I hand-fed him green grapes.

"I have everything here," I replied, "plenty of food, and I promise, you won't need a single tissue. Come as you are."

Realizing once again, I put my foot in my mouth, Dillon laughed loudly. His laugh was genuine, and he probably needed some well-deserved humor.

"Thanks for letting me stay, Zoey. I'm meeting Robbie soon, and I should be to you in less than two hours, and oh, by any chance, did you grab my envelope, it was, um, somewhere, um in the booth?" he asked in a nervous tone.

"Yes, I have your envelope, and your sunglasses too!" I said stoked. "They somehow fell out of your jacket pocket."

"Perfect, that's a huge relief! See you soon!"

34

HOPEFULLY, TONIGHT WAS going to be my lucky night. Sensing I would be sleeping with Dillon this very evening, I had to speak with Emma. She deserved to know the truth, and I needed to come clean about *everything*.

Because of Emma, I'm where I am today. Because of Emma, I decided not to slit my wrists. Because of Emma, I fought through adversity, and toughed out life. Because of Emma, I kept wiping the muck off my face when I was constantly being knocked down into mud puddles. Because of Emma, I knew she would never abandon me, no matter what the cat dragged in. Because of Emma's confidence in me, I became a lawyer, and she was courageous enough to put herself on the hook by cosigning my student loans. Because of Emma, I had my first decent paying job with Abe that springboarded my legal practice. Because of Emma, I have Candace, a great friend, and a cash cow client. And now, because of Emma, during her eleventh hour—life and death situation, I found Dillon, who I knew was my soulmate.

Regardless, this was going to be a hard sell as I risked looking reckless and foolish by staging her false emergency. She would probably think that I was playing another prank. And no doubt once the truth was revealed, Emma would become irate. Fuck it, here goes. Picking up my phone, I was about to dial Ems when it rang unexpectedly.

Who in the hell was calling me at this hour? Caller ID displayed: block call. Aggressively, I replied, "Hello!"

"Good evening, Zoey, this is Dillon's grandfather. Did I catch you at an okay time?"

Holy shit! I'm speaking with the number one terrorist in the world. The one and only, Isosceles.

Just stay calm, and be smart, Zoes.

"Yes," I said agitated on purpose, "it's fine sir."

Cordially, Isosceles requested, "Please, call me, Grandpa."

Don't ask him why, just comply, because I didn't want to piss him off, and provoke his short-wick temper when innocent people's lives were at stake. He already blew parts of Tokyo sky-high.

"Okay, Grandpa, how can I help you?" I asked.

Reversing my question, Grandpa firmly retorted, "Maybe, Zoey, I can help you since my untraceable malware alerted me that my family's top-secret files were sent to you. Do you have any questions I can clarify for you?"

Fuck me! For the first time ever, I'm officially hacked! My entire network has been gravely compromised. Dad would probably disown me for my careless mistake. Fuck, now, Grandpa shadowed and controlled all my computer functions, including my smartphone. And more than most likely, he probably listened to my recent calls (Something, an ethical hacker, like myself, has never breached before.) with Candace and Dillon.

"Yes, Grandpa, there are a few questions I have for you. But first, I do want to let you know that Dillon and I spoke with the feds tonight."

"Thank you, Zoey, for sharing that, but I'm not interested in what transpired. Do not reveal any information that incriminates yourself, okay?"

"Copy that."

Grandpa chuckled, then he asked, "So tell me, Zoey, what concerns you?"

Confidently, I asked, "If you're the number one terrorist in the world, how come I, and the rest of the world, don't know about you?"

Nonchalantly, Grandpa confessed, "Because Zoey, the government only wants you, and others to know what they want you to know. The public could not handle the lingering of a catastrophic event."

"Interesting," I said, pausing to ask the most nerve-racking question of my life. "In Dillon's file it says you may want him dead. Is that true?"

"Negative!" Grandpa revealed. "In fact, Zoey, I'm responsible for restarting Dillon's . . . CPR."

"CPR, I don't understand?" I asked, totally confused.

Grandpa admitted, "Dillon successfully . . . killed himself."

Immediately, I had a horrible twinge in my stomach. "I still don't understand?" I asked, baffled.

"There was absolute pandemonium in his bedroom. The worst words in the world anyone could hear was the announcement of death. His parents were beyond devastated. They were distraught when I jumped in, and restarted the all-out-resuscitation. There's no worse noise than hearing a defibrillator constantly going off. He was clinically dead for a .

. . *very long period of time*. By the grace of God, we brought him back. And since I always wear a body cam, I sent you an edited link of the footage. Now, listen, Zoey…listen very carefully, it comes with a very strict warning!" Grandpa stated forcefully. "Be very careful, the video is extremely unsettling."

The 73-minute video arrived in my inbox from an unknown email sender.

Just to make sure Grandpa was telling the truth, I deliberately pressed play in the middle of the video link.

<h1 style="text-align:center">35</h1>

LYING STIFF ON the snow-white carpet floor, Dillon's lifeless eyes were wide opened. His face was bluish blank, and his mouth was ajar. Partially shirtless (his shirt was probably cut with trauma shears since it was off to each side) on his back, his feet were pointing outwards—opposite directions. Two medics and Grandpa kept taking turns with hand chest compressions and also with the defibrillator. Feverishly, they were working in sync, but unfortunately, to no avail. A pale face Norah was erratically pacing around the small bedroom resembling an agitated drug addict in dire need of a fix.

Dillon's lifeless eyes staring at me were jarring. Hauntingly, they resembled Dad's open, dead eyes, exactly. In the nick of time, I reached for my waste basket and puked.

Dead eyes staring back at you didn't blink back; you automatically lost that bout. If your competitive eyeballs wanted a rematch—same losing outcome. But don't forget to take your unwrapped parting gift—a lifelong mindfuck. Sometimes, you see dead eyes in your nightmare when they playfully blinked back with a devilish sparkle—jolting you from sleeping. Sometimes, they unexpectedly flourished while whisking eggs—dead smack in the whirlwind center. Or maybe you figured out how to compartmentalize them in a rotating hourglass, seeing them in specks of sand briskly moving downward, but mysteriously, they twinkle upward. And if you think smelling wild spring flowers while absorbing natural vitamin D will help alleviate your anguish, not so fast. All you have to do is take a leisurely stroll through a park, and look up at the pure cerulean sky. Believe me, it won't take long before you'll witness dead eyes in the form of unadulterated, cotton-like clouds. For three decades, I still painfully experienced all of those ocular occurrences.

If patience was a virtue, dead eyes would only take a victory lap when they successfully crept into your very being, piercing your soul. And that's where the real havoc begins, especially my havoc—Zoey The Zombie, aka "Zombie Girl." And here's the thing, you never forget dead eyes, because they instantly zapped all your vibrant cells in your body, all 30 trillion of them, into oblivion.

The nonstop flooding thoughts of Dillon dead projected more barf. Suddenly, Norah leaped between the medics and Grandpa, sending them backwards. Frantically, she pounded on Dillon's chest with her interlocked hands. She kept screaming—ranting with each feverish blow, "You never said goodbye to me! You're too young to leave this earth! You never said goodbye!"

Brett hoisted Norah up in a reverse bearhug. Wildly, she kicked and screamed in agonizing pain. Over and over, she cried, "Wake him up! Wake him the fuck up!"

Brett struggled to get her out of the bedroom. You could hear Norah's terrifying screaming through the shut door. Unfortunately, I knew *how* her cruel, soul shattering pain felt. And Norah, if it's any consolation, I never said goodbye to my parents. Those words escaped me because I thought I was going to die with them. Maybe I should have died with them, because right before they perished, I was mad at them. Actually, we were arguing about how I couldn't go to Boston with Emma and her delinquent older brothers to a rap concert. My parents were adamant: over their dead bodies.

Boom! The sound was deafening when the door flung open. Barging in, Norah jumped on top of Dillon's lifeless body, clearing out Grandpa and one of the medics, sending them tumbling backwards. Uncontrolled chaos at its finest. Frantically, Norah was repeatedly pounding on his chest trying desperately to resuscitate her only child.

"Wake the fuck up!" Norah wailed, looking into his lifeless eyes. "You never said goodbye! Wake up, Dillon!"

"I'm very sorry, ma'am," replied one of the medics choking up, "your son . . . is dead."

"Wake him up!" Norah demanded with tears streaming down her face. "Help me wake him up! Please wake him up! Wake up, Dillon!"

"I'm very sorry for your loss," announced the other medic looking at his watch. "Time of death: 4:44 p.m."

Brett came back to the pandemonium with a bloody nose. When he grabbed Norah from behind, he was met with a back kick to his midsection—dropping him.

I stopped watching the most horrifying video of my life.

"Thank you, Grandpa, for saving Dillon." I murmured. "He saved my best friend. You're my hero."

Uncontrollably, I wailed for minutes with my head down. My mind was spiraling with intrusive thoughts and morbid emotions.

The powerful domino effect of one precious life, and how it alters future outcomes—future lives, their happiness—their daily sanity. Compounded with the Medusa cold thought, that jarring mindfuck image of Emma lying face down on the highway, dead like roadkill if Grandpa hadn't resuscitated Dillon—I heaved the little bit I had left in my belly.

"It's okay, Zoey, calm down. Take a sip of water and breathe. Dillon is okay now. He's alive and in perfect health. Calm down, Zoey," Grandpa said softly multiple times, trying to comfort me.

The raw sadness emotion I felt was lost forever, had been reborn.

"Zoey!" Grandpa's raised voice jolted me. He demanded, "I want you to yell as loud as you can, Dillon is alive and doing well! Say it five times!"

Screaming at the top of my lungs, I did exactly that, and instantly felt better. While I was gulping water, Grandpa said, "Your dad is one of my heroes."

What! Why? How did he know Dad since he's been dead for years? Talk about a mindfuck! I must stay focused and ignore his last comment.

I asked, "Why did Dillon lie about his failed suicide attempt?"

Was Dillon that good of a liar?

"Just to let you know, my team and I were watching and eavesdropping on your dinner," Grandpa confessed. "They are trained to detect many important things. Dillon didn't know he died, and *we are never* going to tell him."

"How come you, or his parents didn't get him help!" I barked, demanding an answer. "Or send him to a hospital for treatment!"

"Dillon's very hard to physically control. He would have gone ballistic being confined inside a mental hospital. By the way, Candace is also one of my heroes. I was watching the footage over your shoulder, and I'm in debt to her. She did save his life. And hopefully, Zoey, you will be one of my heroes as well. As her agent, what do you think she may want?"

What? How will I be his hero? I'm not a military person.

"She would love another guy like Dillon, she mentioned it to me multiple times."

"Roger that," said a cheerful grandfather. "What else would she enjoy?"

Wow, was Grandpa a match-maker?

Softly, I asked, "I will ask her if that's okay with you?"

"That's fine, Zoey. I just released your network."

36

FUCK! I KNEW Grandpa copied and downloaded all my sensitive and private information. But for some odd reason, I wasn't too concerned.

Fuck it, let's test Grandpa without lying or revealing anything.

"Thanks, Grandpa, now, in Dillon's file, it states he saved the president's life. Is that true?" I asked with great curiosity.

"Yes, Dillon disrupted my plans to detonate certain landmarks, and assassinate the president. My new target on American soil will be successfully executed within a month. Just to let you know, he didn't lie to you tonight, Zoey. The feds never told him."

"I see," I replied, treating this phone conversation like I was in a heated deposition. "Now, it also states in Dillon's file that he's protected by a special task force from the Secret Service, FBI, and Homeland Security. Is that correct?"

"Yes, but not as you perceive it. Those knuckleheads couldn't properly guard a fish bowl. For some reason, they think I might kill my only grandson, so they tail Dillon unbeknownst to him because he successfully stopped my plans. And they are near him at all times."

Letting out a sigh of relief, I had to regain my composure and focus. How could you not know you're being tailed all the time?

Okay, Zoes, now ask it!

My stomach was in a horrible twisted knot when I asked, "Why are you going to harm a large mass of innocent people?"

"Zoey, most people want to be lied to, but they don't know it," Grandpa rattled-off, without missing a beat, deliberately dodging my direct missile of a question. "Can we make an upfront agreement right now?"

"Yes, Grandpa."

"I know you have been telling me the truth so far which is refreshing," he admitted. "Let's keep it that way going forward, okay?"

"Okay," I replied since he's my new hero.

Casually, he asked, "Are you in love with Dillon?"

I couldn't lie because it was one hundred percent true. I love Dillon Race! And Grandpa probably had seen my Dillon shrine by now, consisting of countless photos and videos. Plus, Grandpa was more advanced than me at technology, which was extremely rare.

"Yes!" I said with utmost conviction.

"Thank you, Zoey," he said. "Would you like to marry him and start a family?"

Please, let the romance gods bless and unite our naked bodies at once so we can get started. "Yes, Grandpa!" I said confidently without any hesitation. "I would love that!"

"That's music to my ears, Zoey," Grandpa said with excitement in his voice. "How can I help you accomplish your goal?"

"I don't think Dillon's one hundred percent into me," I admitted, sounding a little defeated. Then I sighed, "And I think he's doing me a favor. Plus, I'm fourteen years older than him, and he's way out of my league."

37

"**HE WILL BE** in your home soon, and that is a wonderful place to start," Grandpa responded in a very reassuring voice. "I do know one thing for sure, Dillon is smitten with you."

Instantly, my body was energized with Grandpa's smitten comment. I wanted to jump out of my comfortable chair, and start doing cartwheels on a beach. But out of nowhere, my self-doubting, cyclone winds blew me over, stuck out its helping hand, pulled me up, and then sucker punched me in the abdomen.

"Are you sure, Grandpa?" I asked, feeling a little queasy in my belly. "Because he wants to wait, and get to know one another. And he wants to take me somewhere . . . and I'm ready now."

"You must be bold, Zoey, going forward," Grandpa said with vigor, "in order to discover your future."

Pondering Grandpa's last comment, he was one hundred percent accurate. I needed to quickly find and bring my 'A' game.

"By the way, I am a big fan of your father," Grandpa revealed. "I'll never forget where I was when he made the 59-yard field goal to beat Army. I haven't been that happy in such a long time. It is an honor to speak with Navy royalty."

A picture of Mom popped up dead center on my computer screen. Mom found out right before kickoff that she was pregnant with me. She witnessed the historic football game when Dad kicked the record-breaking winning field goal. The picture Grandpa sent was spectacular because you could see Mom standing with a sea of Navy fans with their hands in the air as the football sailed through the goalpost.

"Thank you for the awesome picture, Grandpa," I said, slightly choked up. "You just made my night. Unfortunately, my parents died a long time ago."

"I know dear, I brutally murdered the drunk driver who killed your parents," Grandpa confessed smoothly. "And that drunk bastard was also a low-life piece of shit because he had been arrested multiple times for

102

beating his wife and children. I made him suffer a very slow and extremely painful death."

Thank God Emma was sick that day when we were traveling to Mom's roller derby bout. Boom! We were struck by that fucking drunktard driving a stolen semi-trailer truck. Our vehicle was lifted into the air, and when we landed, we had rolled-over several times, smashing into a tree.

We were suspended upside down. Glass, debris, and the overwhelming smell of gasoline were prevalent. Instantly, I knew that Dad was deceased from the rearview mirror. His dead eyes staring lifeless at me were jarring.

Somehow, Mom mustered up enough strength to unbuckle her seatbelt. Her head hit the roof. Disoriented and in distress, she was gasping for precious air. Mom shook Dad a few times to no avail. Determined to help me, she hurled her body backward, and somehow managed to release my seatbelt.

She so desperately wanted to live, but I couldn't stop the bleeding with my fingers pressing on her throat, and physically, I couldn't lift her to safety. Feeling helpless in the constrained wreckage, I wanted to perish with them. But under no circumstance would Mom allow that to happen. Placing her hand on my arm, Mom gazed into my eyes. She smiled faintly. Frozen for words, I smiled back. Squeezing with the little strength she had left, Mom's last blood-spurting choppy words she gasped in short sentences were: "Dad and I love you. We will always be with you. Stay strong. Emma needs you. Get out now, Zoey!"

Before I could respond back, Mom's eyes closed for the final time.

It's better not to know when it's the last time you're going to see someone you love before they die because it's too emotionally awkward. I kissed Mom on her bloody cheek. "I love you, Mom," I said.

As I looked at Mom and Dad, tears streamed down my face until I was startled by a sudden noise. My parents' teenage love song, "Just Like Heaven" by The Cure, miraculously started playing on the radio.

Immediately, the beautiful melody and lyrics lifted my grief. And at that very moment, I knew that was a sign from Mom, and she was lovingly right, and I had to see Emma. I needed to see her again because I couldn't leave her all alone in this world.

Before I wiggled out of the mangled wreck, I kissed Daddy on the cheek. For the very last time, I said, "I love you more." Tragically, I'll never hear Dad say those special words back to me ever again.

My head was buzzing, and I had bloody scrapes and cuts everywhere on my body. Walking backwards away from our burning car, I prayed my parents would miraculously climb out and appear when our car exploded, lifting me more than five feet airborne. Wishing I was in a nightmare, I sprung up looking back in horror, watching my parents through the ferocious flames being scorched.

The overwhelming metallic smell, and sticky feel of Mom's blood on my hands, face, and caked in my hair made me snap. That's when I ran toward the drunk bastard. The putrid smell of my parents' flesh hovered over me when I took the son of a bitch with his broken bottle of booze to the ground, striking him mercilessly until the cops pried me off.

Weighing less than a hundred pounds, I was thrown in the backseat of a police car kicking and screaming—watching the drunktard stumble, laugh, and plead to the cops and medics on the scene that another person was responsible for the deadly crash.

When my parents perished, I was left all alone in this world wishing someone would save me from life's hardships. My teenage anger that had been suppressed for almost two decades came to a violent rapid boil. Without thinking, I blurted out loudly, "Thank you so much, Grandpa, for killing him! I wish I could have killed him myself! When I heard the news, he was found dead at Colt State Park, I was thrilled he got what he fucking deserved! Not only did he kill my parents, but that was his fourth DUI. And when I see you, Grandpa, and hopefully soon, I will buy you a beer!"

"Your stock keeps rising, my dear," Grandpa replied. "Please, click the live link I just sent."

Without further ado, I went to my inbox, then clicked the live link.

Oh, my God! I gasped!

To my terror-stricken surprise, two women in their mid to late twenties were sitting on their knees next to a large, rounded, open wooden barrel filled with murky water. They were held captive in an enclosed, mid-size, wall-to-wall, light gray concrete looking industrial room with their hands zip-tied behind their backs. The gloomy concrete torture chamber forecasted death.

"You better let me fucking go!" ordered one of the captive girls without any fear in her voice. She repeated, "You better let me fucking go, you fucking dickwad!"

"Silence!" Grandpa ordered firmly. "Or suffer harsh consequences!"

The other young woman looked terrified, but she had a much bigger problem than her captive self because she appeared to be no less than five months pregnant. She was breathing erratically, sobbing to herself with tears streaming down her face. She was trying her best not to utter a peep from her shivering lips.

38

"GRANDDAUGHTER, DO YOU recognize these girls?"

"No, Grandpa," I replied nervously, "I don't."

"My team apprehended two of the four girls who violated Dillon. And just to let you know, we are both on speaker, and they can hear us," Grandpa announced curmudgeonly. "You can speak, and choose their destinies at any time, Granddaughter."

"Thank you, Grandpa, I was going to track them down myself and—"

Abruptly, I was interrupted when Grandpa ordered without any hesitation in his eerie voice, "The devil is disguised in many different formats, and in plain sight, just like a salad bar, or a sinfully beautiful woman. Drown the mouthy one!"

Startling everyone, a very loud, squeaky steel door opened in the far-right corner of the torture room. A stocky looking masked man wearing military fatigues came walking out toward the captive rapists. The looks in their scared eyes spoke volumes.

Aggressively, the military man uprooted the nonpregnant woman by her short hair. She was wearing cream colored shorts, a brown tank top, and sandals. She had to be more than six feet tall with a very husky, buxom build. She looked manly—obesely, probably weighing close to 300 pounds.

"You're going to pay for this!" she yelled fearlessly, trying her hardest to stay away from the rustic barrel. "You cocksucker!"

"Hush, hunny," the military man said mockingly, jerking her closer to the cask.

"No!" she screamed.

Her head was viciously dunked, then barbarically held down into the black water. Gasping, I covered my mouth. After five seconds, her feet were moving erratically in the air when her flip flops abruptly flew off.

Uncontrollably, the pregnant woman was crying. She started screaming—sobbing—repeatedly, "I'm pregnant, please let me go!"

Oh, my God! Was this really happening?! Thinking I was demented in the manner in how I protected loved ones, and it wasn't many, Grandpa

105

took it to a whole other level. Every second that passed resembled an hour. Being experienced in intense legal negotiations, I was trained to keep accurate time counts in my head. Silence during contract negotiations was where the real money was made. Slowly, I started to count past twenty-four seconds. How long would Grandpa continue the water drowning torture?

At exactly thirty seconds, Grandpa commanded, "Stop!"

The military man violently hoisted the young rapist out of the gloomy barrel by her soaked hair. He dragged her body until she was near the wall speaker and a surveillance camera located in the upper left corner of the concrete wall and ceiling. Standing behind her, he planted her feet on the ground, and then placed his hand underneath her chin raising her head upward.

"Who are the other two cowards who did this to Dillon!" Grandpa demanded.

"Fuck you and fuck your granddaughter!" she yelled fearlessly, then purposely, she spat water upward at the speaker and camera. "I'm the daughter of the fucking devil, and I'm not in disguise you piece of shit coward!" she shouted wildly while simultaneously raising her right leg backwards up and into the groin of the military man, dropping him to his knees.

Unbelievable, I couldn't believe the balls on this evil, soaking wet, piece of shit rapist. Brazenly, she spat upward at the speaker while she kicked her captor.

"Hey, Grandpa!" the she-devil rapist yelled without fear in her voice looking possessed in her facial features. "If your pecker still works, and you have a set of balls between your legs, untie—"

The she-devil rapist was interrupted by the temporarily disabled military man when he rolled over, then reached up with a punch, striking her in the lower back. She fell-forward twisting her restrained left shoulder and arm into the concrete wall. Awkwardly, she landed on the unforgiving hard floor.

"You cocksucker!" she hollered in agony. "Be a real man, and fight me face-to-face!" the rapist challenged while rolling on the slab with her hands zip tied behind her back.

Mom and Dad's gruesome death flashed before my eyes. A frozen image of Dad's loving and gentle eyes—open for eternity flashed in my head. Mom's last gasping words as she mothered me one last time lingered in my ears. And I just couldn't escape the metallic smell, and the pasty raw feel of her blood plastered all over my hands and face and caked in my hair. It was permanently etched in my psyche. And now, the haunting mindfuck visual of Dillon's dead eyes staring at me lifeless, ruptured my stitched-up soul.

Yo, Zoey The Zombie, what about Dillon's brains splattered all over the bathtub?

Whoosh, a tsunami of my darkest emotions escaped from the deepest recess of hell. My inner she-devil from my teenage days resurfaced. Immediately, my blood boiled viciously in unadulterated hatred.

Where have you been, girl? It's been a long time. Welcome back, Zombie Girl!

Okay, you devil-cunt rapists, let the fucking games begin.

How about we fight fire with fucking fire.

With the utmost vocal authority, I ordered, "Drown the pregnant bitch!"

39

RISING TO HIS feet, the masked military man appeared to be in groin pain. Bending down, he caught the mouthy rapist rolling away. Uprooting her with a fistful of hair, she was forcefully slammed face first into the merciless concrete.

Screaming in agonizing pain, she was yanked downward, then placed upright sitting on her fat ass. With her back against the concrete slab, she was bleeding profusely from her nose. A few seconds later, she spit out a tooth.

"You have the best seat in the house you fucking bitch," barked the military man hobbling in groin pain toward the sobbing pregnant captive. "Enjoy the show when I drown your prego friend."

With blood oozing from her busted up nose, the mouthy rapist bitch yelled, "Don't you fucking dare! She has pregnancy diabetes!"

"This is where the fun starts!" the military man shouted, mocking the mouthy, less one tooth rapist. "Welcome to hell, you devil bitch!"

Forcefully, the military man grabbed a fistful of hair uprooting the pint-sized pregnant woman. She yelped. Her feet barely touched the concrete floor as he dangled her in a slow circle-walk around the dark oak cask.

"Don't you dare do it!" the mouthy rapist pleaded. "Drown me instead!"

Forcefully, I ordered, "Drown! Her! Now!"

Pleading, "No! Please, no!" the pint-sized expectant mother screamed as her body jerked out of control in horror. "I'm pregnant! I'll tell you—"

Aggressively, her words were submerged when the expectant mother with a medical condition was dunked face-first into the barrel of murky water. Immediately, I started counting precious, oxygen-deprived seconds.

During the first five seconds, the pregnant woman's zip-tied hands and legs were moving erratically. At fourteen seconds, all her body motions stiffened, and then remained that way as I counted lifeless, limp seconds in my head.

"She's fucking pregnant! She has diabetes! She's not moving! Fucking stop! She's not moving!" the soaking wet bitch rapist begged repeatedly with the ruptured, bloody nose. She was screaming, hysterically crying, but not from physical pain, but from the fear of her friend's death. "Fucking stop!"

I screamed—ordered, "Keep fucking drowning her!"

"I will tell you everything. Please stop!" begged the not so tough anymore rapist cunt. "Please stop!"

Nope bitch, you fucked with the wrong woman! And you raped my future husband. And you rapist cunt, I'm immune to have zero feelings at times ever since the death of my parents.

So, ladies, how does it feel to be violated? At twenty-three seconds, I yelled with fucking authority, "Stop!"

Instantly, she was yanked out of the barrel, then placed on her butt. The military man was behind the expectant mother holding her upright with a fistful of wet hair while slapping her face with the other, trying to wake her.

"You killed her! You killed my best friend!"

"I'm going to kill you next, you cunt!" I yelled—promised the missing tooth rapist.

To my surprise, the military man laid the pregnant woman flat on her back, then took off his mask. Immediately, he started mouth-to-mouth resuscitation. After a few hand compressions on her chest, she started to cough-up water. Hysterically crying, she was shown no mercy because she was violently hoisted upright by her hair and then placed on her knees. Her soaked head resembled the slow remains of a recent shut off water hose. Loudly, the pregnant woman kept coughing up water. But what alarmed me the most was when the military man pulled his pistol from his tactical belt. Instantly, his gun was pointed at the back of her head.

Startling everyone, the squeaky, heavy steel door reopened. Another substantial masked soldier conjured—walking briskly toward the not-so-brazen-anymore rapist. Forcefully, he grabbed a fistful of her short hair, and from her sitting position she was barbarically dragged several feet, then placed next to the crybaby rapist.

And also, his gun was pointed at the back of her head.

Perfect timing, and not missing a beat, I fucking shouted with the utmost conviction, "If I don't have the other two names in ten seconds, I will barge through the door, and *I will personally* drown both of you fucking cunts to death in the devil's barrel! Starting with the pregnant rapist!"

The silence was deafening.

Without warning, I bluffed—yelled! "Ten! Nine! —"

Instantly, the count was halted with mutual, terrifying survival screams. The young women sounded like two canaries singing off-key in a death-pod. Both soaking wet rapists squealed like petrified pigs, and gave up the names of the other two guilty accomplices.

"Now, fucking tell me exactly what happened," I ordered firmly while Grandpa remained deathly silent.

Listening to the heinous details that Dillon physically suffered at such a very young age, and the mental abuse he psychologically endured into his adolescence increased my anger to a paramount, dark emotion I'd never felt before.

Don't you worry, Dillon, as promised, these rapists will be punished!

While digesting if I should permanently drown the two and a half women, Grandpa casually asked, "Granddaughter, should I kill them both now?"

"I'm not sure," I said hesitantly, "yet." Instantly, my emotions went one-eighty, from extreme anger—death to compassion—life. With the worst twinge in my stomach, I declared, "I have to think about it."

Grandpa announced, "Granddaughter, you have sixty seconds to decide!"

All of a sudden, slowly, lowering from the ceiling beams, a large-sized digital clock appeared with red numbers. The death countdown was already in progress.

"If there is no answer, Granddaughter," said Grandpa in an eerie tone, "they die!"

The two guilty rapists screamed at the top of their lungs, pleading for their young tainted lives. "Please, Granddaughter, don't kill us!" they screamed and begged repeatedly in agonizing horror. "Don't kill us, Granddaughter!"

Everything seemed surreal, and was happening in slow motion. The two masked military men standing behind the guilty rapists simultaneously cocked their guns.

Somehow, my mouth became cemented. I was so far out of my revenge realm. I never gave anyone the ultimate death sentence. And now, for the first time in my life, I would be responsible for their destinies, including an innocent, unborn baby.

My thoughts were racing. Remember, Zoes, empathy *is* weakness, and so *is* compassion. Don't let your emerging emotions of—*is* this heinous act forgivable determine their rightful outcome. Unquestionably, Zoes, it's death!

Hey, Zombie Girl, let's flip a two-headed coin. Will it be a speedy bullet to the back of their guilty heads—spaghetti splatter? Or pristinely preserve their sorry-ass keisters by turtle drowning them—bottoms up? Tick-tock!

40

SUDDENLY, I THOUGHT what would Dillon want. What justice would he hand down? Truly, I believed he had a weak spot for women. The wicked, fucked-up story I just heard about how he lost his virginity, in the ugliest manor was unforgivable. Those girls treated him worse than a neglected, overflowing porta-potty. His first time should have been special, something he and Stephanie could remember for the rest of their lives, even if their love never went the distance. I really felt the lie Dillon was living with was far worse than the heinous acts itself. Regardless, did the guilty rapists deserve to die?

Dillon probably didn't want Stephanie to know because she would have sought revenge, and thrown her life away. He protected her without her knowledge, and bore more pain by living with a lie at such a young age. It was the daily living with a deep-rooted lie that kept Dillon's psyche toxic. A few hours ago, I saw a strong man crumble before my eyes, and it slayed me. Was that the only reason why he killed himself? Or was that only part of the equation? Was his childhood so fucked up that it compounded his decision to terminate himself? I just didn't know. And God forbid if I get caught, I knew Dillon wouldn't want me to throw my life away.

Zoes, do I want to play God? Do I want to live with the ultimate decision? How would Dillon judge my actions? Could he forgive me for killing them?

After thirty seconds of them begging and screaming for their young tainted lives, the pregnant woman started to vomit. She was hyperventilating while pleading, "Please . . . please . . . don't . . . don't kill me and my . . . my twin babies! Please! Please have . . . have mercy! Have mercy! Please, don't kill my twin babies!"

No Mercy! Kill them now, Zombie Girl! Just give the goddamn fucking order!

Don't listen to her. You're better than this. Don't do it, Zoes!

Kill them now!

With thirteen seconds remaining on the death countdown clock, I instructed, "Grandpa, they will all go to prison. I will infest all their computer devices with incriminating child pornography."

"Thank you, Granddaughter!" they simultaneously cheered—more like roared. "Thank you, Granddaughter! Thank you!"

The ironic thing was the two bitches kept repeatedly thanking me for their upcoming jail sentences.

"Very well, Granddaughter. My team will handle it," Grandpa promised.

Instantly, our live feed ended. Phew! I was so relieved that I didn't hand down four death sentences. And hopefully, for the rest of my life, I'll never have to experience that nerve-racking decision. However, the rapists' despicable actions warranted a suitable punishment, but it didn't command the ultimate death sentence.

"Thank you, Grandpa, for the second-best day in my life," I said, relieved since I didn't kill anyone. "And thanks for using your speedy resources."

"You are very welcome, Zoey. And now, I have a beer thirst."

Fuck, I could use a stiff drink after that harrowing experience. "Roger that."

"Granddaughter, do I have your permission to land my helicopters on your property?"

<h1 style="text-align:center">41</h1>

MY STOMACH WAS rumbling, and I desperately needed to fuel up for our upcoming meeting. So, while I was waiting for Grandpa's militia to arrive, I scarfed down an overstuffed turkey sandwich.

Fortunately, I resided in a secluded, wooded area with a big, open backyard in South Windsor, and routinely hospital helicopters flew over my property. Within fifteen minutes, two ear-piercing military helicopters touchdown.

Waving my hand in a welcoming motion, Grandpa and one other older looking military man entered through the sliding glass door directly into the living room. Briskly walking up to Grandpa, we embraced in an amicable hug. After all, Grandpa *is* my hero for bringing Dillon back to life. Quickly, he dropped his backpack, and excused himself to use the bathroom.

His wing man left a large, brand new, blue wheeled suitcase on the living room floor, and then quickly exited to join six military men sporting high caliber rifles. Two men were guarding the outside sliding glass door, and the other four men were further out into the woods guarding a deeper perimeter.

When Grandpa returned, I noticed he was dressed in camouflage military fatigues wearing a body cam. Despite the fact that Grandpa was very old, he didn't portray it. He looked to be Dillon's height and well-built. Being the number one terrorist in the world, I was taken aback that he didn't frisk me for a weapon. He must have really trusted me.

I handed Grandpa a cold bottle of beer with a glass. "Please, let's sit at the table," I said, pointing. "Are you hungry, I can make you something?"

I couldn't believe that Grandpa was ninety-nine. He was bald with a shiny, slightly freckled head, very fit, and looked—moved as if he was in his early sixties. His skin was youthful, radiant.

"Thanks for the beer," he said, handing me back the clean glass. "Do you have eggs? If you do, I eat them with cayenne pepper."

Jumping to my feet, I replied, "Yes, I have both . . . I will make them for you now," wondering what was in the expensive-looking luggage.

"Please, sit-down, Zoey, and relax," he ordered, then took a swig of beer.

That was very peculiar, why did he ask that?

"Can I get anything for your men, I meant to say your team, like waters, or—"

Interrupting, he said, "No thank you, they are fine."

"Okay, no problem. I can't believe you're ninety-nine," I admitted, a little skeptical. Wanting to know his secret, I asked, "How do you look so young?"

"Here's my aging proverb," he stated. "Aging is for idiots. And for the vast lazy. The fountain of youth resides in moderate alcohol consumption. And the underlining secret to prevent aging is endlessly rooted," he declared in his proverb, and whatever the fuck his last comment meant.

Slowly, I nodded my head.

"Listen, Zoey, time is of the essence," Grandpa said, pointing to his large-faced, military tactical watch. "And we have to cover important ground."

Getting right to the point because he seemed to be rushed, I blurted out, "Grandpa, you and I both know, " I sighed, ". . . this falling in love thing won't be an easy task."

"You are right, Zoey, and again, time is of the essence, for the two of you," he admitted, staring into my eyes. "And I would love for Dillon to play football for Navy."

He must be the biggest fan I'd ever seen. "I don't understand," I said bewildered. "Why is it so important to you that Dillon plays football for the Navy?"

"I don't have enough time to explain because he'll be here soon," he retorted. "It's almost like me asking you about your fixation with Dillon."

Guilty, he had me there. It would take me days to explain my insane obsession.

"But Grandpa, he hasn't graduated high school. And the paperwork filing with the NCAA . . . there's a lot of red tape. How can that all get done in time?" I asked all frazzled.

"You don't have to worry about any details. With my vast and speedy resources, and government influence, I will handle everything for you both," Grandpa assured.

"Okay, it just seems like you would have to pull a lot of strings."

He chuckled, then said, "It does seem like that. However, public officials, especially the ones with influence and power do *not* say no to me. Or they pay with harsh consequences!"

I believed him wholeheartedly. "In Grandpa, I trust."

Grandpa let out a quick chuckle. "Zoey, all you have to do is," he paused, smiling, he said, "just have fun, and let nature take its course."

My lonely, self-doubting, bitch beast residing deep inside my consciousness emerged. And she started to negatively chirp—peck my ear off.

42

LOST IN SELF-DOUBT, and negative thoughts, my eyelids drifted downward. When was the last time I mopped my kitchen floor?

"Zoey," Grandpa said, startling my neglectful chores, "your only focus is to have Dillon fall in love with you. And since you already are in love with him, you are already halfway there. I'm counting on you to make that happen. Do you think you can do that?" he asked. But was that really an underlying threat?

But why did Grandpa want Dillon to fall in love with me? "Grandpa, it's going be a tough battle," I sighed, throwing my hands hastily in the air. "He's out of my league."

"No, Zoey, you got it backwards," Grandpa said pithy, "you are out of his league. Can I make a suggestion to kick things off for you?"

Grandpa wasn't lying. He believed it, and more importantly, he believed in me! Now, I quickly needed to believe it. Okay, Zoes, it's time to start getting comfortable being uncomfortable.

I nodded my head for his input and replied, "Yes."

"Another piece of advice, wear tight yoga pants, or leggings. You have a great figure, Zoey, and wear something that shows off your upper body. And make sure you walk in front of him often. In that suitcase over there," he said pointing with his finger, "are clothing items in your size that Dillon is attracted to."

Grandpa rose from his chair, and I followed his lead. We walked to the living room where the large-sized blue suitcase stood upright. It took him a few seconds to open it.

I was surprised to see an array of neatly folded clothing items, all with visible price tags. There were yoga pants and exercise clothing, skirts, tops, shorts, and stylish short dresses—all with matching accessories. I was very impressed.

"Guys like sex appeal," he confessed with unwavering eye contact. "And you most definitely have a great figure to advertise, so put it to use, understand?"

The high-end quality clothing and accessories probably cost well over three thousand dollars. However, I didn't offer to pay for them because I felt it would offend him. "Yes, Grandpa, I do and *will,* and thank you so much for the clothes."

Smiling, Grandpa said as we walked back to the kitchen table, "You are very welcome, Zoey."

Once we were seated, he reached into his backpack. Grandpa placed his laptop on the kitchen table, then opened it.

"Look where Dillon's eyes are," he said.

I started to laugh.

"There could be mobs of bouncing kangaroos juggling panda bears circling around him, and he wouldn't notice," Grandpa revealed. "And that's why he didn't realize he was being followed by the feds when he was with Candace."

Grandpa's surveillance images were probably taken from a military-grade drone. Dillon's eyes were glued to Candace's ass. Laughing for a few seconds, I thought about Emma's phrase she coined for a person being absolutely fucking oblivious: "virgin clueless." Dillon goggled Candace's ass. Actually, his eyeballs were affixed to it. Grandpa showed me other eye images of Dillon gawking Candace's derriere. If I was a guy, my fixated eyes would be guilty too. No wonder why Dillon couldn't keep a clear thought in his head.

Now, Grandpa's crash course on sex appeal was all making sense; he wanted to give me an advantage—a leg-up if you will. That's what I successfully did with all of my clients—stacked the deck in their favor.

"Let me speed this up for you since we are running out of time, and I must be brutally honest with you. And Zoey, I apologize in advance if I sound crude. Men are easy to understand. They are either horny or hungry, or they want to relax, or be left alone. And always remember the three 'f's' in any relationship. Feed him well, fuck him often, and above all else, just be friends. It's that simple, capeesh?"

Making a mental note about my lack of culinary skills, I said giggling, "Thanks, Grandpa, for the crash course."

"You are welcome. Any other questions, Zoey?"

I needed to know why. It killed me not to know. Ask it again, Zoes!

43

NERVOUSLY, I ASKED, "Why do you plan to do future mass destruction?"

"Zoey, you already asked me that question, how come?" Grandpa asked with a slightly aggravated voice tone.

Now, for the biggest statement of my life. "Because if I can convince Dillon to play football for the Navy, I know we will win more games. I don't want your plans interfering with the media news overshadowing our wins every week." Now, I had to make him feel like he was in control. "But as you said my only focus is Dillon, and I'm sure you'll do what's best." Now, for the knockout punch. "But how sweet would it be Grandpa when Navy plays Alabama without any media distractions in the National Championship Game."

Grinning ear to ear, Grandpa bizarrely glanced at his watch for three solid seconds. "Nothing would make me happier, besides great-grandchildren. And Zoey, I've been alive on this earth for 871,547 hours, and I wish you were in more of them. Tell you what, I will take your last comment under further consideration. Thank you for the recommendation."

Smiling, I warmly said, "You're welcome, and oh, one more thing, Grandpa."

"Yes, Zoey."

Dead serious, I asked, "With your permission, can I call the head coach?"

His eyes widened. "Why, Zoey?" he asked, puzzled.

"Ever since I was a young child, I watched every Navy football game with my dad. To this very day, I watched every game, and last season by far, was the worst play-calling I'd ever seen. And when Dillon is out there, I will not tolerate poor play-calling. It drives me fucking nuts. Since I watched many of Dillon's high school football highlights online, you and I both know when he's on offense, he's good for at least six positive yards. And I refuse for his talents to be foolishly wasted. Can I please see your laptop?"

"Sure," Grandpa said, startled, turning it my way.

I pulled up the Navy-Air Force game from last season. "Watch this play," I said. "It's third and inches, and we have the ball on our own 48-yard line. Our running back for the entire year was averaging 3.7 yards per carry. In fact, in this game he was averaging over five yards per carry. The Air Force was having problems stopping him. We should have ran it for the first down, or called a quarterback sneak. And what do we do, we threw the ball thirty yards in the air—of course, for an incomplete pass! Really? Fucking really! I threw my remote control when I saw that play. And if my dad was alive, he would have been outraged!"

"Zoey, my dear, you are true Navy royalty! And undoubtedly, you are my favorite family member, and *we* must make it official! As God as my witness, I had that exact same play on my notes to go over with the coach. And I will *not* tolerate any more foolish play-calling as well! Tell you what, you get Dillon to commit to Navy, and we will have a conference call with him together. I promise you, my dear."

"I look forward to that, Grandpa. And one last request, please don't harm my best friend, Emma, and her family," I begged with an awful pit in my stomach. "If Dillon and I start a new chapter, she'll probably end our friendship."

44

"I PROMISE, ZOEY, I would never harm them because it would take away from your only focus," Grandpa assured, staring me in the eyes. "I need your head in the game. And for argument sake, Zoey, if it doesn't work out between you and Dillon, there will be zero recourse for your friend. You have my word."

Phew! Because I only have Emma and her family in this world. "Thank you so much, Grandpa," I said with relief.

"You are welcome. And by the way, I deposited a half million dollars into your bank account for loss of income." Grandpa announced, businesslike. "If you feel that is not enough just let me know."

"No, Grandpa, you don't have to do that," I said, pleading with my hands, "it's totally unnecessary, and way too much!"

"It's nonnegotiable!" he ordered firmly. "You are the daughter of Patrick Leary who kicked the greatest field goal in Navy's history. And you should also eat and drink for free, for the rest of your life…that's why I paid for your dinner."

Do not challenge him.

I needed to know more details. "Thank you. And oh, how will Dillon and I be together if he plays for the Navy?"

"Zoey, my dear, one step at a time, and please don't overthink things. Trust me, everything will work out for the two of you when he commits," Grandpa assured, rising to his feet. "Like I said before, all you have to do is be yourself, just have fun, and let nature take its course. I must leave now."

"Roger that, Grandpa," I said knowing the challenge of the task on hand.

Grandpa extended his hand, helping me to my feet. As we hugged goodbye he said, "Next time I see you, I look forward to tasting your eggs with cayenne pepper."

45

DILLON KNOCKED LOUDLY. Rising from my leather chair, my heart was racing. Briskly, I walked to welcome him. Regardless, if tonight was going to be the night I lost my virginity, I had to come clean about all my snooping.

When I opened the door, Dillon sported tan khaki shorts and a dark-blue, tight-fitting tank top exposing his bulging, ripped muscles. I gasped. He looked so fucking hot!

Immediately, we embraced. Near my ear, he said, "Thanks for letting me stay, Zoey. It really means a lot."

"You're welcome, Dillon."

I wanted him so bad, but not under any false pretense. Mutually, we stepped back when he interrupted my next set of words.

"You look more beautiful without your makeup," Dillon complimented, gazing into my eyes with genuine sincerity in his voice. "You look absolutely stunning, Zoey," he said, pausing, "you are timelessly . . . breathtakingly beautiful."

Instantly, my heart melted. That was the sincerest string of compliments I'd ever received. Dillon knew how to make me feel desired.

Fuck it! We both lunged at each other. We were lost in a deep, passionate French kiss for about fifteen seconds initiating my sex hormones to surge.

Like an idiot, I stopped the festivities. I had to because my lifetime friendship with Emma was at stake. We always promised each other that no man would ever interfere or destroy our sacred sisterhood.

"Dillon, I have to be one hundred percent honest with you, before we go any further."

"Can it wait until tomorrow?"

Yes! Dillon wanted me now. Woot!

"No," I said. And that was the last thing I wanted to say.

"Can you please give me the quick version," Dillon requested—more liked begged.

Go for it, Zoes!

"Besides being a lawyer, I'm also a computer hacker," I confessed. "For the last several weeks, I've been snooping in your personal life and business affairs. And I know just about everything about you."

Dillon's eyes started to bulge. He looked startled. His head shifted slightly left, and I thought he was about to say something, but didn't.

Hurry up, Zoes, now sell it for real. It's all or nothing!

Quickly, I extended both my hands. Instantly, he welcomed them with a warm smile. Gazing into his soft blue eyes, I wholeheartedly said with the utmost conviction, "And Dillon, I'm head over heels in love with you!"

46

IF DILLON RAN for the hills, I would completely understand. With our hands connected, he gave me the biggest smile pulling me in for an embrace. Quickly, he kissed my lips.

Very excited, he stepped back and asked, "Where's my envelope?"

Taking Dillon's hand, I briskly walked him into the command center. Once we entered my semi-dark, screen lit only, small office, he released my hand. Curiously, he walked closer toward my chair as I turned on the light. His eyes were glued to my self-sufficient active desk with all the live monitoring screens in progress. His face contorted.

Pointing to my special dedicated bundle of joy screen, Dillon asked in a skeptical voice, "Is that . . . Eloise sleeping?"

"Yes," I confessed.

Did I have a runner? Without saying a word, Dillon looked up in amazement, and spotted on all four corners of my office walls were oversized color pictures of himself—at every age of his life in chronicle order. His eyes widened. I was expecting him to dash and leave skid marks.

Looking around totally perplexed, I handed him the envelope. Immediately, he handed it back, and requested, "Please, open it, Zoey."

After I opened the large sealed envelope, I pulled out three beautiful, black and white hand-drawn pictures of myself at different ages of my life: toddler, childhood, and present—semblance of a teenager. Dillon was an excellent artist. The details in all three drawings of my eyes, face, and hair were impeccable.

My eyes teared up. "They are breathtaking," I murmured, swallowing. "Thank you, how . . . ?"

"I can't explain it, Zoey, all I can say is, during these past few weeks, I've been dreaming about you," Dillon admitted, gazing deeply into my eyes. "And lately, I've been drawing you nonstop."

I was lost for words.

"Tonight, at the restaurant, I purposely had Robbie stop by to drop off my drawings, and take a few photos. Then I had him show our picture to a psychic that I went to many times in the past. And just to let you know, I'm also getting a second opinion from a world-renowned face reader in New York City. I'm just going to say it, Zoey, and I know this is going to sound bizarre," he said, placing his hands in mine. Instantly, I felt the lingles. "The psychic . . . she mentioned that we were married in another lifetime."

Instantly, I lunged at Dillon's mouth. There was a God! We thought and acted alike! After about twenty seconds of savagely kissing, Dillon scooped me up in his strong arms. Feeling like a newlywed, my arms were wrapped around his thick neck kissing his cheek.

My exhilarating heart was literally beating like a rabbit from anticipation! Yes, tonight was going to be the night, woot!

47

GENTLY, HE PLACED my head on the pillows. My bedroom was dark, except for the moonlight peeking in through the blinds. Gracefully climbing on top, our lips instantly magnetized. I loved how he kissed, and for the first time in my life, I had a man in my bed! However, I wanted to visually remember my first time—our special first time.

Stopping our kiss, I looked up at his faint moonlight shadow. "Wait a second," I said, "I want to see everything we do tonight."

After Dillon rolled off to his side, I darted off the bed.

From about five feet away, I flicked on the light. "Now, that's more like it," I said boldly.

Hopping off the bed, Dillon briskly pounced me. Passionately kissing, I pushed—guided him backwards until his butt plopped on the base of the bed. Hovering over him, I halted our kiss. Aggressively, I removed his tank top over his head, exposing his muscular physique. Promptly, I plunged to my knees.

To my delight, I could see Dillon's bulging manhood through his shorts. Forcefully, I yanked off his sneakers—tossed them.

"Zoey, I want you to be first," Dillon suggested. "This is your special night."

"This is . . . *our* special night, Dillon, and I want *you* to be first," I stated firmly, swooping off his shorts and underwear in one swift motion—flung them.

Oh! My! God! Gasping, my eyeballs almost popped out of its sockets. The size and girth of Dillon's penis—Wowza!

Just like me, Dillon was clean as a whistle, and didn't have any pubic hair. In the past, I watched over a thousand blowjob videos, and by far, his dick was king. And going forward, his moniker *is* "King."

For the first time in my life, I was about to give a blowjob, woot! In amazement, I just couldn't stop looking at it, the one and only, King. The eighth wonder of the world was inches away from my eager virgin mouth.

Looking upward into his blue eyes, I sincerely stated, "Dillon, this is my first time, and it's very important for me to please you. Just tell me what you like, okay?"

"Okay, great, I will. Just start off by slowly putting me in your mouth. And be careful of your teeth . . . just be relaxed, and you'll do fine."

Wishing I could remove my teeth, I opened my mouth wide. Nervously, but very carefully, I wrapped my lips around a few thick inches of his giant cucumber, and then I closed my eyes. Slowly, and delicately, I began to move my head back and forth.

Still feeling nervous, but more excited, I was finally giving head! King's swollen shaft felt firm, but his skin felt soft—what a cool contrast! And he felt warm and very smooth—a silky smooth texture. Instantly, I was loving this new, warm, silky feeling of King slowly sliding in and out of my moist mouth. It was absolutely intoxicating to have my lips wrapped airtight around his huge penis.

"That feels really good. Now, put your hand here, and move it slowly like this," Dillon requested with his hand on the lower part of his shaft, slowly tugging it.

Observing Dillon jerk off very slowly, only a couple of inches from my face, was so erotic!

Eager to please, I replaced his hand with mine.

With my eyes closed, I started to bob my head while slowly stroking the base of his cock.

Don't overthink it, Zoes. I can and *will* get used to this because I enjoy this—love this! I *will* please him!

All of a sudden, Dillon ordered, "Look at me, Zoey."

48

BEFORE OPENING MY eyes, I prayed that I was pleasing him. Looking upward with my innocent puppy dog eyes while I was slowly bobbing my moist mouth over his thick velvety shaft, I knew that I was off to a good start. Dillon was trying to control his breathing by slowly inhaling through his nose, then exhaling through his mouth.

Looking downward into my eyes, Dillon softly said, "What you're doing feels . . . amazing."

Wanting to jump for joy since sucking cock was so wonderfully new and infatuating, I was now officially hooked—for life! Plus, I could get used to this because Dillon made me feel relaxed while I gratified him. And I never wanted this new wonderful sensation to ever end.

Pleasuring Dillon with gentle suctions, I started to moan. For the first time in my life, the back of my throat and the front of my mouth, simultaneously experienced utter fullness.

Some bobs were deep—nice and slow, some were medium—mellow and smooth, and some bobs were short and quick. And with a little creativity, some bobs were leisurely in the form of slight side to side head movements—loving the feeling of my cheeks being expanded.

Releasing King with elongated saliva dripping from my mouth, I began to slowly circle the soft, spongy tip with my tongue, followed by gently sucking on it.

Looking upward into Dillon's eyes while tracing my tongue around his plump tip, I announced, "You have the best dick I've ever seen."

"Thanks," Dillon said with a smile, "that feels fantastic, Zoey, just hold on for a second."

Lowering his back flat on the bed, he stretched for a pillow. My eyes were glued to King when he stood up. After placing the pillow on the hardwood floor, Dillon extended his hand and helped me scoot on top of it.

"Please continue," he requested.

He didn't have to ask me twice. Now, erect on his feet with his muscle mass towering above me—this was the holy grail of blowjobs! Even his thighs were bulging with huge muscles.

Eagerly, I carefully wrapped my lips airtight around King. Looking upward with my flirtatious eyes opened, I resumed sucking dick. It didn't take long before my mouth produced a good amount of saliva. My hand and kisser were happily engaged in action, and I *really* loved being in the moment. Dillon was trying to control his breathing through his nose and mouth—yes, he was panting! And I never wanted this feeling to end—for the both of us.

"That feels fantastic, Zoey," he revealed, "and I love when you look up at me. That's . . . sexy."

Yes, I was giving a sexy blowjob! But I needed to do a heck of a lot more than just give a sexy blowjob, knowing full well about the stiff competition before me.

Let's get slutty, Zoes!

Watching countless blowjob videos during the past ten years, I knew deep down that I was capable of pleasuring Dillon on a grander scale. So, I decided to break protocol by taking my kisser off to the side onto his long, thick dick. Seductively, I gazed Dillon in the eyes while I slowly slid my tongue along his giant cock. Very slowly, I kept alternating my salivating tongue all around each plump side, letting out soft, natural moans of pure pleasure.

To further Dillon's viewing pleasure, I began to mix up my repertoire by sliding my tongue underneath his hefty shaft down to the scrotum. And on the way back up on his enormous penis, I was slowly, and lustfully tattooing slurpy smooches.

Blissfully lost in time—engaged somewhere on his thick, robust shaft, I kept slowly sliding my moist tongue along each thick side while gazing upward into Dillon's blue eyes. And every time when I reached the tip of King, I gave that plump, spongy part extra special attention. My favorite thing that I truly loved doing was tracing my tongue slowly around the mushroom tip. Enthusiastically, and playfully, I loved giving it gentle suctions and seductive kisses.

It was questionable if I could fit King in its entirety down my throat. So, I began to perform—play an engulfing cock game of how much thick dick I could jam into my kisser. Since I'm super competitive, I only wished there was lipstick handy to mark each deep-throat attempt. This new, deep bobbing, profusely drooling game—Drooler should come with a lifetime warning because it's highly addicting, making my mouth and insides feel like an overflowing dam. Genuinely, I couldn't help letting

out natural moans of pure penis-sucking pleasure, having the best
slurping and drooling time of my life!

49

DILLON'S BREATHING BEGAN to intensify. Flirtatiously looking upward, I decided to lower my chops onto his large balls while my hand held up his meaty shaft. Seductively, I planted soft kisses on his smooth firm balls. Over and over, I kept gingerly kissing them. Then, I slowly traced my tongue around them. With our eyes locked, and my moist mouth in lustful motion, I had never been so enthralled. And for the grand finale, I decided to get real fucking slutty by delicately placing them—one big ball at a time in my salivating piehole.

"Wow . . . Zoey," he swallowed, trying to control his breathing, "that feels . . . wow . . . amazing."

Yes, I was making him pant as I continued to delicately suck on his smooth-shaven balls.

Dillon's eyes were slowly opening and closing, and his chest had its own soft pulse. His eyes started to blink. Slowly, he said again, "Wow . . . that feels . . . amazing."

I fucking got this!

With King back in my salivating mouth, my fingers were caressing his large balls. My other hand was gently tugging— massaging the base of his sturdy thick cock with the gentle slow motion that he desired.

"I'm going to come soon," he announced, unfortunately.

Looking up with King wedged deep in my mouth, I barely mumbled, "Come in my mouth."

Dillon nodded with a sigh of relief while trying to control his breathing.

Go for it, Zoes! Being very conscious of my teeth, I slowly began to deep throat toward the base trying to fit it all in. I still had a few more inches to go when I started to cough—gag—almost puked—fuck! Abruptly, King exited my drooling mouth. Mortifyingly looking downward at the floor in total disappointment, I kept coughing. Fuck, my first blowjob mistake!

"You don't have to do that, Zoey. Please continue what you were doing before. That felt amazing."

Your wish is my command my future husband, plus I needed to quickly repent from my embarrassing hiccup. With King out of my mouth, I began to slowly lick the spongy tip in a circular motion. My fingernails were playfully caressing his firm big balls while my other hand gently stroked his smooth robust shaft. Yes, I was back on track when I decided to slowly slide my tongue along the left side of his enormous shaft.

"Wow, that feels so . . . incredibly . . . amazing. I'm going to come soon."

To give this type of pleasure to someone you love was a total aphrodisiac.

Stopping all mouth motions, I continued to gently stroke King while caressing his balls. "Please hold off," I begged, looking upward with a feeling of long drool around the outside of my mouth, wishing I could blow Dillon all night long. "I'm having the best time ever!"

50

WHILE TRYING TO control his breathing, Dillon admitted, "I can't make any guarantees."

Doing my best to prolong my new-found favorite activity before it erupted, I halted all motions. Looking upward with sad puppy dog eyes, I begged in my sweetest voice, "Please, do your best."

Catlike, I went back underneath gently sucking on his cum-filled balls while softly stroking King's shaft, of course, lustfully gazing upward into Dillon's blue eyes.

"Okay, okay, I'll try my best to hold off," Dillon replied, stepping back with King inches away from my face. "Let's take a quick break."

Waiting comfortably, and very patiently on my knees, I wondered why wives, or soon-to-be ex-wives—my clients would share with me not giving, or very seldom giving their husbands blowjobs. No wonder why they strayed, and went elsewhere. Startling my thoughts, Dillon placed a cold-water bottle in my hand. Quickly, I took a sip, and couldn't wait to resume!

I'd never been more interested and thrilled in my entire life to give my complete, undivided attention to someone up until now. And for a couple of fun cock-sucking minutes, I kept doing exactly what came naturally. It didn't take long before my head bobbing and hand pace accelerated. And before I knew it, I was savagely out of cock-sucking control with beast mode bobs while my hands and fingers were in tenacious action— working their magic.

For the first time, I noticed Dillon's eyes were rapidly blinking, and his mouth and nose breathing became erratic. His chiseled upper body started to expand and contract. Basic instincts kicked in, and I knew full well to keep King firmly engulfed in my salivating mouth. My fingers were entertaining his entourage while my head continued to move with short—rapid bobs.

Dillon mumbled, "Oh . . . oh, wow . . . that feels," he swallowed, ". . . amazing."

Whoosh! My mouth started to billow—pulsate. King had swelled and throbbed repeatedly.

"Zoey!"

Our eyes were locked when I felt the rapid force of the warm, salty phlegm gush down my throat. I was extremely proud of making Dillon come intensely—massively!

Patiently, I waited several seconds to make sure he was finished. Just to be certain he was drained, I jerked his meaty shaft several times, swallowing more cum.

I didn't have to sell this to myself, because I'm already sold—for life! Now, I wanted to put an explanation point on my first blowjob. Very happily, and again, I slowly jerked King in my mouth a few more times because I wanted to make certain that I swallowed every last earned DNA drop.

When Dillon slowly took King out of my mouth, I noticed a little bit of sperm on the tip. Immediately, I gobbled it up, and then I playfully gave King a few quick kisses. I'd never been happier!

With a colossal smile, Dillon proudly announced, "Wow, Zoey that was . . . incredible . . . amazing! The best ever!"

"Yes!" I said proudly on my knees with a fist pump high in the air. "I want to do it again!"

Dillon began to laugh, then I started to laugh. He genuinely made me feel totally relaxed and very comfortable during my first blowjob experience.

Gazing downward into my proud and happy eyes, Dillon boldly promised, "Drink your water now, Zoey, because you *will* be coming all over my face multiple times!"

51

AFTER A FEW swigs, Dillon helped me to my feet. He was stark naked, and I wasn't. When our lips magnetized, he vigorously showed his gratitude with a passionate French kiss while he squeezed my ass cheeks. In an instant, my shorts were saturated. And before I knew what hit me, Dillon placed my butt on the base of the bed. Quickly, he stepped back, then removed my T-shirt over my head, exposing my breasts.

For the first time in my life, I was exposed to a man—the man of my dreams. Instantly, Dillon smiled which made me feel relaxed and very comfortable in my own skin.

From above, he said, "Zoey, you're absolutely breathtaking."

Wanting to jump for joy, Dillon bent forward, and planted a kiss. Gracefully, he lowered my back on the bed—my legs dangled over the base.

Dillon complimented, "Zoey, your breasts are perfect, absolutely perfect."

Bending forward, he lowered his mouth to my right nipple, gently sucking it. His right hand was gently playing and caressing my left breast and nipple. And the delightful sensations I felt everywhere in my body were stellar.

"Zoey, you're breathtaking. You're driving me crazy," Dillon whispered, switching his mouth to my left nipple.

"You . . . are . . . so sexy," he said, tracing his tongue around my nipple while his hand caressed the other.

Slowly, and softly, Dillon kept alternating hand and mouth positions for a couple of minutes. And I absolutely loved the sucking and gentle pinching sensations.

Stopping all motions, he placed his lips near my left ear. Seductively, with his hot breath, he whispered, "Don't be bashful, Zoey. I really look forward to you coming all over my face."

Lickety-split, I shifted my face to his, and we were savagely kissing. I was lost in lust. Abruptly, Dillon stood upright, and what a stunning sight it was. King was rock fucking hard! Automatically, I wanted to spring off the bed, and resume kneeling on the pillow.

Being the perfect gentleman, Dillon placed two pillows under my head. After a quick kiss, he stepped back, then retrieved the lucky blowjob pillow, positioning it front and center of my welcoming womanhood.

Immediately, Dillon plunged to his knees. Elegantly, he wiggled off my shorts. And the smile on his face inches from my vagina was priceless, probably because that's all I sported. However, I immediately felt self-conscious down there. My breathing became erratic. Suddenly, too many random thoughts—questions invaded and ran through my self-doubting mind: Did I smell? Would I like it? What if I tasted weird? Or worst-case scenario, what if I didn't orgasm?

Very gently, I felt Dillon's hands in mine. Softly, he squeezed them. "Just relax, Zoey, and enjoy it. You can close your eyes if you like, just breathe and relax."

Instantly, Dillon made me smile. Wholeheartedly, I trusted him. After a couple of deep breaths, I felt relaxed. "Okay, I'm good," I said with a couple of playful hand squeezes.

Dillon slid my upper body back a smidge, then lifted my dangling legs onto the edge of the bed. My knees were bent upright.

Just breathe, Zoes.

My heart was racing when Dillon gracefully spread my upper thighs wide apart.

52

LOOKING DIRECTLY AT my pussy, Dillon's tongue slowly circled the outside his soft lips.

"You look absolutely breathtaking, Zoey," Dillon assured. "Just breathe and relax."

And before I could utter a word, I felt a warm, soft kiss on my clit, followed by Dillon's slow tongue movement. I gulped because I never felt anything electrifying wonderful like this before. His tongue felt like a tender, wet tickle.

His slow tongue rhythm on my clit kept wonderfully tickling my insides. It didn't take long before the moist gratification struck every feel-good hormone in my body like a lightning bolt—pleasurably perfect.

"Zoey, I love your scent," Dillon whispered. "You're driving me crazy."

Now, I could let go, and be in the moment. Softly, Dillon's tongue leisurely licked my clit up and down, then circled it all around. Wow! Now, that's what I'm talking about! Where's this pleasurable sensation been my whole life?

Surprisingly, Dillon slid his large hands underneath onto my buttocks. Immediately, he began to squeeze with mild force. His moist tongue felt terrific, gratifying my aroused clit. Now, the delightful sensations everywhere in my body felt like warm, ripple ocean waves gently splashing—refreshing my exposed sun-kissed skin. Oh, the way his skilled tongue tenderly caressed my clit was the best pleasurable feeling ever!

Pausing the best feeling in the world, Dillon gazed upward deep into my eyes, and proudly announced, "You have a magnificent ass."

"Thank you."

By watching Dillon lick my clit, I knew he *really* loved gratifying—delighting me. I loved how he softly grunted while keeping eye contact. And I loved how his soft, moist tongue slid slowly up and down, then all around—in every pleasurable direction. And I absolutely loved the way Dillon's strong hands felt squeezing my ass. Hopefully, his hands would leave a noticeable and permanent imprint on my glutes. Proudly, I would exhibit them at a clothing-optional beach as the property of Dillon Race. All the hours squatting at the gym, and not skipping leg day workouts, paid off.

For the first time in my life, I wasn't in control of my sexual pleasure, and now, I prefer it this way. Feeling totally relaxed, I finally closed my eyes, and placed my arms over my head, enjoying the rippling body waves of delightful tongue sensations and firm ass squeezes. It was pure bliss.

Softly, I began to moan, surrendering myself to Dillon's skilled tongue rhythm and powerful ass squeezing. And it didn't take long before my moans became louder. Undeniably, I was getting close to the edge of my first big O that didn't originate from my own fingers.

Dillon must have sensed it or read my mind, because he playfully paraphrased my own words when he said, "Please hold off, I'm having the best time ever."

Simultaneously, we both started to laugh. Quickly, we took a drink, and in no time, Dillon resumed the best feeling in the world. With my eyes closed, his tongue was circling and licking my clit a little bit faster which I was absolutely loving.

After a couple of forceful ass squeezes, Dillon repositioned his right hand onto my left breast. In no time, my left nipple was skillfully being entertained. His dexterous fingers traced the outline of my nipple, followed by gentle pinches, it felt amazing!

Lickety-split, his tongue speed increased. The pleasurable waves were swelling my insides with warmth. "Oh, Dillon!" I blurted out. "What you're doing feels amazing."

In a slow, low, husky voice, he said, "I'm glad you like it. You taste so good!"

Dillon's rapid tongue pace all over my swollen clit intensified my moaning—his grunts became louder. One dexterous hand was forcefully squeezing my butt-cheek, and the other continued to gently—skillfully pinch my erect nipple.

His soft, moist tongue felt like a delightful whirlwind all over my aroused clit. My breathing became heavy and erratic. And I wasn't thinking clearly about anything. Splendidly, I was only feeling the overwhelming lightning bolt sensations striking all of my pleasurable nerve endings in my body.

All of a sudden, my body was flooded with stiff tension traveling from my neck all the way down to my tingly toes. And I just couldn't keep up with Dillon's tongue pace. The tightness—the clenching sensations and the—

I shrieked, "Dillon! Oh, my God! I'm . . . I'm . . . coming! Dillon, I'm coming! I'm coming, Dillon!"

Dillon! What did you just do to me?! You are my king—for life! My orgasm felt like a massive prolonged sneeze exhaling out of my mouth, mind, and pussy—simultaneously! Wow, what a rush! A total, mind-boggling experience! Spinnacles—the greatest orgasm that felt like—you fill in the blank! All the tension in my entire body vanished. Trying to catch my breath, my legs kept trembling.

53

WHEN I OPENED my eyes, I smiled at Dillon, my new lifetime king! I couldn't believe he delivered that overwhelming, sensational, mind-blowing orgasm out of me—in multiple areas! And he never even asked what I liked. He just knew *how* to satisfy my entire body beyond my wildest dreams. I'm more in love with Dillon now than ever before. Now, he unequivocally had me wrapped around his tongue—for life!

"That truly was the best orgasm I've ever had, thank you," I honestly and proudly proclaimed.

"You're welcome. *It's my pleasure*," Dillon said, smiling from below.

My mind and body were in a euphoric state when I playfully reminded him, "I thought you promised . . . multiples."

Instantly, Dillon's grin became the spacious width of his broad shoulders. With his head slightly raised above my pussy, he said, "Indeed, I did."

Gazing into my eyes, and in one quick, slick motion, Dillon flicked his tongue, puckered his lips, blew me a lustful air kiss, and then he dove the fuck back in!

Attaboy!

Not aware of his second tongue gear, and biting off more than I could chew, once again, I was instantly lost in cunnilingus bliss. If Dillon was a superhero, he would be dubbed "Oralman." Rapidly, his tongue was traveling north and south, east and west, and circling all-around my wet, aroused clit. Fuck, I wasn't sure what direction his tongue was roaming when his licking speed intensified. And I absolutely loved the licking swash sounds and the soft grunts Dillon was making while gratifying me.

Now, with both thumbs and index fingers gently pinching my erect nipples, Dillon made me feel fantastically fucking out of control everywhere in my body. I felt a lot looser without any tension. And I had warmness in my belly. And the electrifying lightning bolt sensations were intensifying—getting warmer throughout my body. I kept moaning, saying his name loudly and proudly, and mumbling I didn't know what.

Genuinely, Dillon loved giving oral sex since I kept noticing the smile in his eyes as he grunted and licked—pampered my clit. His grunt sounds were the perfect side dish to the main dish—his terrific tongue technique. When he convincingly said, "You taste . . . so good, Zoey. I can do this all night long!" I forcefully came all over his unshaven face screaming out his name multiple times.

My legs were trembling out of fucking control! My upper body kept twitching. My head was humming—whooshing. This orgasm felt like a huge wave crashing down on top of your head and pinning you underneath steamy, hot water—blissfully trapped in time. Spinnacles!

When Dillon stood up to retrieve his water, King was profoundly erect. How on earth will it fit in? Regardless, my body must make room for him—dessert. But how? Feeling lightheaded, I was invisibly glued to the bed, my body couldn't budge—I was sexually spent.

Being a perfect gentleman, Dillon held a water bottle to my parched lips. After a couple of sips, he pecked them, then returned to his knelt position.

This time around, I knew better not to utter a word of encouragement to the king of cunnilingus. But it was too late when he confidently announced, "Zoey, I promised you multiples, and you *will* receive . . . all of them!"

54

FEELING ONLY HIS warm breath on my pussy, Oralman had every feel-good nerve ending on my clitoris purring. Whoosh, my body's delight zoomed vertically. The unselfish cunnilingus pleasure Dillon kept gratifying felt like I was front and center on the tippy top, free-fall ride of my life. Suspended at the top of Mount O, I was about to weightlessly plunge into another mind-blowing, G-force orgasm.

Without feeling his mighty moist tongue, that I wanted so desperately to resume on my begging clit, Dillon methodically rolled and gently squeezed his fingers on my sensitive, erect nipples. Slowly, the gentle nipple pinching increased in intensity and became wonderfully more delightful.

With finger finesse, Dillon teased and pinched both nipples, pleasurably perfect. Then, he would mix up the routine by gently squeezing my full breasts. His tender large hands felt amazing as he softly squeezed and slowly moved them in an upward circular motion. Leisurely, Dillon kept alternating this wonderful, pleasurable feeling. And every aroused nerve ending sensation in my body was back at high alert.

I knew my breasts, especially my nipples were super sensitive, but it's not on the same level of pleasure-pinching delight when Dillon was in control. Bottom line: Dillon's nipple playing method was skillfully and methodically superior. In less than a minute, I was quivering and moaning loudly. I just needed the full royal tongue treatment.

"Please, Dillon, use your tongue!" I begged loudly. "I . . . I . . . love the way you lick my pussy!"

He began licking slowly—too tender. But I needed it faster—much faster! Forcefully, I grabbed the back of his head and rammed his face into my pussy.

Shut the front door! Where the fuck did that come from, Zoes?!

Lickety-split, Dillon obeyed, and in no time, his tongue was at full throttle. That's what I'm fucking talking about! Lick my clit fucking fast, baby!

The persistent swash sounds made me wetter. Amplified by his animalistic grunting, my body's feel-good hormones escalated to the top of Mount O. The unselfish oral pleasure Dillon kept gratifying was superior than anything I'd ever physically experienced. I kept moaning in awe—delight. "Yes, Dillon, yes!"

Methodically, his tenacious tongue kept licking my engorged clit in every pleasurable direction as his dexterous fingers pinched my erect nipples perfectly.

Whoosh! From head to toe, my body was stiffening. My breathing became erratic. "Oh, Dillon . . . that feels amazing! Don't stop!" I ordered.

"Glad you love it!" he grunted. "Your pussy tastes amazing!"

His last comment combined with his relentless—terrific—tenacious tongue speed propelled me over the edge. "Fuck, Dillon! I'm going to . . . I'm coming! Fuck, Dillon . . . I'm coming! I'm coming, Dillon!" I shrieked, plunging rapidly—violently coming all over his 18-year-old face!

Uncontrollably, my body kept sprawling—twitching all over the bed.

Best! Night! Ever!

"Zoey, your clit is extremely swollen, and I want you to come again!" he demanded forcefully. "All over . . . my face!"

Catching me off guard, Dillon grabbed my hand and firmly placed it on the back of his head! Are you fucking serious?! Like the king of cunnilingus needed further instructions. It didn't matter because lickety-split, his moist, soft tongue resumed pampering my clit!

Attaboy!

Lost for words, I giggled.

Dillon kept up the rapid tongue pace and gentle nipple play for about two minutes when he delivered another over-the-top, out of this galaxy, I'm his for life—spinnacle orgasm. I kept shaking out of fucking control while profoundly screaming his name. Now, he owned me for life. Where do I sign?

Drop the mic!

Boom!

55

DILLON STOOD ON his feet, and King was rock fucking hard—a spectacular sight! But I was still panting from the orgasm aftershock sensations combined with sexual exhaustion. And also, from the amazement of what was about to penetrate my body.

Dillon placed his penis on my clit. Slowly, he was sliding—guiding King from my clit down to my virgin entrance. Dillon kept doing this pleasurable feeling repeatedly. It didn't take long before Dillon drove me sexually crazy. Desperately, I wanted us to be united as one. However, I kept marveling how King would fit. It would take a miracle.

Alright, Zoes, it's now or never!

Gazing upward into Dillon's eyes, I took in a deep breath. Smiling, I nodded in approval. Smiling back, Dillon bent forward, lowering his upper body and soft lips to mine. For about ten seconds, we were lost in a slow, deep, passionate kiss. And before I knew what hit—pierced me, Dillon was deep inside!

How on earth did Dillon gracefully part my vagina like the Red Sea? Miraculously, King fit! And the temporary discomfort resembled a quick pinch. A miracle must have happened and in more than one way since we were officially united as one! All of my dreams were coming true. Thank you, God!

It must have been Dillon's saliva—his testosterone from our kiss that sparked my second-wind. Without warning, Dillon began to slowly move back and forth, and I wasn't used to this new wonderful feeling—fullness. My insides for the first time were stretched to full capacity, yes! Without a doubt, Dillon completed me emotionally and physically.

Promptly, I had to get my head back in the game. Successful blowjob—check, four mind-blowing orgasms—check. Okay, Zoes, I think I can handle this intercourse thing.

Gingerly, Dillon pulled out, then stepped back upright. Immediately, I noticed some blood spotting on King. Regardless, and holy cow, I still couldn't believe I was able to house the royal highness.

Dillon asked, "I don't have a condom, do you?"

With my eyes fixated on King, I replied, "No."

"Are you on the pill?"

Zoes, look into his eyes.

Gazing up into Dillon's blue eyes, I said, "No."

Shit, my nonvirgin eyes drifted downward again.

Very concerned, Dillon asked, "How do you want to proceed?"

Gazing into his eyes, I boldly stated, "I love you, Dillon. And I would love to have a baby. And it would be an absolute honor to have yours."

Instantly, Dillon smiled. "I love you too, Zoey," he announced genuinely. "It would mean the world to me for you to be the mother of *our* baby."

Yes, for the first time, Dillon sincerely told me he loved me! And I knew he meant every powerful word he just proudly stated. Now, I'm officially the happiest woman alive!

Elated, I proclaimed, "Come as you are!"

56

WE INCHED OUR way to the top of the bed. Gracefully, he lowered his muscular torso and soft lips to mine. My heart raced with anticipation. Very slowly, Dillon entered, gently stretching my insides. Moaning in pure pleasure with our mouths magnetized, I wrapped my hands around his broad shoulder and thick neck.

Gingerly, Dillon moved his body forward, and I felt every smooth inch of King further inside. Instantly, an overwhelming feeling of wetness submerged. It felt like a warm bubbly hot tub gently massaging all my feel-good nerve endings. As each second passed, my body temperature kept getting warmer.

Dillon freed his mouth, gazed downward deep into my eyes, and genuinely announced, "I love you, Zoey."

With the utmost conviction, I desperately wanted to reciprocate, "I love you," but he captured my mouth.

Just hearing Dillon convincingly say those three magical words dramatically intensified the wonderful sensations running through my entire body. For the first time in almost twenty years, I was loved by someone new in this world.

Lost in the moment, and time, my body kept getting hotter. Dillon's groin was magnetized to my clit giving those extra sensitive nerves electrifying delightful sensations. It felt like a magical swarm of fireflies were turning up the dopamine thermometer in my filled insides—heating up and lighting up all my aroused hormones.

With his muscle mass on top of my body, I couldn't budge a smidge. Willingly, my body and mouth were pinned, and I wouldn't want it any other way. His slow, deep thrusts were perfect—perfect rhythm. Blissfully, lost in a deep passionate kiss, I wanted to yell—praise at the top of my lungs, "I love you, Dillon Race!" When his deep thrusts became faster—more forceful, I had another stellar orgasm!

Shaking uncontrollable underneath Dillon, I somehow freed my mouth. I shouted, "I love you, Dillon!"

"I love you too, Zoey. You feel," Dillon said panting, gazing into my eyes, ". . . you feel…amazing."

"You do, too."

Running my fingers through his wavy brown hair, he said with his hot, sex-breath, "I'm going to come soon."

Dillon's back and forth thrust pace was wonderfully relentless. It was giving my insides uncontrollable wetness—wet waves of delight.

"I love the way you feel inside of me," I said, absolutely loving the constant ramming momentum, the nonstop feeling of fullness as he kept stretching my vaginal walls.

"You feel amazing, Zoey!

"You do, too," I concurred—moaned, trying to catch my breath, wanting to tell him—

Whoosh, the dial of my inside thermometer surged. The wonderful feeling of a warm wave inside my body gracefully crashed—I came again!

The prolonged orgasm sensations ricocheted blissfully everywhere in my body. And to my delightful surprise, I felt another big sneeze on the horizon.

Repositioning himself, ever so slightly by raising his torso, gave my body some wiggle room. Hovering over me, his mouth recaptured mine. Instantly, our breath became one. Dillon's thrust pace quickened. The constant ramming of our bodies colliding was driving me absolutely over the fucking edge. Every stuffed—filled inch of my pussy was rhythmically expanding and contracting. Moaning into his mouth, I was quickly at the brink again when I felt King swelling—throbbing.

Gasping, he halted our kiss. "Zoey!"

"Dillon!"

Whoosh! In perfect harmony, we orgasmed simultaneously.

57

CONNECTED AS ONE, Dillon collapsed on top of my body. I prayed for his sperm to successfully disperse throughout my uterus, ovaries, and if I forgot anywhere else, where needed for immediate fertilization. Within a few seconds, he rolled off reaching for his water.

Resting comfortably on his back, we were smiling at each other. Extending his hand, Dillon nimbly pulled me into him. Yes, for the first time, we were finally cuddling! My arm was draped across his baby-smooth chest while I was relaxing on my side—nestled perfectly into his cozy, warm body. Gazing into each other's eyes, I initiated a well-deserved quick smooch.

"That was amazing!" Dillon proclaimed.

"Well, you were pretty good yourself," I said, joshing around, waiting for the ceiling to release and sprinkle the overdue confetti.

Dillon was laughing.

"When can you go again?" I asked giggling while glancing at a flaccid King.

"So just pretty good, huh?" he said, dishing it back with a chuckle. "Next time, I will try . . . harder."

We both let out a quick laugh. Even though this was my first time, I knew sex didn't get any better than this. God willing, Dillon was hopefully my first and last lover. Gazing into Dillon's eyes, I announced, "It was better than great, and well worth the wait."

He said, "I like the way that rhymes."

We both started to laugh with quick, playful pecks.

"I love you, Dillon," I said, giving him a quick kiss.

"I love you too, Zoey," he declared, giving me a quick smooch.

Giggling, I flirtatiously admitted, "Seriously, Dillon, I have over ten years of sex that I need to make-up for."

"Okay, I hear you, Zoey. It seems like the pressure is all on me. If you want to go again, all you have to do is keep priming the erection button until it pops up."

Simultaneously, we burst out laughing.

Dillon closed his eyes, and planted a soft, slow kiss on my lips. Instantly, I was ready with waves of wetness. As the seconds passed, our kiss deepened, escalating my jubilant hormones. And as time passed, I was more in love with Dillon. It was more than the greatest, mind-blowing sex. We connected on a deep, emotional level. And just as important, we had fun and laughed.

<h1 style="text-align:center">58</h1>

PLACING MY HAND on King, he felt damp, and at half-mast. Slowly, I began to tug him. A few seconds later, I was tenaciously stroking him—voila! I was very proud of myself for resurrecting his majesty to full mast. And trust me, King had my full, undivided, wet attention. The erection of all erections was a wonder to behold!

Catlike, getting on my knees, I straddled on top of Dillon. Gracefully, I lowered myself down his thick, robust shaft. Miraculously, I swallowed King whole.

Just breathe and relax, Zoes, this mild discomfort will pass. My hands were resting on Dillon's ripped abs when I slowly began to maneuver up and down, then back and forth.

Yes, now, I was in total control of the greatest sensation I'd ever felt. The initial pleasure was body and mind electrifying. It felt like I was sitting on top of a huge joystick of pure wonderful bliss. And I controlled the speed, the direction, the intensity, and body temperature of my desired delight. Oh, fuck, his big, thick dick felt incredible in every direction I maneuvered.

And the spectacular view from riding—towering above Dillon, wow! From his six-pack abs, chiseled chest, and massive arms, what a sight! Occasionally, I would bend forward with my long hair in his face for a quick smooch, and then shoot back up with my hair flipping.

"Zoey, you're absolutely driving me crazy," Dillon grunted. "You . . . are . . . so sexy."

There's nothing I loved more than sincere body compliments. Please keep them coming hun because the way you feel inside—amazingly blissful, I never wanted it to end. I loved pleasing him and myself. The deep fullness feeling of riding all the way down and then back up, along with the amazing view of Dillon's muscular physique below sent erotic heat waves of delight throughout my insides. Lost in the heat of the moment while rapidly bouncing up and down, I blurted out, "I love riding your cock!"

Panting heavily, he said, "I love the way you ride it."

Yes, after all these years, I was finally taking the joyride of my life on a big, thick, blissful joystick! Working on it. Grinding it. Enjoying it. Fucking loving it! My favorite pleasurable feeling was King fully engulfed deep inside while my hips moved in the tempo and direction that I desired—slight side to side, semi-circle motions, then slightly forward and backwards.

After a few grinding minutes at the helm, Dillon requested, "Do me a favor, Zoey, and turn around. I want to see your sexy ass."

Smiling, I playfully said, "Since you asked nicely, your wish is my command."

Climbing off, I turned around with my ass auditioning near his handsome face. Without further ado, I hopped the fuck back on!

Fuck yeah, Zoes!

Truth be told, I loved to the nth degree the initial feeling and the 'pop' sound when King first entered. It was a new, deep, feel-good, sensational thrill that I all of a sudden craved, like none other. My new rush, my brand-new addiction, my new sexual high was when I first felt the grand entrance of King. My eyelids would slowly fade—disappear like a sunset gracefully plunging into the sea while I softly gasped in anticipation for the perfect amount of lovable pain which lickety-split turned into delightful pleasure. This feeling of complete, utter fullness was truly the best high in the world.

59

THE WEIRD THING was that I always got off watching reverse cowgirl porn, but it wasn't the same feeling—pleasurable sensation of traditional cowgirl, which I enjoyed a lot more, by a landslide.

"Your ass is so sexy!" Dillon said, gawking at my backside. "I love the way you bounce up and down…you turn me on!"

I replied, "You turn me on!"

My rhythm increased during the next few minutes which made Dillon grunt. Occasionally, I would look back on the gratification we were both receiving from the fruits of my grinding labor.

Breathing heavily, Dillon said, "I'm going to come soon."

Maybe it was the distance away from Dillon's face that was responsible for me not being in the aroused state for another big O. Quickly, I picked up the grinding speed (Giddy-up, Zoes!) in order to climax together, but it was too late when I felt King billowing—throbbing.

"Zoey!"

Whoosh! I felt Dillon's ejaculation spurt deep inside my pussy. Liftoff! Swim sperm swim, and at Godspeed.

Bummer, maybe I'm being selfish because I didn't orgasm. My body felt like it was trapped in sexual purgatory. However, I was extremely proud that Dillon came massively with the live image of my 32-year-old ass working, grinding, and bouncing in front of his handsome eighteen-year-old face! Looks like I ad-libbed and passed the ass audition with flying colors!

Fuck! Yeah! Zoes!

Immediately, I was hoisted up, and then gracefully, he placed me flat on my back. Instantly, Dillon smothered my mouth. Yes, the dose of testosterone I needed was back fueling—revving up—heating up my body's delight!

Stopping our kiss, he gazed into my eyes and said, "You amaze me, Zoey, and I would never leave you hanging."

Dillon's right hand started to gently and methodically pinch my nipples. Looking directly into his eyes, I began to moan. In less than a minute, his left hand slid downward. Ever so softly, and slowly, one of his large fingers was dexterously caressing my aroused clit.

Compared to my touch, his touch was more arousing and superior. Moaning in the utmost delight, I decided to close my eyes, and let Dillon do what he does best: deliver another mind-blowing, spinnacle orgasm!

Dillon's head and mouth dropped to my breasts. He was partially on top of me going nipple to nipple, gently nibbling on them while his skillful finger caressed—pampered my clit ever so perfectly.

My insides were soaked. And I'm not sure if it was from the combination of my secretion and his sperm. It felt like a warm, overflowing river. In the most relaxed body and mindset, my fingers ran wildly through his thick wavy brown hair. In a split second, all the fireflies were heating up and lighting up every wonderful, feel-good nerve ending in my body. In the utmost delight, I kept repeating, "That feels amazing, hun."

And yes, once again, Dillon, aka "The Clit Maestro" thunderously delivered!

Boom!

WHAT A WILD past ten hours. The best ten hours of my life! Before we retired for the evening, we quickly changed the sheets, and I filled Dillon in about meeting his grandfather.

Dillon fell asleep first with my head resting comfortably on his chest—listening to his heartbeat. From ear to ear, I was glowing— beaming. For the first time in my life, I was unequivocally in love! And I knew Dillon was in love too, woot!

Feeling safe and protected was a wonderful feeling that I forgot about a long time ago. And thanks to Dillon, for the first time in almost twenty years, I had that identical, blissful feeling resonating throughout my body. It resembled the exact same marvelous feeling that I had with my parents when they kissed and tucked me in for the night. Lingles and linnacles.

"Good night, Mom and Dad. I love you," I whispered out loud, like I always did, every night.

Then, I drifted into a very deep, peaceful sleep.

60

THE WONDERFUL SMELL of bacon, yes bacon, was aromatically floating its way down the short, narrow hallway into my sunny bedroom. Rolling over, I reached for Dillon. Fuck, he was gone! Did he leave me high and dry, early this morning? I really hoped not! He couldn't have, someone had to cook the bacon to begin with, as another mouthwatering whiff created happy pandemonium in my empty belly. Flipping over the other way toward the nightstand, my eyes widened because the alarm clock displayed the time of 1:11 p.m. Holy moly, I can't remember the last time I slept this late!

Leaning up against the bedside lamp next to the alarm clock, I noticed a black and white drawing. Talk about being embarrassed, how long was Dillon watching me sleep? Nevertheless, Dillon's drawing was absolutely stunning. He drew me on my side looking elegant and very peaceful. The picture outlined my sleeping face, and long hair flowing gracefully upon the sheets, impeccable! Dillon's new Rembrandt masterpiece shall be framed at once.

After another yummy whiff, I remembered never having any bacon to begin with. Dillon had to go shopping in order to cook it! From a near distance next to the bureau, I noticed two laundry baskets. They weren't in the bedroom before we retired. Quickly, I jumped out of bed, then smelled the perfectly folded bed sheets which were as clean as a whistle. Also, to my delight in the other basket, Dillon washed and folded my regular soiled clothes which I'd been neglecting for over two weeks. Unbelievable, he was making me look like a slacker.

Peeking out my bedroom door, I vaguely heard Dillon talking with someone, perfect. Quickly, I darted into the bathroom and then hopped in the shower for a quick rinse.

Brushing my teeth while drip drying, I noticed Dillon's toothbrush was on a piece of toilet paper located behind the hot water knob. Since he's not going anywhere for the rest of his life, I placed his toothbrush in the glass cup where I stored mine. Admiring the new novelty—snap, I remembered the happy dream I was awoken from. It was the first peaceful dream in almost twenty years with Mom and Dad. The three of us were at the beach—happy as clams with our feet submerged in ankle-deep ocean water. I was young, and young at heart. Gracefully, Mom and Dad held each of my hands while I was jumping and splashing, having a carefree time. Amazingly, a baby dolphin and its mother swam up and playfully sprayed the three of us frolicking in the shallow water. *We felt free!*

That's when I overheard Dillon's voice, and snapped back into reality. But the weird thing was, I knew that I was in reality, now. And miraculously, I could *feel* my parents' spiritual presence—their unconditional love. I *felt* their invisible, loving touch on the outside of my skin. Blissfully, I *felt* their lingles resonating inside my body. It felt exactly the same way last night when I asked Dillon to be my first.

After another yummy bacon whiff—okay, Zoes, focus, Dillon made us breakfast, woot! Already in the few minutes I'd been awake, and without being near me, many times he had made me smile. And Dillon did wonderfully make a woman out of me, many spectacular times! He was kind and very gentle, and I knew it was because of our first time.

Deep down, I knew Dillon was a thoroughbred lover. And I wanted to experience everything with him, wanting the full, royal treatment. When the time is ripe, I would ask about this so-called branding ordeal, and what that entailed. But more importantly, would Dillon brand me?

61

WHEN I ENTERED the living room, Dillon was exercising. He was wearing only white baggy shorts and sneakers. His shirt was draped over the edge of the couch. Luckily, I'm not spotted because his head and body were facing the sliding glass door. I watched in awe. Rapidly, he was doing regular and clapping push-ups. Yup, by watching his amazing muscular physique in action, I wanted another round of amazing sex. The proof—dampness was in my brand-new, white yoga pants.

Getting on all fours, I crawled to my future husband. Using the top of my head, I gave him a playful love nudge. Cheerfully, I said, "Good morning."

Dillon paused his push-up near my face. Smiling on a slight angle, he said, "Good afternoon, beautiful. I hope you're hungry."

Dillon called me beautiful! Immediately, I had lingle sensations everywhere in my body. He closed his eyes, and I followed suit. Automatically, our lips magnetized. Oh, yes, his soft lips I loved, and I loved how he kissed, and I loved how Dillon made me feel—alive.

Quickly, I surrendered by turning over. Lying on my back with my legs brushed to the side, I inched my face to his. Immediately, we were lost in each other's bliss. My hands were slowly and gently squeezing the outside of his bulging triceps. We kissed slowly and softly for I don't know for how long. Head over heels in love, I never wanted this moment to end.

Dillon's arms started to shake causing our lips to separate. I couldn't believe he could suspend his push-up in a mid-pause, plank positioned for that long. Dillon rolled over on his back trying to catch his breath. Smiling, he gracefully dragged my upper body on top of his pulsating chest.

Gazing directly into my eyes he said, "Thank you, Zoey, for the best night ever. I know this is going to sound corny, but I have to tell you . . . last night you made me feel like it was my first time. Thank you for healing me. I love you, Zoey."

The floodgates in my eyes streamed down my face. "I love you too, Dillon," I murmured.

Lowering my wet face into his chest, he planted a kiss on top of my head. Immediately, I felt the lingles. At that very instant, I wanted to ask Dillon to marry me. But I haven't proven myself fully to him yet, and even if it took a million years, I would wait patiently. Without a shadow of a doubt, Dillon Race *is* the one.

He's my linnacle.

62

WAS I ON a cruise ship? The spread of food Dillon bought, and elegantly prepared was extravagant. The selection to choose from was mind-boggling: bacon, eggs, sausages, waffles, hash browns, a colorful fruit assortment displayed beautifully in a wicker basket, and oddly, perfectly golden chicken tenders.

Was Dillon trying to fatten me up for the kill? Remembering the stories Candace shared, Dillon ate for three, famished adults. Also, Candace admitted within a month from the time she met Dillon, she packed on her perfect, multi-million-dollar modeling figure, a quick ten love-pounds. Not on me he won't!

Placing a golden chicken tender inside a folded waffle, Dillon added a strip of bacon, a section of a hash brown, a drop of maple syrup, and a dab of whipped cream. Sitting across from one another, he carefully extended his hand holding the well-crafted waffle concoction. "Open your mouth, and try this."

Facing each other, I joyfully opened my mouth, and then the party flavor kicked off. "Mmm, delicious, thank you," I said, having a palate blast.

"You're welcome, now promise to keep your eyes closed for a moment," Dillon said excitedly.

"Promise."

The suspense was killing me with my eyes closed. Rising from his chair, I wanted to peek so badly, but didn't. He returned in eleven seconds flat, placing a solid-thin, light object in my right hand.

He said, "Keep your eyes closed, and open your mouth."

With my eyes closed, Dillon gently placed another amazing bite of the waffle concoction into my mouth. Softly, I chewed and swallowed. "Yummy."

"Now, open your eyes, and take a sip," he ordered.

This was so fucking sexy, and so much fun. And now, it was an all-out-of-control, party flavor with a champagne mimosa! Dillon had to purchase expensive crystal flutes and superb-tasting French champagne because I never owned either. His attention to detail was impeccable.

"Thank you, wow!" I cheered, leaning in for a quick kiss.

"You're welcome, now please close your eyes again."

Once I closed my eyes, I heard Dillon's chair slide back. Immediately, my business mind started to count. Fourteen seconds later, Dillon returned, and I instantly smelled the overwhelming lush scent.

Once seated, he said, "Okay, beautiful, you can now open your eyes."

"Oh, my God! Dillon, they're beautiful! Absolutely gorgeous!" I announced, flabbergasted. "Thank you, hun! I love you!"

On top of the counter, I was looking at the most beautiful, lavish crystal vase hosting more than two dozen, in full bloom, long stem red roses.

"You're welcome, and I love you too," Dillon said with a quick kiss.

There must be ants in his pants because he pushed back his chair, again. He walked to the freezer retrieving vanilla ice cream.

"Now, try this," Dillon said, placing a warm, chocolate chip cookie with a dab of vanilla ice cream on top into my mouth.

I took a bite of the best gooey chocolate chip cookie in my life. Immediately, the sensational rush of rich dark chocolate started to dance in my mouth. The vanilla ice cream added an extra taste bud party boost sensation like nothing I'd ever experience—savored. Unbelievably delicious!

"Oh, my God! Where did you get this?"

"I made them special for you," Dillon announced with a broad smile. "It's my grandma's secret recipe."

"It's the best cookie I've ever had. Thank you, hun," I said honestly as we continued to feast.

Hopefully, Dillon was fueling up for some wild afternoon sex. He definitely had well-earned it. He still hadn't shaved which made him sexier, if that was even possible.

Knowing what I knew now, Dillon was worth the wait, in every conceivable way. Yes, at first, it was solely sexual, and undeniably, he rocked my world. However, it was Dillon's heart and actions outside the bedroom that made him totally irresistible. If I never had sex again, which I hoped wasn't the case, I would be well-satisfied.

63

FINALLY, AFTER ALL these years, I'm breaking bread, and having a fun, in-person conversation in my home with the opposite sex. When Dillon stood up to fetch himself a mimosa, I still couldn't believe I lost my virginity to him. By far, Dillon was the sexiest man I'd ever laid eyes on. With this new, wonderful string of luck of mine, hopefully, in the twinkling of an eye, I can parlay it into a positive pregnancy test.

"How come you did all this?" I asked in total amazement because *I should have* done all of this while he slept.

Sitting back down with a warm smile, he replied, "I'm just trying to earn my keep, and not get kicked out."

Amazingly, in a very short period of time, Dillon went shopping, made a delicious brunch, bought expensive champagne, red roses, washed and folded all of the laundry, and had me shaking all over the bed last night. "You couldn't get kicked out if you tried!"

Dillon was laughing.

After a few seconds, I sternly said, "Unless you violate the only rule in my home."

"And what is your only rule?"

Meaning every word, dead serious, I declared, "I forbid you from jerking off, and that's nonnegotiable."

My new goal was to always sexually satisfy Dillon any way he wished. He well-earned it last night when he told me he loved me, and he sealed the deal by making his grandmother's special homemade chocolate chip cookies. Add in bacon, champagne, red roses, and his delicious cooking into the delightful mix of things—Dillon was a lifetime keeper!

With a distressed look on his face, Dillon said, "Uh-oh, I wish you told me that beforehand. Can we please start tomorrow?"

Oh, my God, while I was sleeping, I wasn't tentative to his sexual needs!

"Are you serious!" I hollered, feeling defeated.

With a shoulder shrug, he confessed, "I'm sorry, but I didn't want to wake you because you looked tired. And I only did it twice . . . well, actually, three times if you count the time I was waiting for your laundry. But not a lot came out."

What the fuck, not a lot came out! I needed every last drop of his magical, baby-making fluids. Not for him to jerk off, and waste it on some spin cycle. It seemed like Dillon really was a real-life jack-in-the-box with nonstop popping erections.

Not even a full day yet, I was failing miserably! I remained speechless.

"I'm sorry, and it won't happen again," he said remorsefully.

"I'm *very* sorry you had to take care of yourself," I announced in a very concerned—defeated tone. "You should have gotten me up anyways. Please promise me, hun . . . you'll wake me up going forward."

"Relax, Zoey," Dillon said, laughing for a few seconds. "I'm just messing with you . . . you should have seen your face."

"You just gave me a heart attack, and you really had me fooled. Please, Dillon, let me take care of all your sexual needs. It's *very* important to me, promise?" I asked, more like panicky begged, not wanting to ever sexually disappoint Dillon—my king—my everything.

Dillon nodded, and I knew he discovered my sensitive nerve—concern of pleasing him. "I promise, Zoey," he assured, leaning forward for a quick kiss to seal my unwavering commitment.

64

HOW ON EARTH did Dillon prep and cook all of this delicious food? "What time did you get up?" I asked in total amazement.

Shoveling eggs into his mouth, and in-between bites, he replied, "A little after eight."

"Why so early?" I asked while thoroughly enjoying his cooking which was lightyears better than mine.

"I had a vivid dream of you as a child."

Now, my interest was piqued. After I swallowed a delicious bacon strip, I asked, "What happened in your dream?"

After swallowing his food, Dillon revealed, "You and your mom were building a sandcastle on a sunny beach. And for some bizarre reason your mom was wearing roller skates. You looked to be about five or six years old. And there was an orange triangle flag with a blue . . . smiling face in the middle of it planted in one of the sandcastles. And your dad was wearing some kind of candy necklace," he said, pausing to take a sip of the bubbly. "From a few feet away, you waved at me and I waved back. And your mom skated . . . actually she glided on the sand over to me with a smile, and gave me a hug. Then she turned around so we faced you, and then she very quickly grabbed my wrist, and raised my arm high in the air."

On my 13th birthday, Mom had 'the sex talk' with Emma and me. She mentioned to the both of us when the right person came along that she would let us know.

"Please continue," I requested.

"Your dad asked me to go in the ocean, and I hesitated because I'm afraid of sharks. He assured me that I would be fine. So, your dad and I were on our own surfboards, and we kept paddling on our stomachs away from the shore. And oh, two dolphins were following us, and jumping around which I thought was pretty cool. When I looked back at the shore, I could barely see you and your mom," he paused, reaching for my hand. Then Dillon revealed, "Your dad wanted me to tell you . . . 'he loves you more.'"

162

Oh! My! God! Dillon just miraculously channeled—conveyed those most precious words in my heartfelt vocabulary! In my wildest dreams, I never thought that Dad would ever say them again to me. Instantly, my eyes started to tear. Daddy and I always playfully said to one another "I love you more." That was our special morning ritual we said to each other before he left for work.

Reaching for a napkin with my free hand, I said, "I'm sorry that I'm being emotional."

"No, I'm sorry, Zoey," Dillon said softly, gently squeezing my hand. "I'll stop."

Instantly, from the soft squeezes my body became flooded with the nostalgic feeling of love I felt at dinner last night—the lingles. Lost for words, because I never wanted this jolt-tingling, love-popping sensation to evaporate. It felt like Pop Rocks in my carefree, adolescent mouth.

"It's okay . . . please tell me more about your dream." I murmured, maybe too timidly.

"I'll tell you later, eat up," Dillon ordered, releasing my hand. Luckily, the pop-loving lingles kept encoring.

My mind raced as I took another mimosa sip, but it was too late, the cat's out of the bag. What's going on here? What's my parents' important message to me from Dillon's dream? Oh, my God! It seemed like our dreams paralleled. Also, he dreamt about dolphins. Now, I remembered more about my dream. Dillon was sitting high up in the big white chair. It was definitely Dillon on lifeguard duty protecting us because he wore Daddy's candy necklace that I handmade.

Grabbing another napkin to wipe my watery eyes, I softly requested, "It's okay, I'm fine, hun, please continue."

65

AFTER WIPING AROUND his mouth, Dillon said, "After I asked your dad a question, he handed me a candy from his necklace, and he made me eat it. Your dad wanted me to promise him something."

Breaking off our eye contact, he began to stack eggs and hash browns on his fork. It didn't take long before he was inhaling his food.

Desperately, I wanted to hear more about his dream. "What was it," I asked.

Without any response, or eye contact, Dillon took a very slow sip of champagne.

"Please continue with your dream," I requested.

It seemed like Dillon was stalling because he wiped around his mouth a couple of times. Looking downward, he started to slowly cut into his chicken tender. Still ignoring my question, he started to eat.

How on earth did Dillon know this actually transpired? Mom and I loved sand sculpting. For hours, that was our special activity we did together at the beach. And we did have an orange flag with a blue, smiling face planted in one of our sandcastles. Even by some remote chance he saw the picture of Dad wearing the candy necklace I made him, how would Dillon know what Dad and I said to each other? And how would he know about Mom's love for roller skating? That was impossible. And on that sunny beach day in Rhode Island, Dad was about to swim with the necklace on, and I stopped him just in the nick of time. And before I had a chance to ask a slew of questions the doorbell rang.

Instantly, Dillon sprang up, dashing to the front door.

Robbie waltzed inside carrying a gorgeous, shiny-silver, rectangle-looking object that was beautifully wrapped. Attached, dead center of the presumed gift was a substantial red bow.

Robbie was talking in a whirlwind. "Hey, Dill, you were right, and you're not going to believe it. And oh, before I forget, Mafalda wanted me to tell you she double checked the purchase order and it looked good, but she made a couple changes. And oh, she also wanted me to tell you,

164

she has everything under control. And oh, she's requesting you to take a couple of days off. Oh, hey, Zoey, good to see you again," Robbie said genuinely.

Internally laughing, Robbie looked like a typical teenager who was Dillon's age. However, Dillon looked twelve years older than him. Robbie appeared to be more than six feet tall, a solid two hundred plus pounds, and in excellent shape.

"And good to see you too, Robbie. Are you hungry?" I asked.

"Starving, I've been running around all morning, and haven't had lunch yet," Robbie replied.

"Please, help yourself," I said, walking to the counter to retrieve Robbie a plate and utensils.

Reaching up to grab a plate, I noticed Dillon's eyes were glued to my ass—where they should be! Immediately, I was smiling, thanks, Grandpa!

Thank God, Robbie was here to help us eat this wild feast suited for an army. And I'm glad he wasn't bashful helping himself to a variety of food. His plate was stacked to the brim.

Sitting across from us, Robbie inhaled a few quick bites, then he said, "Hey, Zoey, did I miss any of your favorite food items because Dillon had me buy just about everything under the sun?"

66

LOOKING AT DILLON with a raised eyebrow, I warmly replied, "You did perfect, Robbie. Thank you for everything."

Robbie said, "You're welcome, Zoey."

"Robbie was my very first employee," Dillon boasted. "And he's also my best friend. And when he's working, he's the best go-to-person that gets the job done perfectly, and on time."

"Well, thanks, Dill, but I think Mafalda is going to fire me because she's upset you pulled me, and two others, and—"

Quickly, Dillon interrupted, "Relax, Robbie, she can't fire you without speaking with me first. Do you want me to call her?"

So that's how Dillon embarrassed me in my own home. He orchestrated helpers—elves running around town doing all sorts of errands—spending money like wildfire. Wow, now, I needed to quickly step up to show my gratitude for all of Dillon's thoughtful acts of kindness.

With a concerned look on his face, Robbie said, "No, I'm good. Now, please don't get upset, but I had to jump through hoops, and pay top dollar to bump your facial reading request to the front of the line. His wait list was over four months out."

"I gave you a green light," Dillon said businesslike, "and I told you to get it done, so it doesn't matter how much you paid."

Now, I was curious. Being the ultimate snoop, I was dying to know. They looked at each other for a few seconds without speaking. Emma and I had done the exact same thing hundreds of times knowing what the other was thinking.

Nervously, looking downward, Robbie cut into his sausage. "I'm just going to tell you, Dill, I spent forty thousand dollars."

Oh, my God! Dillon paid forty thousand dollars! It was that important to him to know. Dillon was piling on massive—copious points on our love-scoreboard. And I had a big goose egg—zero points in my own house. Dillon was easily winning by a landslide.

"Relax, Robbie, you made the right decision," Dillon said reassuringly. "Now, please show us the video."

67

SITTING ON DILLON'S lap with one arm draped over his shoulder, we were waiting patiently for the verdict. After kissing his unshaven cheek, I took another delicious mimosa sip. After Robbie pressed play on his smartphone, he handed it to Dillon, then attacked his mountain of food.

The facial reader was an Indian man in his fifties. He spoke understandable English with a soothing Indian accent. The long and short of it was, the facial expert confirmed that Dillon and I were happily married in another lifetime, and we lived a long, happy life as soulmates. However, there were no children in our past lifetime. In our past life, Dillon was older, and we resided on a farm. We worked the fields together from sunrise to sundown.

The facial reader predicted in our present life that we would happily grow old as a married couple, and we would be blessed with many children and grandchildren. Also, the facial reader with a smile pointed his finger at Dillon's picture, and with conviction in his voice made a bold prediction that Dillon would be famous worldwide. I really liked this facial reader a lot.

The dam burst down there. Smiling at Dillon, I leaned in for a kiss, almost spilling my bubbly. Nailing my mouth to his ear, I ordered, "I want you, now!"

Speaking Polish, Dillon and Robbie walked to the sliding glass door. With their backs facing me, Dillon pointed outside. It sounded like he was giving Robbie instructions. This lasted for about a minute, and I knew Dillon was up to something, and I must be in the know. They hugged, and before Robbie left, he approached me.

"I'm very happy for you, both," Robbie whispered near my ear. "You guys make a great couple."

With my hands patting his back, I replied, "Thank you, Robbie, for everything."

I liked Robbie a lot.

Speaking Polish, Dillon showed Robbie the door.

Instead of pouncing on me, Dillon walked to the kitchen table. Erratically, he started to take dishes and food items off the table, placing them onto the counter. Some dishes were placed in the sink.

He looked nervous because his hands were slightly shaking. Totally ignoring me, Dillon continued to clear food items off the table. But why did his demeanor change? And why was he avoiding my presence while acting suspicious and nervous?

Now, I was getting nervous from the way Dillon was behaving. Was he an anal clean freak that I didn't know about, and had to clean up before we had sex? Or was Dillon now spooked from the revelation from the facial reader? Or worse, was he now having second thoughts about us?

Oh, shit, I just remembered.

From a near distance, I asked, "Hey, Dillon, getting back to your dream with my parents, what happened?"

68

PLACING A PLATE in the sink, Dillon stopped the running water. Bending forward, my neck was at a slight side angle when I noticed his eyes were closed. Dillon placed both hands in his front short pockets while taking deep breaths. When his eyes opened, his face was pale.

Walking directly my way, his facial features showed fear while his eyes kept blinking. He looked extremely nervous. What's going on? Fuck, I sensed that Dillon was about to tell me sayonara.

He extended his hand. Nervously, I accepted. Catching me off guard, Dillon led us into the center of the sunny living room.

Once we faced each other, he took my other hand. Gazing into my eyes, Dillon cleared his throat. "Zoey, I asked for your dad's permission if I could marry you. Your dad made me promise him that I would always take care of you. And I gave him my word I would, until my very last breath. He shook my hand, and gave me his approval. With our hands locked, his free hand pointed up at the bright-blue sunny sky. When I looked up, I saw two dolphins jumping over us. And when I looked back at your dad . . . he mysteriously vanished."

Shocked, speechless, and with tears of happiness, I stood frozen. Dillon released my hands, then dropped to one knee. Gracefully, he took my left hand. The nurturing loving feeling of Dillon's hand resembled the loving sensation—lingles that I received from my parents.

Was this really happening?!

Smiling on one knee, looking upward, Dillon, in the most romantic way said, "Zoey, from the first time I saw you in my dreams, and the first time I saw you in person yesterday, I knew you were the one. Every night, I want to kiss you before we go to sleep, and I always want to wake up by your side. Will you make me the happiest man in the world, and marry me?"

69

FLABBERGASTED, I PROUDLY shouted, "Yes, Dillon, I will marry you! Yes!"

Dillon's hands were trembling. Shaking, he reached into his short pocket. And to my surprise, he once again took my left hand. Slowly, he slid a ring on my finger—fitting perfectly! Looking at the ring, my hand and body were shaking. Oh, my God! It was Mom's engagement ring exactly how I remembered it! And in mint condition! How on earth did Dillon get it? How!

Helping Dillon to his feet, he had happy tears in his eyes.

"I promise you, Zoey, I will always take care of you," he announced, clinching his unwavering commitment with a quick kiss. "I love you."

In less than twenty-four hours, Dillon had made all my dreams come true! It was kismet. We were happily engaged!

"I love you more!" I said stoked. Now, I really need to prove it, every day for the rest of our lives.

Scooping me up in his strong arms, he walked back to the bedroom. I kissed him over and over on his stubbly cheek while glancing at Mom's platinum ring—my engagement ring in absolute amazement!

The center round diamond appeared to be at least three carats. It was secured by four prongs, and it was bright white—sparkling to the heavens! Also, on each side of the center diamond set in four prongs were three smaller round stones consisting of emerald, diamond, and emerald. The emeralds were of the finest, vibrant green color I'd ever seen, and the smaller diamonds on each side were as bright as the center diamond. And my engagement ring fitted perfectly up against Mom's wedding band—they were finally reunited! A magnificent, remarkable family heirloom for future generations. How did Dillon find Mom's ring—my ring?

Gently, he placed me in the middle of the bed. Baffled, I asked, "Dillon, how on earth did you get my mother's ring?"

"I will tell you the story during our first intermission," Dillon promised as he swiftly removed my sports bra and yoga pants—flung them!

"I can't wait to hear it!"

"Zoey, you have the sexiest body I have ever seen!"

70

AGGRESSIVELY, I REMOVED Dillon's shirt. Lickety-split, he stepped backwards, then stripped naked. Lunging forward, I pulled him on top of me. Instantly, we were passionately kissing as an engaged couple.

Within seconds, my insides were gushing from either his testosterone, or sincere body compliments, or knowing there's no better feeling in the world than what was on the horizon. Stoked, I was lost in a wonderful whirlwind of lust, love, and feeling blissfully alive as an engaged woman!

Immediately, Dillon scooted us to the top of the bed. Stopping our kiss, he gazed down into my eyes, and admitted, "I've never been so nervous in my life. And I'm so happy you said, yes. I love you more than life itself."

Instantly, I smiled. Dillon didn't realize that I was a sure thing. He could have thrown the ring outside deep into the woods, and I would have cheerfully retrieved it jumping into his arms. However, catching me by total surprise, Dillon perfectly orchestrated our special engagement, and asked me to marry him in the most romantic way. He made me feel like a queen, and truly touched my heart and soul in a way no one had, or ever would. In a few short hours while I slept this morning, Dillon, on my turf, moved heaven and earth! He made me feel like the most special woman on the planet. I'm forever his.

"I love you, Dillon. Thank you for choosing me to be your wife," I said looking up in awe with a quick kiss. "I love my ring, and I'll never take it off. And every day, I promise to *always* make you happy."

"You already do, Zoey. And I promise," he said with our eyes locked, "to always be faithful to you."

Those very powerful, heartfelt words spoken from an angel in disguise, cemented my trust, my love, my heart, my happiness, my orgasms—his, and every conceivable fiber of my existence for eternity.

<h1 style="text-align:center">71</h1>

AS THE HAPPIEST engaged woman on the planet, Dillon surprised me by muff-diving. Lickety-split, my soon-to-be husband buried his handsome face into his new favorite place!

Yes! Now, I was, my body was totally relaxed anticipating the initial tickle sensation. Softly, he kissed my pussy. Seconds later, he was gently pinching my erect nipples. Then, the best feeling in the world commenced: my clit being skillfully licked—pampered. Fuck yeah! The combination of his nipple play, and ravishing tongue felt amazing. And I loved the low, husky, grunting sounds Dillon made while he gratified me, it amplified everything. My fiancé, yes fiancé, really took great pride catering to my utmost delight.

"I'm addicted to your scent," he said. "And I love the way you taste. *You* make me rock hard."

In no time, Dillon had me moaning. "That feels . . . incredible, hun."

His right hand stopped playing with my nipple, and for the very first time, I felt a finger slide inside my pussy. Slowly, his finger started to move back and forth while his moist tongue traced my clit. Immediately, my body temperature began to climb and bubble.

"Mmm, oh, my . . . God!" I said, gasping. "What are you doing to me?"

"Since you're dripping wet, I'm going to give you the best orgasm you ever had. Guaran! Fucking! Teed!"

His tongue speed increased, and somehow, he slipped another finger inside my wetness. If giving oral was an Olympic sport, Dillon would hands-down win a gold medal.

Dillon stopped licking my clit. "Do you like how it feels?" he asked, looking upward while finger fucking me.

"Mmm . . . fuck, Dillon . . . mmm," I said in between moaning. "Oh, yes, hun! That feels fucking amazing!"

"I love how wet you are," Dillon admitted. "It makes my cock, Rock! Fucking! Hard!"

The gushing sounds, and the feeling of his two fingers rapidly fucking me was paramount. When Dillon resumed his terrific tongue technique, I felt the big sneeze on the horizon.

"Oh, I can't wait for you to fuck me!" I blurted out lewdly, loving how his tenacious tongue and fingers pleasured my pussy. "Don't fucking stop!"

I felt his tongue press deeper into my clit. Savagely, he was feasting on his afternoon dessert. For the next several minutes, Dillon's grunts were getting louder and more animalistic while he continued to skillfully lick and pamper my pussy. Fuck yeah!

Coming up for a quick breather, he said, "Your pussy is dripping wet. And you taste . . . so fucking good!"

"Oh, fuck, hun, I love the way you lick my pussy!" I ordered, "Don't stop!"

Dillon's thumb replaced his skilled tongue. Vigorously up and down, and all around, he was deftly thumbing my wet, engorged clit while his other hand—two fingers continued to methodically massage my insides.

He asked, "Do you love the way I make you feel, my future wife?"

72

"MMM, WHAT YOU'RE doing to me feels fucking amazing, I love it!"

"I'm glad you love it!" he replied.

Suddenly, Dillon repositioned his two fingers upward in my vagina, hitting the most sensitive erogenous nerve I ever felt. "Oh, fuck . . . hun!" I shrieked.

Skillfully, using his left thumb, he gently, but rapidly rubbed all around my super-sensitive swollen clit while his right two fingers were perfectly caressing 'that' most sensitive nerve with blissful vigor. I was all out panting and wriggling.

"Zoey, your pussy is soaked. And I love how your clit is puffed out. Say my name loudly when you come!" Dillon ordered.

"I will . . . I promise, hun."

Lickety-split, Dillon's moist tongue was back on my overstimulated clit, and I knew it wouldn't take long.

"Oh! Fuck! Dillon!"

His licking pace was wonderfully relentless. His tongue-tempo was so rapid that it made swash sounds. Quickly, coming up for air, I heard Dillon say in an authoritative, husky voice, "Your pussy taste so fucking good! I love licking it!"

His last comment spoken in a low and rough tone immediately heightened my arousal. The feel-good warm sensations in my body came to a boil. The pleasurable ripple wave gliding in my direction was cresting. Every ecstatic hormone splashed blissfully in my body. It felt like a big kahuna wave hovering over my head. Suddenly, it peaked, "Dillon! I'm . . . almost . . . fuck . . . don't stop! Dillon . . . yes . . . hun! Don't stop! I'm . . . going to—" then, gracefully crashed—whoosh! "I'm coming . . . fuck Dillon, I'm coming! I'm coming, Dillon!" I proudly shrieked as the soon-to-be Mrs. Race during my first squirting orgasm! A juggernaut!

Loudly, I kept praising Dillon's name, and rattling off a few choice profanities. Sprawled all over the bed, trying to catch my breath, my entire body kept jerking out of control for I didn't know for how long.

What the fuck did Dillon just do to me? Oh, my God! Dillon, aka The Clit Maestro, aka Oralman, and now, aka "Fingerman", had successfully found my G-spot!

"I forgot, my future wife, did I," Dillon playfully paused, then asked, ". . . did I promise you, multiple orgasms?"

Don't answer that, Zoes; it's a trick question.

Every time, when Dillon used the word 'wife', it automatically placed my body in the most euphoric state. In less than two minutes, Dillon had me shaking all over the bed in another mind-blowing, fluid release, oral and finger orgasm. And yes, it was the best, fucking, ever! The big kahuna of all orgasms! Besides the greatest body pleasure known to mankind, Dillon truly loved delighting—pampering me, he genuinely got-off on giving finger and oral sex. The proof was when Dillon stood up with his gigantic erection.

"I'll be back in a moment," he said, grinning while my body was still jolting from orgasm aftershocks. Spinnacles!

Coming back from the bathroom with a semblance of water on his face, Dillon said with the biggest smile, "Thank you for my first facial."

"I'm so sorry, hun," I said embarrassingly, not knowing I was capable of intense, rapid fluid release.

Smiling, Dillon said, "Relax, hun, don't be. I loved it, and I wouldn't want it any other way."

We called each other hun!

73

GRACEFULLY, DILLON CLIMBED on top. My hands rested on his chiseled chest.

"Please, put it in slowly," I requested, looking up at my future husband in pure gratitude. "I love the initial feeling."

"Your wish is my command, my future wife," he said.

I absolutely loved the sound of the word 'wife', it was never getting old. To my surprise, he lifted my legs sky-high, resting on his broad shoulders. Slowly, with his right hand, Dillon was guiding—rubbing his penis—the chubby, plump tip all over my clit down to my impatient, wet entrance. Leisurely, he kept sliding his meaty tip up and down, over and over. King was driving me sexually crazy—they both were!

"Okay, mmm, I'm . . . ready!" I begged.

Ignoring my plea, Dillon kept repeating the pleasurable teasing motion. "Please, Dillon, please," I said, begging. "I'm ready, hun!"

"Are you sure, my future wife?" he asked in full, total control of my pleasure.

I've never been this horny in my life. "Yes, I'm sure, please, Dillon!" I begged louder. "I've never been surer in my life, please, hun!" I yelled in sexual agony, jonesing to be fucked.

"I will do it, " Dillon said, pausing with a playful smile as he teased me to my sexual brink, "for a . . . quick kiss."

Supporting his arm behind my back, he raised me slightly upward. Bending forward to meet in the middle, I lunged upward. Savagely kissing, I managed to mumble into his mouth, "Fuck me!"

King was paused on my yearning entrance.

Breaking off our kiss, I loudly pleaded—begged, "Please, Dillon, I'm fucking begging you, please, hun!"

I would have signed everything over that I'd ever owned, given back the million dollars, and mortgaged everything to the hilt (for the third time) to feel him inside.

Very slowly, Dillon put King's plump mushroom head into my wetness. Immediately, I felt a pleasurable 'pop'—yes! What a royal rush! The best sexual feeling ever!

"Oh, Fuck! Thank you, hun! You feel amazing!" I said totally relieved, loving the feeling of the much-needed sexual adrenaline rush.

"I love how wet you are, Zoey," Dillon announced, slowly moving deeper inside—stretching my vaginal walls. "Your pussy is dripping, and you feel incredible. You're driving me fucking crazy."

"Please, hun, take it out," I ordered, gazing into his eyes, wanting—demanding more of the royal rush—sexual adrenaline. "And put it back in!"

Not only did Dillon obliged, but he did it a few more slow times earning him copious brownie points. Slowly, he started to move back and forth stuffing—pumping my insides with his big, thick dick. And it didn't take long before his thrusting intensified.

I loved the feeling of being pinned into the bed and receiving a fantastic fucking. I loved the feeling of my pussy being repeatedly pumped, filled, and stretched to capacity—marveling how King miraculously fits. I loved how Dillon pulled all the way out, and quickly rammed back inside my wetness. I loved the slapping sounds our bodies made. I loved how he took control and grunted. And I absolutely loved the animalistic look in his eyes as he unquestionably marked *his* territory.

Dillon's repeated fast and deep thrusts was exactly what I needed and craved, making me come loudly and violently. My vertical legs were uncontrollably shaking—bucking into his upper body. Spasming out of control, Dillon somehow placed my legs onto the bed.

Instantly, and gracefully, he sandwiched his body flat into mine. Our perspired bodies welded, perfectly. Capturing my mouth, our breath became one. Willingly, I was pinned, and unquestionably his for life. Blissfully feeling helpless, Dillon continued to ravish and have his way with me. And I loved every fucking second!

Now, Dillon had another alias added to his virtuoso list of sexual accolades: The Pussy Whisperer.

74

REPOSITIONING HIS MOUTH next to my ear, he whispered, "I never want you to forget our first time as an engaged couple. I love you, Zoey."

"I love you too, Dillon."

Getting back on his knees, Dillon lifted my legs sky-high. Without a doubt, King was my sexual oxygen. Loudly, I begged, "Please put it in, and fuck me hard!"

Mounted and ready for copulation, he placed King partially inside. With his hands gripped to my ankles, he separated my legs wide, bending them toward my shoulders. Once again, I was willingly pinned into the bed. And with the look in Dillon's eyes, I knew I was in for a fierce fucking. After 32 years, it felt exhilarating to be fucking taken—claimed!

Slowly, and in full control, Dillon was building momentum. In a rough, low, husky voice, he asked, "Zoey, your pussy is soaked, would you like it faster?"

Without hesitating, I loudly ordered, "Yes, hun! Full throttle! Fuck me hard!"

Oh, my God, what an incredible feeling it was to feel his big, thick cock thrusting deep inside my pussy. And yes, Dillon—the sex machine, delivered with deep, fast thrusts. Much faster and rougher than our first time. This *is* what I was fucking waiting for! Feeling submissively pinned into the bed—loving it, I had no control from this point on but to take a rigid fucking.

I loved feeling every thick, long inch of King stretching and fucking me pleasurably senseless. I loved the feeling of his strong hands and muscular body on my skin while he fiercely pounded. In low, choppy breaths, he salaciously said, "I love . . . how tight and wet your pussy is."

"Oh, fuck, Dillon, don't stop!" I ordered. "I'm almost there! Keep fucking me hard!"

Dillon continued the rapid pounding pace. The sex-sounds from our bodies colliding—slapping, slap—slap—slap, combined with our moaning, panting, grunting, and sweat, I kept blissfully surrendering to rapid, uncontrollable—I didn't know how many mind-blowing orgasms.

Dillon's deep thrusting was at full throttle. His breathing became shorter—

"Zoey!"

Whoosh, the forceful ejaculation of Dillon's orgasm sent wonderful, feel-good warm sensations throughout my insides. My grand wish was for one of his studly swimmers to successfully reach and rendezvous with my welcoming egg for immediate impregnation.

Sexually spent, I felt like the luckiest woman alive. "Wow!" I boasted, "that was mind . . . fucking . . . blowing! The best ever!"

Still trying to catch his breath, Dillon collapsed on his back. Smiling, he pulled me into his warm body. "I promised you, I was going to try . . . harder."

"Well, you succeeded beyond my wildest expectations," I said gazing into Dillon's eyes while we were cuddling. "I'm faithfully and forever yours."

75

GAZING IN ABSOLUTE amazement at my engagement ring, I was slowly moving my hand all around, rocking it side to side. In awe, I was watching the diamonds and emeralds sparkle from all different angles.

Startling me, Dillon asked, "Do you love your ring?"

"Love is an understatement. From the bottom of my heart, thank you so much for giving me the best engagement ring in the world. I thought that I would never see my mother's engagement ring ever again. So how did you find it?"

With a playful smile, he closed his eyes. "I will tell you after I take a nap."

"Rule number two in my home is no napping!" I said loudly, playfully nudging his chest. "I need to know, Dillon! The suspense is killing me!"

With his eyes closed, he chuckled, "Hey, you said earlier there was only one rule."

"Since this is my house, I can change my mind, and add in new rules at any time I deem fit! Dillon, I need to know right now!"

Laughing, Dillon opened his eyes and briefly kissed me. "Okay, I will tell you, but I have to apologize for bringing up my past, okay?"

Now, this should be interesting. "Okay, no problem," I replied purposely, slowly nodding my head.

"I didn't know the woman wearing roller skates was your mother until I saw your tattoo last night," Dillon admitted. "And the dream that I was awoken from today, I started to put the pieces of the puzzle together."

"What puzzle pieces are you talking about?" I asked—snapped impatiently for more crucial details.

"The first time I saw your mother was during my failed suicide attempt, when I was dreaming. In my dream, I was with my deceased grandmother sitting at her kitchen table, when your mom skated in and interrupted us. My grandmother and your mom were staring at each other, and somehow communicating. And I don't know what they said to each other. Then, my grandmother walked over, kissed my forehead, and

182

then she mysteriously vanished," Dillon admitted, reaching for his water on the nightstand.

"Then what happened?" I asked, eager for the scoop.

"Without any warning, and lightning fast, your mom flipped my chair over, got on top of me, and was forcing fire tasting cookies down my throat. The cookies burned my throat, and for some odd reason my arms and legs were immobilized, and I couldn't fight back. She kept shoving smashed fire cookies down my throat and forcing fire cookie crumbs up my nose. It was the worst dream ever because I couldn't shake her off of me. When I woke up, my mouth and nose were still burning. Your mother was the other person who saved me."

Instantly, my eyes swelled. That was the most fascinating and compelling dream I'd ever heard. How do I respond to something supernatural?

Choked-up, I said, "Mom knew you were meant for me, that's why she saved you."

Thank you, Mom! You have always been my hero!

Our lips briefly touched. "I agree," he concurred.

Gazing into one another's eyes, my thoughts started to race. Oh, my God! Now, I'm putting the puzzle pieces together. Mom didn't want Dillon to cross over! Or did he cross over?

Softly, Dillon whispered, "There's more to the story when you are ready, hun."

Totally spellbound, I said, "I'm ready, hun!"

76

AFTER TAKING A couple sips of water, Dillon said, "The second time I saw your mom in one of my dreams was when I was living with Candace. During my dream, I was fishing with your dad, of course not knowing he was your dad at the time. And this was my first-time ever fishing, and I was at ease with him. Your dad and I were having a relaxing good time until your mom, out of nowhere, forcefully grabbed my wrist, and the next thing I knew, I was wearing roller skates and skating with her. And I had never been on skates before," Dillon admitted, taking a quick drink. "Your mom and I were roller skating on a road overlooking the ocean, and I couldn't break off her grip. Then, she yanked my head, and made me look at her ring for the longest time. When I awoke, I sketched the ring, took it to a jeweler, and had your mom's ring custom designed, which was over a month ago."

I was fucking shocked and speechless, there was no way on earth Dillon could ever fabricate this type of a detailed dream. Dad, for the most part fished alone, that was his special quiet time away from the world. One-time, Emma and I accompanied Dad, and we were bored out of our minds, and in less than two hours, Mom had to come get us. And on a rare occasion, Dad would invite someone, but he really had to enjoy their company. Well, it seemed like Dillon passed Dad's fishing test which was impressive.

"My mother died wearing her new derby skates. She was breaking them in. Anyway, please continue."

Dillon had fear in his face when he admitted, "At first, I thought the ring was supposed to be for Candace, until the woman who manhandles me in my dreams, visited me again."

Immediately, I burst out laughing.

"What's so funny?" Dillon asked, petrified.

"My mother was six feet, two inches tall and weighed 200 pounds. She was extremely fit because she loved powerlifting. Get this, she was the captain of her roller derby team, and she used to manhandle just about

184

anyone in her path. With ease, she used to hurl her opponents, and sometimes the refs around."

"Well, that explains a lot because in my third dream with her, she was on a rampage, and kept pushing me to the ground and picking me back up. And you have to understand, your mom doesn't verbally talk to me. She gives me a thumbs up or thumbs down, and sometimes she gives me this 'fear-stare look' and I have trouble keeping eye contact with her, and I just want to escape," Dillon admitted sheepishly without eye contact.

77

AFTER I LET out a loud laugh, I said, "My parents had their occasional tiffs, and on a rare occasion when Mom was really upset, and in one of her crazed moods, she would be up in my dad's face, and even he couldn't stand to be around her. He would take me for a long car ride around Ocean Drive until she cooled off."

"Wow, no kidding," Dillon said, slightly relieved, but still looked a little bit puzzled. "Your mom intimidated your dad sometimes, really?"

"Oh, yeah, it's not only you, hun, my mother didn't discriminate. And get this one, Emma practically lived at my house growing up, and treated her like a daughter. And if we acted up, my mother used to put the fear of God into us. All she had to do was call us by our first and middle names with her big hand in the air about to strike us, and we knew to stop, or else. One time, when we were little and being really bad, we were making messes everywhere in the house, and we forgot to clean the kitchen, so she grabbed us by our collars, shoved us in the car, and drove us to Providence. And you're not going to believe this, she dropped us off all alone in the heart of the city at the bus station for a long time. We were terrified. Well, anyway, please continue—what happened in your dream?"

Dillon had a bewildered look on his face. "That sounds like something my dad would have done to me. So anyway, your mom showed me a picture of Candace with a thumbs down. Then she showed me a picture of you with a thumbs up," Dillon said softly with a genuine smile. "That's the first time I saw your face, and that's when I started drawing you."

"That's so sweet, hun."

Dillon took a sip of water.

All of this was so fascinating. After a quick peck, I asked with great curiosity, "Any other dreams with my parents?"

Immediately, Dillon looked away. And I knew, I struck his sensitive nerve again. Now, I need to know. It killed me not to know. So, in my softest, sweetest voice, I assured, "It's okay, hun. I'm not going to judge you."

"Um, you . . . you . . . um, promise, Zoey . . . because . . . um?" he asked nervously, stuttering.

78

THE SUSPENSE WAS killing me. "Dillon, you're going to be my husband soon, and I love you," I said with a quick smooch. "You can tell me anything you want to about your past, okay? I promise, hun, no judgement."

Slowly nodding his head, he confessed, "About a week ago, Stephanie came over unexpectedly, and we slept together. It was the wrong thing to do, and I gave her the wrong impression, and I deeply regretted my actions. Later that night, she left, and when I went to bed, and while I was dreaming, your mother visited me, and went berserk. She forcefully dragged me by my neck to a bowling alley, and threw me down each and every lane as your dad watched from afar, ignoring me, while sitting at the lounge bar," Dillon said, taking a quick sip. "And every time your mom threw me down a lane, she showed me a picture of you at a different age. She kept showing me her ring, and a picture of your face, before she forcefully threw me into the pins. And for some strange reason, she always extended her hand and dragged me back up, just to throw me down again. The next morning, I woke up very sore from head to toe, and on the floor with all the sheets ripped-off, and I was about five feet away from the bed. And also, I don't like admitting this, but some nights, I feared going to sleep because of the roller-skating lady."

Immediately, I burst out laughing.

"I don't find this funny, Zoey. This ghost thing, or paranormal stuff, or whatever you want to call it, doesn't sit well with me. I didn't know she was your mother until last night. This morning, when I woke up from the dream of you at the beach with your parents, your mom for the first time didn't kick my ass. She actually was supportive, and very nice to me," Dillon said, sort of relieved.

"Thank you for your honesty," I said with the utmost sincerity. "My mother's MO was whenever she knocked someone down, she would extend her hand and help them back up. Well, I now think Mom is very fond of you."

188

"Well, that's a huge relief," Dillon said, "and oh, there's one other thing I need to fill you in on about Candace. I'll tell you after my nap."

79

WAS DILLON OUT of his fucking mind? He already knew how to push all my hot buttons. He understood, I wanted to know as of yesterday. Now, this was going to be interesting since it involved Candace.

"Mom will be waiting for you with an Irish fist if you take a nap," I said harshly with squinted eyes. "And you just got on her good side. Do you want to risk upsetting her!"

"Good one, Zoey," he said hesitantly, letting out a quick nervous laugh. "You . . . you got me there!"

Playfully poking him in his chest with a stern face and a raised eyebrow, Dillon squealed, "Okay, okay, I will tell you. Last night, when we spoke, she mentioned that if we were both not married in fifteen years, that we should get married. I didn't respond back because she surprised me, and quickly ended the call. I just wanted you to know, and of course, that's not the case anymore because we'll be married soon for the rest of our lives."

Dillon's honesty was refreshing, and I would rather be in the know than him not telling me at all, or worse, flat out lying. Regardless, and at once, I must have a heart-to-heart conversation with Candace. Dillon's alive today because of her keen intuition, and I'm truly forever grateful.

"Thanks for informing me," I said. And now, for the million-dollar question, I asked, "How come you didn't accompany her to Paris?"

"When Candace was presented with the modeling opportunity, I saw a major shift in her personality and demeanor," Dillon admitted without any sadness in his voice. "She reminded me of my mother."

"I don't understand," I said, confused. "How did Candace remind you of your mother?"

"Growing up, when I would occasionally see my mother, she really wasn't mentally there. She would always be thinking about her upcoming title fight, and ways to beat her next opponent and training all the time, or she would be thinking about her new business location. It's a very competitive, Type A personality, and they're never satisfied with

190

being in the moment," Dillon said businesslike. "Mafalda is the exact same way. All three of them are high strung, and I refuse to be someone's afterthought. And even if I went to Paris to be with Candace . . . her mind would be elsewhere. She would always be thinking about work, or the next photo shoot, or her next business deal, and I would just be her familiar support crutch."

It was unbelievable that Dillon knew about different personality types at a young age, and I was impressed with his street-smarts. And he was one hundred percent accurate about Candace's work-drive because she was a nonstop business beast. Knowing Mafalda worked around the clock because I snooped on her emails, she was a business bad-ass. Hopefully soon, I will meet my future mother-in-law and weigh in.

"If you never won the lottery, would your answer still be the same, would you have gone to Paris?"

Dillon started to chuckle.

"What's so funny?"

"I asked myself that exact same question many times. And to give you an honest answer, I would have gone with her because my home life was that miserable," Dillon answered honestly. "And I would be forced to live with one of my parents until I left for college."

So, it seemed like money did buy a certain level of happiness. And being financially well-off, provided a comfortable time freedom for someone to carefully vet their soulmate. It's funny, I asked Candace the exact same question during one of her meltdowns. I asked her if the modeling gig never manifested, would she have left Dillon, and her reassuring answer was never in a million years! And deep-down, I knew she would always love him. But the real question was, did Dillon still love her in some manner?

Come on, Zoes, fuck, after all, Candace saved his life! And he just told me he would have gone.

Since I needed to know the skinny about my future husband, I asked, "If Stephanie hadn't broken up with you, what do you think would have happened to you guys?"

"We probably would have gotten married after college. Our goals were for her to hopefully make it to the WNBA, and for me, to hopefully make it to the NFL. And our dream was to have a big house somewhere, but now, when I look back at it all, I was in an abusive relationship. It was her way or no way."

Bringing out my inner arsenal of legal questions, and knowing full well that Stephanie assaulted Dillon many times last night, I asked, "What do you mean you were in an abusive relationship?"

Dillon closed his eyes. "If she didn't get her way, she would sometimes hit me, or throw things at me, but the worse abuse was when she would verbally degrade me, and tell me I was a piece of shit and yell all sorts of mean things. And she would withhold sex from me if she was mad. And I'm embarrassed to admit this, but she bullied me for years. And I blame myself for letting it happen."

"I'm so sorry that happened to you, hun, and I would never do any of those things to you, I promise," I said assuring, nestled securely in his arms when our lips quickly met.

With a faint smile, Dillon said, "Thanks, hun, that means a lot."

"Did you ever call the police?"

"No, however, last night she kicked in my glass door that goes out to the balcony. And when I got home, she was already inside waiting for me. Then she started to hit and belittle me. For the first time, I was dialing 9-1-1 when she kicked my cell out of my hand and—"

Interrupting, I interjected, "That's against the law."

"Really, it is? I never knew that."

"Yes, it is, hun, do you still want to press charges?"

Dillon said, "No, because I made it very clear that I wanted nothing to do with her."

"If you change your mind, I have it all recorded. Actually, I watched it all unfold. You could have Stephanie arrested and brought up on a slew of charges, such as, breaking an entry, destruction of property, assault and battery, and interfering with a police call. She even intimated your neighbor, the old woman. She could be a witness."

"You saw that!" he said, startled. "How did you see that?"

"Unfortunately, I did, hun. My special skill set is hacking, and I can easily hack into a surveillance system. When I saw you for the first time when you came to Emma's rescue, I was head over heels in love with you. I've been watching you for weeks provided there was a camera."

"That's creepy. Did you watch me in my apartment when I showered, and *stuff*?"

"I wish!" I admitted, giggling. Dillon started to laugh. "Only at work, and at the gym, and the grocery store, and I almost forgot about The Den. That's all."

"That's all?" Dillon said laughing when he gave me a quick smooch. "I guess if I could take a peek and watch someone of interest I probably would too. So, getting back to Stephanie, I don't want to press charges because it would ruin her basketball scholarship that she put her heart and soul into during the past four years. And I don't want that on my conscience. Once she leaves for California, which is very soon, she'll be long gone."

"Okay, I understand. Then with your permission, hun, can I call Stephanie on a recorded line, and warn her that if she assaults you again there will be severe legal consequences, and possibly, even jail time."

"Really? You would do that for me, hun?" he asked, surprised.

"Hun, I would do anything for you. I love you with all my heart."

Dillon's eyes started to tear. I reached over for the tissue box which I now realized was purposely missing because I didn't want to give him any ideas or encouragement to jerk off.

"Besides my grandma, you're the first woman in my life who truly has ever had my back," Dillon admitted. "That's why I love you with all my heart, and you mean the world to me. Yes, please contact her, I will text you her number, and oh, also tell her to never contact me again. You're the best, hun!"

Inwardly, I was laughing because I already possessed *all* of Dillon's complete contacts. "No, you're the best, hun," I said with a quick peck, feeling the lingles.

"Ask me another question."

I asked, "When you drove by us yesterday, and saw me for the first time, what went through your mind?"

Instantly, Dillon smiled, and said, "I was relieved! Well, actually, at first, I was shocked. I thought Emma was playing a joke on me because—"

Interrupting, I asked, "How come?"

"Because I thought I would have to attend my senior year to find you because I kept dreaming about you. I was going crazy trying to find you, and I had no idea you were Emma's best friend. Please take this as a sincere compliment, you look like a typical teenager."

"Looking too young can also be a curse," I declared, "because many people only see the outside, and not what you're truly capable of doing."

"Well, I partially disagree, hun. Who wants to get old?"

"Okay, I see your point too, and I partially disagree as well," I said. "So why were you sitting on the foyer floor near the elevator last night, looking depressed?"

With a puzzling look, Dillon asked, "You saw that too?"

"Yes, I did, sugar," I said jokingly, trying to sound Southern.

Reaching for his water bottle, Dillon let out a hesitant, awkward chuckle. That's not the positive reaction I was hoping to receive from my lame sugar joke. Unfortunately, I knew his sensitive nerve was once again, struck.

Softly, he said, "I prefer to not answer that."

In my sweetest voice, I assured, "No judgement, okay."

Dillon closed his eyes, and said, "It had to do with a lot of things, including Emma."

Under no circumstance was Dillon getting off the hook! I needed to know right now! Very softly—sweetly, I said, "It's okay, you can tell me, hun, no judgment."

"When Candace left for Paris, I was in rough shape. A couple days later, Ed and Emma invited me over for a swim and a cookout. And you know, Zoey, I . . . I . . . just can't."

The suspense was killing me. Softly, and very soothingly, I said, "You know, Dillon, being a divorce lawyer, I heard it all. It's okay, and safe for you to tell me."

"Okay, okay, you have a magical gift of getting everything out of me. When it was just Ed and I outside attending the grill, he thanked me again for saving Emma's life, and credited me for getting them back together. Then he left for a minute and got us two more beers. When we touched bottles, he mentioned that Emma was, as he put it . . . she was doting on me, and he was comfortable with that. He also said she takes a lot of time and pride choosing her outfits, and *really* looks forward to seeing me. Ed actually said, and I can't make this shit up, he . . . um wanted to watch Emma and I have sex. And I, um . . . was taken aback because that's fucked up. I'm not in any way into that kind of weird stuff," Dillon admitted with a frazzled look on his face. "I could never let my wife or my significant other screw someone else while I watched. That's really fucked up!"

OMG, now, I heard it all! Talk about being fucked up, that was 1,000 percent fucked up! My gut feeling was right, Emma was in love with Dillon. Fuck! How could you not be?

"So, what was your response back to Ed?"

"Since I was extremely uncomfortable with his statement, I told him I should get going. He immediately put his arm around my shoulder, and begged me to stay because it would upset Emma if I left abruptly. He also said that Emma didn't know about his bizarre fantasy, and he apologized."

"Anything else happened when you were there?"

"Wow! You don't miss a beat, hun, do you?"

"Hun, as *your* attorney, it's my job to keep asking questions until I get what I want, which are truthful answers, got it?"

"Okay, got it. At the end of the evening, Eloise was getting cranky and tired, so we all decided to say goodnight. Emma took Eloise upstairs to bed, and Ed walked me out to my truck. In the driveway, he gave me his permission, that if I wanted to sleep with Emma . . . I could."

I stated, "That blows my mind!"

Remaining silent, Dillon nodded his head in agreement.

"Okay, so why were you sitting on the foyer floor?"

"You're relentless, Zoey," he said, turning his face away. "Let's stop."

"Let's not! Please continue."

"For the past couple of weeks, I noticed Emma was getting flirtier. And yada yada."

I burst out laughing for a few seconds. "In our relationship, hun, there's no yada yada gibberish, got it!"

"Are you sure, Zoey . . . you want to go down this road?"

"No judgement, hun."

"Okay then, I thought I was going crazy during these past few weeks dreaming about you and your parents. I didn't know if it was real or not. I expected Emma's best friend was going to look like someone in their thirties, and when it was you, I couldn't believe it, I couldn't believe it was you!"

"Please keep going," I requested with a quick, open-eye peck. "I'm still waiting patiently for the main course."

"Remind me to never get on your bad side, and owe you an explanation."

"I couldn't have said it any better, hun," I replied with a quick laugh. "Dillon!"

"Okay, okay, you saw how she was dressed last night, and I'm not trying to sound conceited, but she probably dressed that way to get my attention. She knocked you over to get to me. And when we hugged, it was her most aggressive hug ever. Her fingernails dug into my back, and you know she was crazy about me from the way she acted. Do you not agree, hun?"

Trust me, hun, you don't know the half of it. And yes, she did dress that way for you—*slutty*. She's named sex toys in your honor—one requires batteries. And if you only knew about her extramarital get-out-of-jail free hall pass she was just awarded—Houston we definitely have a—let's stop this, Zoes!

I said, "Yeah, hun, I saw it too, and I was embarrassed how she acted. And yes, it was blatantly obvious she was goo-goo over you."

Dillon started to laugh.

I asked, "What's so funny?"

"Goo-goo, you're killing me."

"Glad to make you laugh. Let's get back on track, hun. What was going through your mind when you were sitting there?"

With closed eyes, he said, "God, you don't let up, do you?"

"No, I don't, hun," I said, feeling safe in his arms. Knowing this was going to be awkward, I softly and sweetly requested, "Please continue."

"Okay, if it wasn't *you* who showed up last night, I was going to ask *her* if she wanted to have only a physical relationship," he admitted, reaching for his water. "When I was sitting there, all my thoughts and emotions were all coming together in a perfect storm. And I realized how lucky I was to find you when I did because if I didn't, I would have asked her."

Dillon's honesty was extraordinarily refreshing. And he deserved an A-plus for his rhetoric. He was clever to use the word 'her' instead of Emma and 'physical' instead of sex. My soon-to-be husband was cool and calculated.

Be cool, Zoes, and act like this was no big deal. And let's save *those intrusive questions* for another time.

Giggling, I asked, "Was that really hard?"

"Yes, it was," he chuckled. "Any other questions I can clear up for you?"

My future hubby could take the heat in the hot seat, I was very impressed. Let's start from the beginning. "Why was your childhood so awful?"

"The best year of my life growing up was when I lived with my grandparents. I was six at the time. And when I lived with my parents, my mom was always gone, and my dad for the longest time, worked the third shift. Most nights, when he was away, I slept alone in an apartment with a gun in my bed."

"With a gun in your bed!" I yelled dumfounded. "Get the fuck out of here!"

"I kid you not. My dad taught me how to use a gun when I was seven. He ordered me to shoot anyone except for him if someone came into our apartment. The order was to shoot them fucking dead, with more than one bullet. One bullet in the chest, and the next two bullets point blank in the head. One time, he switched my real gun for a BB gun, and being only seven-years-old, I didn't know the difference. And one night he charged in wearing a ski mask, and I shot him," Dillon started laughing, "in the balls."

I was laughing with Dillon when I asked, "Are you fucking serious?"

"I'm not joking, I can't make that shit up. He was irate because I didn't hit him squarely in the chest like he taught me. And oh, get this, if my bed wasn't made perfectly every day, and if his breakfast wasn't waiting for him on the table when he returned home from his graveyard shift, I got the belt."

For thirteen lucky years, I cherished my awesome childhood, and loving parents. Every night, I felt safe in my room. In the event of a nightmare, I would run down the hallway and jump into their welcoming king-size bed. One time, when I barged in, I interrupted their wrestling match. Mom was on top—winning. Oh, shit, Zoes, talk about being virgin clueless—they weren't wrestling! Anyways, I could have burnt down the house, and Dad wouldn't have said, "Boo." He never once hit me. However, Emma and I knew better not to push Mom's hot buttons because we would feel her wrath. Mom really was the enforcer in the family. She kept Emma and me in line, but she also had a heart of gold. As long as you didn't cross 'her line' you were good.

My eyes swelled. "I'm so sorry that—"

Interrupting, Dillon said, "Please don't shed any tears on my inept parents. At least, I was fortunate to have one good year as a child with Grandma and Grandpa Race. They lived in Rhode Island, and my grandma taught me how to cook and do laundry, and do all sorts of stuff when I lived with them. Growing up, she was my hero."

"Why did you have to live with them?" I asked.

"To this day, my parents never told me the reason. The day they picked me up, I cried all the way back to Connecticut."

"Well, I'm glad you came back, and rescued my bestie. And Emma told me your grandmother was once an Olympic runner, is that true?"

"Oh, yeah, it's true, and in her heyday, she was the fastest woman sprinter in the world."

Talk about coming from a great athletic gene pool. "Wow, that's very impressive. So, what was your grandfather like?" I asked with great curiosity.

"Very strict!" Dillon snapped. "I feared him when I lived there. Every morning, I had to make my bed perfectly, and my bedroom had to be spotless when he did his daily inspection. Also, he would make me exercise with him. And he would throw a regular size football at me very fast. And it hurt catching it. He told me numerous times that he would love to see me play football for the Navy."

"Why is it so important to your grandfather that you play football for the Navy?"

"I'm not sure, but one-time when we were throwing the football, I threw a tantrum. I told him that I would not play football for the Navy because I was afraid of being too far out in the ocean on a battleship.

And I didn't want to be attacked by sharks or a giant octopus. And he went crazy. He took off his belt, and was chasing me around the yard. My grandma ran out of the house, and had to stop him from whipping me."

What's wrong with the Race family? Like a fool, I started to laugh into his muscular chest. "I'm so sorry, hun, that was very rude of me," I admitted with an apologetic kiss, still softly laughing. "I don't mean to laugh, but the way you tell your story with battleships and sharks and running for your life is adorable."

Whew, thank God, Dillon started to laugh. "Glad to make you laugh," he said with a quick smooch. "So, if you don't mind me asking, how did your parents die?"

Wow, Dillon was cerebral in the manner he asked questions. He knew from me laughing at his story gave him an opportunity to ask something extremely personal. I explained my tragic story in detail, along with my foster care aftermath. Dillon was visibly shaken to his core with Mom's last words. Like me, Dillon felt justice when I explained the drunktard was tortured. However, I didn't tell Dillon that his grandfather was the executioner.

Since I just divulged my parents' death in full detail, I knew it bought me additional cred. "Tell me something else about you or your family that I don't know."

"Robbie says . . . I'm a really good singer."

"Sing me a song, hun, and I'll give you my ruling."

"I need to be in a certain mindset to sing. Well, anyways, you're not going to believe this one, my parents are still married."

"Really! I honestly thought they were divorced since they didn't live together."

"Yeah, everyone thinks that."

Embarrassingly, I asked, "Do they still, you . . . know?"

With a straight face, Dillon asked, "You . . . know?"

"Do they . . . ?"

"Do they . . . what?" Dillon teased until he burst out laughing.

"You're a jerk!" I screeched with a soft playful slap to his chest.

"You asked for it, hun! And yes, they still do, but only when I'm there."

"Ew, stop it, hun!"

"You nasty, Zoey!" he said laughing. "And since you asked, you ought to know the walls in my mother's condo are razor thin . . . it sounds like they are killing each other."

"Ew gross! Stop it, hun!"

Connected as one, we were belly laughing.

With great curiosity, I asked, "So, how often do you see a psychic?"

"Grandma Race took me many times when I lived with them. She used to take me to Fall River, Massachusetts to her favorite psychic. And I used to sit and watch in amazement. And if I behaved well, she bought me pastries."

The childhood bribe system has always been alive and still thriving as I let out a quick laugh. I remembered Dillon's adorable pictures when he was a little boy, imagining frosting and chocolate smudged all over his cute face.

"When was the last time you went to a psychic?"

With a big smile, Dillon replied, "Right after my first drawing of you, I took it to the same psychic my grandma and I went to in Fall River because I always liked her, and she said we were married in another lifetime."

I gave Dillon a quick smooch. "Is there anything else I need to know along those lines?"

Gazing into my eyes, Dillon profoundly stated, "Yes, and I don't know how to explain this, hun," he paused briefly for a sip. "Last night at dinner, right before you asked me to be your first, I saw two images, one on each side of you. I can't say for sure if it was your parents, but I can tell you this, I had a very warm, tranquil feeling resonating inside of me. And it felt absolutely amazing."

80

OH! MY! GOD! Amazingly, Dillon felt the lingles too! Dillon was my liaison to my parents! Truly, Dillon was my everything—my linnacle! With happy tears in my eyes, I announced, "And just when I thought I couldn't get any happier, you keep amazing me, hun. I swear on my parents' souls, I had the lingles too. I love you."

Confused, Dillon asked, "What are the lingles?"

Softly giggling, I admitted, "It's when true love resonates blissfully inside your body. It's the best feeling in the world."

"Yes, I definitely had the lingles last night, and I have them right now, and you're right, it's the best feeling ever."

"And hun, you are my linnacle."

"What does that mean?" he asked, baffled.

"Love's pinnacle."

Smiling he said, "And hun, you're definitely my linnacle, too."

Immediately, our lips magnetized. Blissfully, we were lost in a soft, deep kiss. The man of my dreams was an understatement. Dillon was a lot more. Best lover—check, great friend—check, liaison to Mom and Dad—check, honest person—check, great protector and keeps me safe at night—check, great cook—check, best future husband—check. Check—check—check—check to infinity. Candace was one hundred percent accurate, Dillon checked off every box, perfectly. And he free-willing chose me to be his wife! Now, I had to discover all of his important boxes, and make sure to check them off, perfectly.

Breaking off our kiss, Dillon confessed, "Zoey, there's one last thing, you have to forgive me in advance if I have an affair with *my* attorney. I just can't resist her—she's . . . so fucking sexy."

Immediately smiling, I sprang up lunging on top of Dillon—sandwich flat. We were lost and locked in a passionate kiss when I felt King. Instantly, I leaned back with my hand shoving him inside my wetness— loving every thick, deep sensational inch. Before I could rise up and take control—start riding dick, Dillon effortlessly flipped us over. Connected as one, I was pinned and his.

Gazing upward into his kind blue eyes, Dillon said, "There is something else, Zoey. Since we will be married soon, you will receive half of my likeness, including what I have now, and that's nonnegotiable."

Instantly, my eyes swelled. "Dillon, that's—"

81

INTERRUPTING, DILLON SAID, "The only reason why I didn't ask you know who to marry me was because of money. She fought me on everything I spent on her. And it put a wedge in our relationship."

Impressive, Dillon was clever not to use Candace's name deep inside.

Sternly, he reiterated, "I asked you to marry me, Zoey, because I love you, and what I have now is also yours. Again, it's nonnegotiable."

Dillon's heart was made from pure, wonderful goodness. Overwhelmed, flabbergasted, and aroused by being firmly told what to do, I said, "Thank you, Dillon, that's the most generous gift anyone has ever given me. I love you."

"I know you love me, and you give me the lingles."

Speaking my love language, Dillon forever won. And at that very moment, I decided to unplug our love-scoreboard—for life. I just couldn't compete with his kindness and overwhelming generosity.

Just let go, Zoes, and have some fun. Flirtatiously, I said, "Did you know, hun, I'm going to have you sign a sex-prenuptial?"

Playfully, and rock hard—throbbing inside, he said, "Really now, how . . . *come!*"

Loving the back and forth banter, I said with the biggest smile, "Because I have over a decade of sex to make up for, and you're going to have to . . . try to keep up with me."

Matching the size of my smile, Dillon started to slowly thrust. "Well, I need to run everything by my lawyer first." Thrusting faster, he playfully asked, "And how am I supposed to satisfy the two of you?"

"You better quickly figure it out," I announced in a challenging tonality. "Just remember, my future husband, I always, fucking come first!"

Abruptly, Dillon stopped thrusting, pulled out, got on his knees, and then flipped me over—flat on my stomach. Authoritatively, he whispered in my ear while firmly squeezing my butt cheeks, "I love your ass, and you will be coming loudly, real fucking soon. I . . . guaran! Fucking! Tee-it!"

Oh boy, did I bite off more than I could chew? Dillon's strong hands kept firmly squeezing my ass making my insides gush. Briefly, he stopped to widen my legs, then quickly went back to the pleasurable firm squeezes. Softly, I started to moan thinking about King—wishing for another hard fucking.

82

DILLON HAD TO read my mind because he slipped in a finger. Slowly, I was being finger fucked. In less than fifteen seconds, his second finger entered.

With my face resting flat-down in the pillow, I was softly moaning. "That feels amazing, hun."

In no time, Dillon's two fingers were ravishing my insides—my moans became louder.

When Dillon's finger pace became rapid, he forcefully ordered, "Look at my cock while I finger fuck you!"

Tilting my head sideways, King was profoundly erect. Badly, I wanted to be reconnected with my mouth mate. Slowly, and seductively, with my moist tongue, I traced the outside of my lips. In a begging voice, I said, "I want to blow you."

Instantly, I was flipped over. Resting comfortably with two pillows underneath my head, Dillon slid his left knee near the top of my head, the rest of his body paralleled the right side of my body. Turning my face slightly to the right, King was directly above my face. Dillon's hand guided King into my welcoming moist mouth. Finally, I was reunited with my mouth muse!

Placing my right hand on King's lower shaft, I was doing my best to bob my resting, tilted head with off-kilter suctions.

Looking downward, Dillon challenged, "Let's see who comes first!"

Looking upward with King engulfed—stretching my jaws, I cock-mumbled, "Game on!"

Within a few seconds, Dillon started to vigorously play with my clit which sent delightful shivers throughout my body. He would mix it up by sliding in two fingers, fuck me intensely for a about fifteen seconds, then take them out to play with my swollen clit. Dillon's fabulous finger technique was absolutely driving me sexually crazy. And he definitely had the advantage in this orgasm challenge because of my lack of mobility.

And then The Clit Maestro with his free hand decided to caress and pinch my erect, sensitive nipples. It was almost game over. Gazing upward into Dillon's eyes with King wedged deep in my drooling mouth, I knew he would win because I felt the big sneeze. And this intense sneeze lingering deep inside felt like a category 5 hurricane.

Sprawled out, softly moaning, I slowly started to squirm. Instantly, my body's thermometer was cranked to the max. I closed my eyes trying my best to delay my orgasm. However, Dillon's fingers hit fourth gear. Vigorously, he kept circling over my supersensitive clit. And yes, all the active swarms of fireflies were heating up and lighting up my insides. My body's temperature spiked, and was almost at a rapid boil.

Forcefully, Dillon demanded, "Come for me, Zoey!"

My erect, sensitive nipples were being pampered—pinched perfectly. His virtuoso fingers flawlessly caressed my clit. Just let go, Zoes, I'm forever his.

The intensity of my orgasm was fucking off the charts. Shaking uncontrollably, my orgasm screams were muffled with King jammed down my throat.

Placing two fingers back inside my soaked pussy, he guaranteed, "I'm going to make you come again!"

Nailed into the bed with King lodged deep in my throat, Dillon started to vigorously finger fuck me. And the delightful nipple pinches amplified my sexual arousal. My insides felt incredible, like a nonstop lightning bolt striking every feel-good nerve ending. Quivering, my orgasm aftershocks were a mere afterthought while I was being tenaciously finger-fucked.

And yes, in under a minute, Dillon, my king, had me violently coming again!

My legs couldn't stop trembling when King—rock hard sprung out of my mouth. Shaking, I yelled, "Oh, my God, Dillon! What are you doing to me?!"

Ignoring me, Dillon bent down, taking my mouth hostage. The sounds of my moans were captive only to his mouth. When I finally calmed down, he released my mouth.

Quickly climbing off the bed, Dillon was erect on the floor. He placed his large hands on each side of my obliques, then effortlessly flipped me over like a pancake. He hoisted me up, and then positioned me near the base of the bed—on all fours.

Without any warning, without any permission, and without ejaculating, for the very first time in my life, my future husband *is* going to take me from behind. And I wouldn't want it any other fucking way!

83

FOR THE LONGEST time, I fantasized about being on my hands and knees. In a high-pitched silly voice, I asked, "Are you gonna do me like a doggy?"

Laughing loudly, Dillon rubbed King on my clit down to my eager entrance. Already saturated, I started to moan.

Slowly, Dillon put King inside—inch by thick, robust inch into my river-soaked pussy—stretching my insides to capacity. "I'm all the way inside of you. How does it feel?"

"Oh, my God!" I said, gasping. He was so fucking deep inside, I thought King was going to exit through my mouth! "You feel amazing, hun!"

"You feel amazing, hun," Dillon concurred. Slowly, he started to move back and forth. "Zoey, your ass is so fucking sexy. You drive me absolutely fucking crazy!"

Let's get kinky, Zoes!

Flirtatiously, I said, "If you like my ass . . . spank me once. And if you *love* my ass . . . spank me twice!"

Lickety-split, my left butt cheek received its very first welcoming slap. Gasping in slight pain—more pleasure, immediately, my right cheek felt the same soft pleasurable sting. Yes, my very first sting-a-ding! He loved my ass, that's what I'm talking about!

With slow, gentle thrusts, Dillon sent wonderful sensations throughout my body. King was beyond deep inside my gushing wetness, and I loved the way his balls struck my clit. Without any warning, both butt cheeks received more pleasurably spanks: sting-dings. But this time with more vigor, making me yelp.

Speeding up the deep thrust—the tempo, Dillon was in total control. I loved the natural—raw sex-sounds our bodies repeatedly made as we kept colliding. These raw sex-sounds amplified my body's delight.

"I love your cock deep inside my pussy," I blurted out lewdly. "It feels so . . . fucking good! Fuck me harder!"

206

"I love how tight and wet your pussy is," Dillon said in a low, rough voice. "You look so fucking sexy on your hands and knees. I'm going to fuck you . . . real hard now!"

Dillon's pace was rapid, deep, and intense. My moans coincided perfectly with his grunts—loving the sounds we continuously broadcasted. With each deep grunted thrust, my knees were slowly separating further apart. It didn't take long for Dillon's forceful momentum to collapse my upper body into the bed. Submissively, I was pinned on my chest and on the front of my shoulders with my arms by my side. My face was flat down—pancaked into the sheets. Ta-da! Without further ado, my ass was perfectly arched in the air for my future husband's viewing pleasure.

I loved being fucked hard from behind. And I loved being forcefully taken, it was blissfully animalistic. Truth be told, I loved being submissive. And I loved the sex-smell, the stickiness, and the sounds we mutually howled. And I loved how Dillon controlled everything. For the next couple of minutes with my face buried in the bed, I was fiercely being fucked. My moaning became louder—correction—out of fucking control while I squeezed and bit the sheets.

When Dillon slowed down the pace, I felt the perspiration from our bodies while my ass kept receiving sting-dings. And yes, hands-down— no pun intended, being taken and fucked hard from behind was now my favorite position!

84

WITH TWO CONVINCING sting-dings, Dillon lewdly ordered, "I'm going to stand still, and watch you fuck my cock!"

There was something extra special about Dillon being in full control of my pleasure, especially when being submissive. And everything Dillon sexually promised, he always over delivered. Getting back to my original, on all fours position, I slowly started to move back and forth. After a few seconds of me getting used to fucking King, I increased my back and forth momentum since I loved how it made my insides feel—full and wonderfully stretched.

"You keep amazing me, Zoey. That feels incredible, you have the sexiest ass. Twerk for me!" he ordered with a convincing sting-ding.

After letting out a shriek, I dropped to my elbows with my hands stretched forward. After another swat, I started thrusting my ass up and down—twerking for about a minute with King deep inside, receiving pleasurable sting-dings.

Without any notice, Dillon took control and started to fuck me. "I'm addicted to your entire body," Dillon said in a husky tone. Grunting from behind while thrusting faster, he revealed, "Especially, your . . . tight pussy."

Convincingly, he kept spanking my ass while he intensely fucked me from behind. Whoosh, without any warning, my vajayjay released and vocalized her very first, and extremely loud queef, aka a pussy fart. Remembering the stories that Emma shared over the years, it was common during vigorous sex.

Dillon stopped all motions once he heard the loud, embarrassing, vaginal hiccup. His right hand slid around my waist, then down to my aroused clit—caressing it while his left hand was squeezing my ass.

Fuck, I queefed, again. Why be bashful? Just fucking ask for it—demand it, Zoes! "Fuck me hard!" I yelled—ordered.

Dillon placed his large hand on my ass. Slowly, he was building momentum. Looking sideways at the full-length wall mirror while being fucked from behind, he looked so fucking hot with all his ripped muscles engaged. He was in full control when I received another sting-ding.

But I needed to be fucked faster. "Fuck me harder! Please!" I moaned—begged. "I'm addicted to your thick cock!"

Loudly, he demanded to know, "Tell me how much you love my cock!"

"I love your big . . . thick cock. I want it in my pussy all the time!" I shouted. "Please, fuck me hard!"

He started to fuck me deep and fast when he lewdly asked, "And what about my cock in your watering mouth, do you love blowing me?"

"Oh, fuck, Dillon, I love your big . . . thick cock in my mouth and blowing you. It's my new favorite activity. Oh, fuck, hun, I love pleasing you any way you wish. Make me come all over your cock," I begged lewdly. "Fuck my pussy...hard!"

Coming to a halt, Dillon forcefully grabbed my hair, yanking me backwards. His other large hand—fingers were tightly squeezing my chin and throat. Convincingly, he turned my neck sideways, then leaned forward, and before I knew it we were passionately and savagely kissing.

While controlling my head and neck, Dillon abruptly stopped our kiss. Gazing deep into my eyes, he forcefully asked—correction—with the utmost authority, he demanded to know, "Whose fucking pussy is this!"

85

"I LOVE YOU, Dillon," I announced truthfully. Gazing lovestruck into his blue eyes, I declared, "It's unequivocally your pussy! And it will *always* be the property of Dillon Race!"

Fervently, he kissed me. After about ten seconds, Dillon announced, "That's the best fucking answer I've ever heard! I love you, Zoey!"

We resumed kissing, however, I needed to be fucked—hard! After a few seconds, I halted our kiss beseeching, "Please, fuck *your* pussy hard!"

After giving me a quick smooch, Dillon placed my head gingerly in the bed with my arms stretched out resembling a yoga pose. My ass was perfectly arched in the air when I received sting-dings. Within seconds, Dillon started to give me what I craved—begged for: deep, hard, fast thrusts. And it was the best pleasurable sensation I'd ever felt as our bodies kept forcefully colliding—slap—slap—slap.

Dillon, the man I love, was in full control of my body's delight. Moaning and groaning, my hands were squeezing the covers. His large balls kept intermittently striking my clit, sending heat waves throughout my insides. Lost in lust—the heat of the moment, I lewdly blurted out, "Make me come all over your cock!"

Lewder, Dillon ordered, "Play with your clit while I fuck you, and you'll come!"

Reaching backwards, while Dillon was thrusting, I did exactly what I was told. And for the record, I loved being forcefully told what to do. For the first time, we partnered for my sexual pleasure. Abruptly, he pulled out King, then delivered two more forceful sting-dings on my lobster bottom.

Feverishly playing with my clit, I queefed again. Faintly, I giggled.

King reentered, and in no time, Dillon was full throttle.

"You feel fucking incredible," he said. "I can feel your pussy squeezing my cock."

The nonstop momentum of being forcefully rammed, the incredible feeling of King expanding my insides while he grunted, combined with pleasuring myself—I came loudly praising Dillon's name.

My orgasm was totally out of fucking control. I was shaking uncontrollably on my stomach for about a half minute, and I couldn't remember what I was saying.

Somehow, we ended up sideways on the bed. And when I thought it couldn't get any better, from behind, Dillon hovered over me, positioning his knees on the outside of my almost closed thighs. Face down, my entire body was pancaked—nailed into the bed. My hands were stretched out and comfortably restrained—interlocked in his huge hands.

Slowly, he entered King back into my wetness. Once again, Dillon was in full control. I couldn't budge a smidge, and I wouldn't want it any other fucking way!

He whispered in my ear, "I love you, Zoey."

"I love you too, Dillon."

I will always be his.

Slowly, Dillon started to move back and forth. With his hot sex-breath he kept kissing the back of my neck and the side of my ears. Then all of a sudden, his thrusts became faster—deeper. Feeling pleasurably overstuffed with his thick cock continuously ramming my insides, he had me moaning uncontrollably.

Loving how Dillon took control while he was heavily panting, it didn't take long before I kept orgasming out of fucking control.

Surprisingly, Dillon hadn't come yet.

86

MY INSIDES NEEDED a much-needed breather, so I instructed Dillon to relax.

When I returned from the bathroom, Dillon was on his back with two pillows comfortably behind his head—spread-eagled—erect.

With a perfectly warm, damp washcloth, I gingerly cleaned King, making him glisten.

Lying flat on my stomach, with King front and center, I started to show my mouth appreciation for all the wonderful, thunderous orgasms Dillon had unselfishly gratified.

Slowly, I took King deep into my kisser. Then I began to stroke his base with one hand while the other was caressing his large balls. It didn't take long before Dillon's breathing became erratic, and I knew at any moment he could ejaculate.

Changing up my strategy to delay his orgasm, I started to tease the meaty tip of King with soft circle licks, playful kisses, and gentle suctions.

Gazing into my eyes, Dillon requested, "Please, hun, use your mouth more."

He wanted me to oblige, yeah, right. Two can play this sex game. Game fucking on! Ignoring Dillon's plea, I decided to go underneath. Slowly, and seductively, I began to suck on his swollen, cum-filled balls—one at a time. Looking directly up into his eyes with one of his smooth, big balls in my salivating piehole, I purposely slurped and moaned, and was behaving like a disobedient, cock-sucking spoiled brat.

The look in his distressed, sexual eyes spoke volumes. Loudly, Dillon begged, "Please, Zoey, I want to feel you sucking my cock more, please, hun!"

Fuck no, hun! I must loudly hear, but more importantly, I must *feel* your sexual agony—keep fucking begging!

Just to solely tease Dillon, I placed King into my mouth, only giving him a few bobs. Abruptly, and coldly, I stopped the desired suctions he so desperately craved, then went below. Immediately, and once again, I

212

began to very slowly, and seductively suck on his cum-filled, aching balls.

Loudly, Dillon beseeched, "Please, Zoey! Suck me some more! I love the way you blow me! Fuck, you're giving me . . . blue balls! Please, hun!"

So, how does it feel, Dillon—my future husband to walk a mile in my agonizing begging shoes for once? Now, it was your fucking turn to beseech to the heavens, and beg for sexual relief!

Purposely, I kept ignoring Dillon's frantic requests as I unquestionably marked *my* territory. Payback *is* a bitch. Leisurely, I started to slide my tongue along his lengthy, robust shaft—behaving slutty while staring him down. Deliberately, I teased him to the edge of his aroused sexual threshold.

Panting, Dillon ordered—correction he loudly squealed, "Please, Zoey, put me in your mouth . . . I'm begging you, please! You are driving me fucking crazy!"

Being in full control of his overdue and very impatient orgasm, I quickly sprung to my knees. Immediately, I placed my left hand on King, giving him gentle, but firm enough tugs to feel my presence. My right hand was intentionally, and firmly on Dillon's throat, squeezing it.

Looking downward into Dillon's distressed, blue-ball eyes like a possessed, wild woman, I asked—correction—with the utmost authority, I demanded to know, "Whose fucking cock is this!"

Gazing upward into my eyes while panting, Dillon wholeheartedly admitted, "I love you, Zoey. It's unequivocally your cock! And it will *always* be the property of Zoey Leary!"

Debating if I should pin Dillon's verbal commitment to a legal document with his inked signature that I now owned King—*my* new prized possession—piece of penis real estate, I gave him a quick smooch.

Feeling like an empowered empress, I loudly announced, "That's the best fucking answer I've ever heard! I love you, Dillon!"

"Please, Zoey, I love you . . . I'm begging you!"

Feeling elated that King would always be mine, I plopped down on my stomach, and then happily gave Dillon exactly what he craved—begged for.

87

LOVING THE FEELING of being cuddled into Dillon's warm, cozy body, he declared, "I can't believe . . . you branded me."

Now, he had my full undivided attention. Startled, I asked, "What are you talking about . . . I branded you?"

Gazing into my eyes in awe, Dillon admitted, "No one has ever branded me before. How on earth did you know how to do that?"

Dead serious, I convincingly said, "In my dream last night, my mother told me to sexually dominate you, and not to take any of your fucking shit!"

Immediately, Dillon's eyes widened, and his facial features displayed fear. It was priceless.

"Know this, Dillon, I was Daddy's little girl—the apple of his eye. And Mom protected me with a vengeance! In your sleep, *they will* come for you!"

Dillon looked scared shitless. Very slowly, he cleared his throat. Nervously, he swallowed, then he said, "Um, I'm so sorry, Zoey, if I . . . um—"

Quickly changing my facial features to the most happily engaged woman on the planet, I interrupted, "I'm just messing with you, hun!"

Dillon gasped. With a huge sigh of relief, he said, "Oh, my God! You just gave me a heart attack!"

Giggling, I said, "Well, you pulled the wool over my eyes earlier with your jerking-off prank. And I felt horrible for not pleasing you. And I'm sure you heard the saying before . . . payback is a bitch."

Dillon flashed a smile, but the look in his eyes exposed a deep concern. "It bothers me, if I hurt you . . . you know, when we were doing it before, I'm truly sorry, Zoey, if I—"

Interrupting my future husband with a quick smooch, I boasted, "Relax, hun, you didn't hurt me. And for the record, that was off the charts."

"Promise me, hun," he said nervously, "that you'll let me know if it's too physical, okay?"

"I promise, hun," I replied, sealing it with a kiss.

"Just to let you know, Zoey, I would never forgive myself if I ever hurt you in any way."

Dillon truly loved me. "That means the world to me," I said.

Our lips briefly touched. And just to make one hundred percent certain it was, what I thought it was, I asked, "So how did I brand you?"

88

GAZING INTO MY eyes, Dillon admitted, "You made me say, my cock belongs to you—the property of Zoey Leary. And I meant it, every word."

"You damn right your cock belongs to me, for life!" I declared with authority. "And just to be certain, I'm going to have you sign an airtight contract!"

Reaching for his water, Dillon was laughing. "I'll be happy to sign it once I have my attorney approve it."

I laughed for a few seconds, then in a very excited, high-pitched voice, I asked, "And you're telling me no one has ever branded you before?"

"No one, Zoey. I swear, you're the first. You're my one and only, sex goddess."

Well, this glowing sex goddess wanted to jump for joy for branding my future husband. "Yes!" I shouted triumphantly.

Dillon was laughing when I asked with excitement, "So does that mean that I'm branded too!"

Aroused and with authority, Dillon positioned his smothering muscle mass on top, and then into me—*convincingly*. Welded into the bed, he firmly claimed with his hot sex-breath glued in my ear, "Yes, you're officially branded the soon-to-be Mrs. Race. And never forget, Zoey, *it will always be my pussy!*"

Without thinking twice, I declared, "I swear . . . I promise you—it will *always* be *your* pussy. It's the property of Dillon Race!"

He said in a husky voice, "That's my girl!"

Lost in a slow, French kiss with King deep inside, my thoughts started to race as he unquestionably marked his territory, *again*. Sex didn't get any better than this. Dillon *is* a sexual stud, a thoroughbred stallion between the sheets. And without warning, the radioactive—negative consequence remark Dillon barked at his dad imploded my train of thought—whoosh! Who else besides Stephanie did Dillon brand? Did he brand the model goddess herself, Candace? Did he brand anyone else that I needed to be concerned about?

And like me, did they beseeched in agonizing, sexual pleasure to be fucked? Did they willingly surrender their privates to Dillon—for life? And if they did, would they ever recover, and find someone else to replace my king? Furthermore, would I always have to worry and be on guard that Dillon's exes would miss what they once sexually experienced, and periodically check-in for an overdue check-up? Would they try to hit him up via text or call from a mysterious number, or be brazen enough to show up unannounced every now and then in hopes to rekindle their once happy, sexual past?

Choose your poison very carefully, Zoes. Did I want to be bitch-slapped hard across the face with the brutal truth? Or kissed softly on the lips with an infused lie?

89

WHILE I WAS tidying up the kitchen, I kept glancing at my sparkling engagement ring and the spectacular, absolutely breathtaking, three dozen—in full bloom, long stem arrangement of red roses. The grand finale fireworks display of 'I love you' red roses could have been on the front cover of a bridal magazine. Dillon had to pay a small fortune for them to be perfectly nestled in the high-end designer crystal vase. Besides Dad buying flowers for Mom, Emma, and me on a rare occasion, Dillon was the first man to ever buy me flowers. And this kick-ass, elegant arrangement of red roses knocked my socks off!

From a near distance, I kept noticing Dillon peeking out the sliding glass door. Very curiously, I asked, "Hey, hun, are you up to something because you keep looking at the backyard?"

Dillon didn't answer, proving he was guilty. Playfully, I said, "Hey, hun, I asked you a question, and rule number three in my home is…you must answer all questions honestly, and or to the best of your knowledge and belief, and at once!"

Smiling, Dillon walked over. Facing each other he pecked my lips, then he said, "I don't want to ruin the engagement surprise."

Now, I had to know as he kept shaming me on the unplugged love-scoreboard. "Dillon, you already gave me way too much. The man of my dreams asked me to marry him. And now, I have the most beautiful engagement ring in the world on my finger. You bought me beautiful red roses and champagne with crystal flutes. And also, you did way too much around the house. You did all the laundry, drew me a spectacular picture, and you cooked a delicious meal. You don't have to do anything else for the rest of your life."

However, I needed to up my game and put in a lot more effort. Real. Fucking. Fast. And give back to Dillon in every conceivable way since he's given me so much love and tangibles in the quickest period of time.

With a playful smile, he asked, "Does it really bother you that much when you don't know something or waiting for a surprise?"

I burst out laughing for a few seconds. "My parents had to spike my eggnog with a mild dose of an antihistamine, and a splash of booze when I was a child to put me to sleep on Christmas Eve. If they didn't, I would be tormenting them all night long. So yes, it drives me fucking insane not knowing!"

Dillon was belly-laughing. When he calmed down, he asked, "So, you won't get mad if I reveal the surprise?"

I gave him a quick snarl. "Dillon, I—"

"Okay, okay, relax, Zoey, I'll tell you."

Bouncing on the balls of my feet, very excited, I gave Dillon a kiss.

Slowly, he started to walk backwards down the hallway toward the bedroom. "Don't get mad, but I made a deal with the feds to use their private jet. And I'll tell you the rest after I take a long nap."

What kind of deal did Dillon make with the feds without my consent? Maybe I should teach him a lesson once and for all by putting him over my knee, and whack him with sting-dings.

Hopefully, this new deal he made didn't matter, but if it did, I would have to forgive him because there was no better feeling in the entire world than being head over heels in love.

90

NOT ONLY COULD Dillon drive me sexually crazy between the sheets, but outside the bedroom, he could playfully dish it out as well. Charging after him full throttle, Dillon turned around plowing into the bedroom. I went airborne, pouncing on top of his muscular back with my arms draped over his shoulders—my hands slid down his rugged chest. With all my might, I drove him to the bed. Tussling to position myself on top, he effortlessly flipped us over. Once again, I was pinned and his.

Gazing up into Dillon's soft blue eyes, I asked, "How much do you weigh?"

"You know, Zoey, it's very offensive to ask a guy," he started to laugh, "how much he weighs."

My soon-to-be husband was also a comedian. "No, it's not! Seriously, Dillon, you're so muscular, and solid like a mountain. Please, tell me, I just want to know."

"Around 270 pounds, maybe around 275 pounds depending on what time of the month. Sometimes, I might be retaining water."

We couldn't stop laughing for about ten seconds.

"Why do you want to know?" he asked.

Feeling slightly defeated, I admitted, "Because I can't budge you, and you keep easily pinning me. And I'm not used to being tossed around."

Dillon let out a quick laugh, and after a quick smooch, he asked, "Does it turn you on, that I can take you at will?"

"Yes, it does!" I admitted, thirsty for more great sex. "I've never been on a private plane before. And where are you taking me?"

"Last night at dinner, I promised you that I would take you anywhere in the world. And I would never break my promise to you," Dillon assured, gazing into my eyes. "So, I will only reveal part of the surprise. In the next hour or so, we will leave from here, and head to the airport. I'm taking you somewhere special."

In the shortest period of time, Dillon had always made me feel very special. Looking upward beyond thrilled, I asked, "Where are you taking me?"

Smiling, Dillon announced, "We're off to the Bahamas for a few days. We're going to swim with the dolphins."

My eyes started to tear. "Dillon, I'm so—"

Instantly, he captured my mouth. But my mind was spinning. Dillon had me in a delightful whirlwind. However, there was so much to do in an hour. Frantically tapping his muscular arm, he released my mouth.

"I have to pack!" I howled. "Hold on! I can't go, I don't have a passport!"

Dillon smiled and very relaxed, he asked, "Zoey, do you think that I would ever let you down?"

"God know, Dillon, but—"

Interrupting, he said, "Ms. Forte has our passports waiting for us on the plane, and your new clothes are waiting for you as well," Dillon assured. "I told you that I would handle everything. You have nothing to worry about . . . just relax, hun."

"Dillon, I don't know what else to say, except thank you from the bottom of my heart. By far, today is the happiest day of my life."

"It's mine, too, Zoey," Dillon concurred when his phone rang.

Reaching into his short pocket, Dillon pulled out his cell. It was Emma calling to check-in, fuck! Exhaling a deep breath, I gave Dillon a hesitant, go ahead head nod to answer.

"Are you sure, hun?" he asked with a shoulder shrug. "Do you want to wait?"

Fuck, I knew this was a bad idea, but I had to get this over with. Nervously, I requested, "Please, put her on speaker."

Dillon climbed off the bed, then extended his hand to help me up while his cell kept ringing. Once my feet were planted on the floor, he said, "Now, this is going to be interesting."

Interesting to say the very least. My lifetime friendship was at stake. And this call was going to be one for the ages. God, please help me!

Dillon answered the call. Upbeat, he said, "Hey, Emma, how's your day going?"

91

IN PERFECT HARMONY we walked hand in hand toward the open space kitchen—living room area.

Upbeat, and on speaker, Emma replied, "Hey, Dillon, my day is going good. And don't you sound cheerful today. And oh, how did your dinner go last night with Zoey?"

"Today is the best day in my life!" Dillon boasted with a quick peck while his arm was tightly around my waist. "And dinner went fantastic! We had a great time, and a great night. And we're now happily engaged, and off to the Bahamas!"

"Yeah, yeah, do you really think I'm going to fall for that one? So, how did it go with Zoey last night?" Emma asked again, thinking he was yanking her chain.

Now, Dillon's hand was firmly squeezing my ass. That's what I'm talking about!

"Seriously, Emma, I know this may sound suddenly crazy, but I asked Zoey to marry me, and she made me the happiest man in the world and said, 'yes!'"

Abruptly, Emma barked, "Zoey, can you hear me!"

Immediately, the butterflies swarmed into the pit of my stomach. Okay, Zoes, the time had come. After taking a deep breath, I broke off Dillon's ass squeezing.

Facing each other, Dillon gave me a reassuring nod. Confidently, I replied, "Yes, I can hear you perfectly, Emma. And it's true, this is not a prank. Dillon and I are officially engaged. And we want you to marry us."

"It's funny, I had a . . . you know . . . never mind. Anyways, you're both telling me, you guys met for the first time, quickly got to know each other, fucked each other brains out, instantly fell in love, and now, you're both engaged. Are you fucking kidding me!" Emma yelled in total bewilderment.

Quickly, Dillon interjected, "And off to the Bahamas!"

Was Dillon crazy to antagonize Emma, and rub her face in our tropical excursion? However, he wasn't aware Emma could be extremely rigid when provoked. He's only seen her fun, flirtatious side.

"Off to the Bahamas, yeah, right!" Emma fired back. "You both have gone mad! No! No, you're not!"

Oh, fuck! I knew from the sound of Emma's tonality that she felt scorned. Knowing how Ems processed emotions, and in her mind it should be her accompanying Dillon, not me, on this paradise getaway.

Gazing into my eyes, Dillon declared, "Emma, this is fate, and I know without a shadow of a doubt, Zoey, is the one."

Emma scoffed, "Yeah, right."

"You know, Emma, how bizarre would I have sounded last night at dinner if I said to you, and Zoey, 'and by the way, I've been dreaming about and drawing Zoey, and I don't why,'" Dillon stated with his hand in the air, trying to plead his case. "You would have thought I was crazy."

"Dillon!" Emma blared. "I'll get back to you in one moment!"

Emma's voice tonality just roared back to Dillon was going to set the awkward mood of this uncomfortable conversation. Instantly, I knew her boxing gloves were coming off. Emma *is* about to go ballistic—bare-knuckles on my guilty rogue ass.

92

AT THE TOP of her lungs, Emma yelled, "What the fuck, Zoey Stella!"

Oh, fuck! Emma used my middle name in a screech that I never heard before, and was charging down the warpath. Unfortunately, Dillon had no idea what was on the horizon. Scared shitless, I remained silent.

"I gave you simple instructions, and now, this happens!" Emma declared, howling and fuming. "What am I supposed to tell his mother, Zoes, when I have lunch with her tomorrow? 'And oh, by the way, Norah, as a way of saying thank you to your son for saving my life, I introduced him to my best friend who happens to be my age, and they're now engaged.' For Christ's sake, Zoes, she's only a few years older than us! She's going to fucking kill me!"

"Emma, I guarantee you'll not be physically harmed in any way," Dillon said reassuringly, but very thoughtlessly.

Clearly, Dillon didn't realize that was a rhetorical statement. He was playing a slow, old-timer game of careless checker words, whereas, Emma was playing a speedy, methodical chess game of carefully chosen words as the grandmaster. Nevertheless, Dillon had missed his cue to remain silent, and had no idea of the F5 Emma—shitnado storm directly in our path.

"Okay, Dillon," Emma snarled, "walk me through this!"

Since Dillon had no idea that his head was about to be severed, I had to protect him. That was the very least I could do for my future husband. If Emma wasn't an adrenaline junkie who needed to be thrilled most of the time, she should have been a trial lawyer. In my opinion, that was Emma's true calling because she's a great interrogator.

"Emma Erin, direct your questions and comments to me going forward!" I ordered confrontationally while I looked at Dillon with hand waving gestures at the throat and mouth, along with nonverbal words that I wanted to handle this argument.

Ignoring my request, Dillon snapped back, "Walk you through what, Emma? Zoey and I love each other!"

Fuck it, I wanted Dillon to know I agreed, wholeheartedly. "It's true, Emma, Dillon and I love each other!"

"You're both fucking virgin clueless!" Emma blared. "Now, Dillon, look at Zoey, and tell her what you asked me at the hospital!"

"That was a private and confidential conversation," Dillon retorted, "that we agreed upon!"

"Since you're now engaged to Zoey, my . . . best friend, and for the record, our lifelong friendship is now on the line, everything we discussed in the past is out in the open!" Emma snapped back at the top of her lungs. "Do you want me to tell Zoey what you asked?"

Fuck, once Emma inhaled a whiff of blood, or even worse, tasted the smallest drop, there was no going back. She won't stop until her prey is terminated.

Fuck, now, Pandora's box creaked open with dust particles of Dillon's past, floating invisibly in the air, creeping into my very being.

Unauthorized by the two of us, their private conversation was about to be divulged. The awful pit in my stomach turned soupy sour resembling acid reflux.

93

DILLON WAS HESITANT. And from his facial expressions, I concluded the question was of a very sensitive nature. I knew Dillon knew what question Emma was referring to. Now, the rumbling in my gut started to twinge.

"I asked you many . . . questions," Dillon replied nervously, and purposely stalling for precious time to choose his response carefully, "at the hospital."

In a very challenging manner, Emma said, "Let's start with the question you asked me when you were in your thirties."

Now, this should be interesting to say the very least.

"That's not fair, Emma!" Dillon pleaded. "I'm a completely different person now."

When it came to carefully chosen strategic words, Emma never played fair. All of a sudden, my anxious, aching growl in my abdomen was coming to a boil. Emma always had and quickly went for the jugular, and since Dillon had never seen this vicious pit bull attack side of Emma before, he was about to get verbally devoured.

"Look right into your fiancée's eyes, and tell her what you asked me!" Emma ordered. Deliberately, she paused causing my body to shiver. "Or would you rather have me tell Zoey!"

Fuck me, from the very beginning, I knew this conversation was a horrible idea. Looking directly into my eyes, Dillon took both of my hands, and confessed, "I asked Emma when I was in my thirties, would I want a younger woman . . . in her twenties."

Instantly, and hastily, I released *our* hands. And for the first time in our new relationship, I had trust issues. Dillon looked extremely hurt, his eyes started to tear. Abruptly, with his cell in hand, he turned and then walked away.

Immediately, I felt horrible for betraying his trust. At least, Dillon had the courage to speak the uncomfortable, harsh truth. Consciously, Emma remained silent to let Dillon's last statement rattle, and seep deeply into my battered brain.

Snap, Grandpa's comment: "Most people want to be lied to, but they don't know it," popped into my head. And I didn't want to be lied to. Whether I liked the answer or not. And technically, I shouldn't be upset with Dillon because we were not involved then. And for the record, I wasn't aware of the context of why he would ask that type of a question.

Briskly walking to Dillon, I forcefully turned him around pushing his back up against the wall. Yes, he welcomed my embrace!

I whispered in his ear, "I'm so sorry, hun. I'll never doubt you again. I love and trust you. Please, forgive me."

Thank God our lips briefly touched.

"That's correct, and what was my response back to you?" Emma asked kindly, but was really egging him on.

Please, Dillon, don't fall for her false sense of verbal generosity as I knew all too well that the wallop, verbal strike was on the horizon.

"You said with my looks that I should wait to get married. And *you* wouldn't be involved with someone if the other person looked a lot better than you."

Did Emma know something about Dillon that I didn't?

"That's correct," Emma confirmed, "and why did you tell me within a 72-hour time frame you slept with four different women?"

Holy shit! In just three days, Dillon slept with four different women! What the fuck! And I guarantee all the women flocked to him beforehand with their panties in one hand. And afterwards, when they experienced the best, mind-blowing sex that I experienced, I bet they all willingly had a signed, lifetime contract in the other hand dictating their privates belonged to Dillon.

Again, I couldn't be upset or hold a grudge since Dillon and I weren't involved then. But why was Emma portraying Dillon to be some kind of manwhore?

Remaining silent, and absorbed in deep thought, Dillon started to pace in a circle. And from Emma's tone it seemed like she was trying to put a powerful, doubtful wedge in our new relationship. She *is* trying to hijack our engagement. Undeniably, Emma *is* madly in love with Dillon. She's fighting for him! And unquestionably, she's jealous of our upcoming wedding.

"Well, Dillon!" Emma demanded with an authoritative voice. "I'm waiting for your answer!"

Breaking his slow, circle walking pace, Dillon popped a squat on the floor. With his back against the wall, eyes closed, knees upright, and one hand on his forehead, he softly pleaded, "You know, Emma, that's not a fair—"

Abruptly, Emma cut Dillon off, and interjected, "Look at Zoey, and add twenty years."

With one very powerful comment, Emma clipped our lovebird wings. Eerie chills entered my very being. Goosebumps were noticeably visible on my forearms. Emma, aka the "Wicked Word Warrior", never played fair with deliberate, bombshell word daggers. And unfortunately, for us, she wasn't finished turding.

94

DILLON REMAINED SILENT. He portrayed a featherweight with carefully chosen words—well out of his verbal fighting weight class. Whereas, Emma was the undisputed reigning heavyweight world champion of strategically chosen jagged words that would emotionally and mentally scar someone for a lifetime.

Unfortunately, I'd been down this losing road with Emma in the past, and witnessed her verbally beat her ex-boyfriends, including her husband with toxic, hurtful words, and profound statements. Indisputably, I knew Dillon was seconds away from a first-round knockout punch.

Purposely, Emma danced around the ring in silence wanting her last verbal statement—punch of adding twenty years to my existence to sink into Dillon's bruised brain.

"She'll be . . . 52! And you'll be . . . 38. Let me clarify that for you . . . Dillon. Zoey will be fifty . . . two! And you'll be . . . distinguished at thirty-eight, and even better looking. And if you think women throw themselves at you now, it will get easier for you. Let me paint a very bountiful, robust picture for you. Teenage girls, women in their twenties, and going on up, throwing themselves at you. And you're telling me, you're going to go home at the end of the day to your," Emma paused deliberately, then she sarcastically asked, "older wife?"

The referee started the count. Dillon's unresponsive busted up mouth was on the canvas.

The silence on both ends was deafening. My thoughts raced. Oh, fuck! I never thought that far ahead. Would Dillon still desire me twenty years from now? Or would he want a young, fertile spring chicken in his life when he was thirty-eight? At fifty-two, the other woman would be thirty years younger!

"How dare you, Emma, compare me to my father!" he protested, getting back to his feet. "In every relationship I've been in, I was faithful! Are you accusing me of being a cheat?"

Emma dodged his question similar to a boxer dodging a punch. Purposely, she remained silent. Emma wanted her newest horror movie of disturbing aging visuals starring Zoey Stella Leary to slowly seep into Dillon's psyche, and scar him for a lifetime.

Catching me off guard, Dillon pulled me into his upper body planting a very powerful, convincing kiss on my lips. Case solved! Dillon would always be loyal! And I would do everything in my power—in my newly acquired sexual prowess to make damn sure he's always satisfied.

"Hey, Emma! I'm telling you that I'll always be faithful to Zoey, and take care of her until my very last breath because that's what I promised her, and . . . Mr. Leary."

Oh shit! Fuck me! Dillon should have never said that!

95

EMMA'S HIGH-PITCHED LAUGHTER resonated in the background. Very much amused, she asked, "So tell me, Dillon, how did you promise, Mr. Leary?"

"In my dream last night," Dillon said very confidently, "I promised Mr. Leary that I would always take care of Zoey, and he gave me his approval."

"Now, I heard it . . . all," Emma replied flippantly. "Do you believe any of this, Zoey?"

I knew she thought we were both batshit crazy. "That's enough Emma Erin," I pleaded with my arm around Dillon. His dream was amazingly spectacular.

In a very challenging manner, Emma replied, "You're next, Zoey Stella!"

During the past fourteen years, Emma and I only had a handful of disagreements, and very quickly we'd always reconciled. However, this argument was worlds apart. Hopefully, I could hold my own, and explain my point of view more convincingly than Dillon.

Ready for battle, my gloves came off, but the sour pit in my stomach disagreed. All the happy deep memories we shared during the past thirty years began to erupt magma. This lava slithering down our friendship mountain started to torch the landscape of our sacred sisterhood.

Running into the kitchen in the nick of time, I puked into the trash bucket. The end of our lifetime friendship had officially come to an abrupt ending.

The worst imaginable chills invaded my insides. These putrid, sour, sharp, painful feelings of anguish were probably what Candace experienced when she left Dillon. And these morbid emotions were worse than the death of a loved one because the person you still care about and deeply love, was still alive.

Why did love and grief have to coexist, and hurt so fucking bad? Why did grief lay patiently dormant like undetectable, rogue cancer cells reappearing years later—multiplying—wreaking havoc? How come the power of love's bustling youth couldn't trump old man grief's slow aftermath? And would the hopeful sunrise of love ever reappear and flourish? Or would love sunset, and become trapped in grief's genie bottle?

What would love's innocent sentence be? Could love ever be eligible for early parole, and swap sentences with grief? Or would love be held indefinitely in grief's solitary confinement? And the ultimate question I would love to know the answer to: Could love ever escape from grief's chains, and reign supreme again?

The worst possible outcome would be love's warm brightness succumbing to grief's cold dark wrath. And then I would become a hopeless basket case—a lifelong victim of grief's daily thoughts. The best possible outcome would always be an ongoing internal struggle, and came with many strings attached and with no guarantees, which I was willing to accept. Could I forge a semblance of a positive mindset, and alter the ongoing daily outcome, the nonstop daily love-grief seesaw internal battle with positive memories? I just didn't fucking know.

Just remember, Zoes, up until now, Emma had Ed and Eloise to go home to at the end of each precious day. And I had no one, until Dillon came into my life. Our lifetime friendship boiled down to the brass tacks of love and jealousy, and unfortunately, only one winner. And I was reluctantly, but willing to pay the ultimate price, and sacrifice our lifetime friendship for true love.

"Hey, Emma," Dillon said, shattering the silence, "you said at the hospital that I should stay single until all the fun was out of my system!" he blurted out frazzled. "And I'm telling you, it's one hundred percent all out!"

Dillon might as well have handed Emma a giant club-like stick wrapped in rusted barbed wire, and stood piñata still while she struck him verbally senseless. Intentionally, she remained silent.

"Come on, Emma," Dillon pleaded, grasping at straws, "you know that I'm telling you the truth."

"I'm sure you are. Now, tell, Zoey, what bold statement I requested of you!" Emma ordered. "Wait, I'll do the honors."

Emma delivered the final knockout punch, and I was up next. God, please help me choose my words warmly and wisely. Even if Emma struck hard and dirty, I must refrain from stooping to her vicious verbal rabbit hole. Under no circumstance shall my tongue become viciously vengeful. After all, this was my grand master plan to begin with, and the new bed I willingly made.

My goal was to leave a door opened, even the tiniest crack would have to suffice. And after the dust settled, I would apologize profusely, and constantly slay Emma with love and kindness. I would snail mail her handwritten letters with colorful pictures of us enclosed, reminding her of all the happy times we shared, and beg nonstop for her forgiveness—until she caved.

"I'll tell you, Emma, what you requested!" Dillon said with a raised voice. "You wanted me to take you home, and spend the night!"

Getting on the balls of my feet, I pleaded in Dillon's ear, "Please, hun, let me handle this!"

"That's right, now, go ahead, and tell Zoey what happened when we were inside my house!" Emma ordered. "Tell! Her! Dillon!"

Lost for words, Emma's ugly tonality screeched into my soul, imploding my nerves. Fuck, now, the ugly serpent truth was about to surface. And strike viciously.

And now, our conversation was officially upgraded to a first-class train wreck.

96

DILLON CLOSED HIS eyes, then replied, "I went over to you, and right away you put your hands up, and stopped me."

"That's right," Emma said in full control of the verbal round. "And why do you think I stopped you?"

"And why do you think I was there to begin with?" Dillon fired back in a challenging tonality, finally landing his first successful verbal strike.

"I don't understand, you—"

Cutting her off mid-sentence, Dillon said, "I agreed to take you home, Emma, because I felt sorry for you. I was your only visitor at the hospital."

And for the second time, Dillon dodged Emma's remarks while verbally punching back from a different viewpoint stance.

In a very insulted voice tone, verbally swinging back, Emma shouted, "Are you saying that you were treating me like a pity-fuck!"

"Those are your words, Emma, not mine," Dillon proclaimed with the utmost sincerity. "I just didn't want you to be alone since I know loneliness all too well."

He could have kept tattering Emma, but Dillon chose compassion instead. He verbally outclassed her, and from his facial expressions, he genuinely felt bad.

Like most of us, Emma always took everything to heart when it came to love and relationships. She remained mouse silent. But I knew Emma was on the canvas looking up at Dillon with a busted lip.

Pressing something on his smartphone, Dillon asked, "Hey, Emma, can you see me?"

Oh shit! Fuck me! Dillon should have consulted me first before he went video rogue because Emma loved to tell people eye to eye to fuck off. This conversation was about to derail at any moment.

Avoiding eye contact, she replied, "Mm-hmm."

We both see a somber Emma sitting at the kitchen table tapping her finger on a water bottle. I hoped she wasn't thinking about her next verbal attack.

Dillon asked, "Emma, in all honesty, right before I pulled over to help you, did you have severe tightness in your throat?"

"What does that have to do with anything?" Emma asked, frazzled.

"It would mean a lot to me, Emma, to know your answer," he softly— politely said. "Did you have tightness in your throat?"

"Yes!" she admitted, agitated.

"I did, too," Dillon admitted.

"I don't understand!" Emma said, frazzled about to blow her boiling steam engine top. "What does that have to do with anything!"

Where on earth was Dillon going with this? With his line of questioning, he kept throwing rocks at her hornet's nest. He'd better hurry up, and quickly get to the point before Emma blew a fuse.

In a soft, very soothing tone, Dillon asked, "During the mayhem, was there a person from your past or present that came to your mind?"

97

EMMA WAS MUTE. After six, very long, silent seconds, she replied, "Yes."

"Who was that?" Dillon asked softly.

"Mom. Well, I always called her, Mom," Emma admitted. "I mean, Maureen, Zoey's mom."

"What do you mean?" Dillon asked perfectly in a soft, neutral tone.

"The Leary's always treated me as a member of their family . . . like a daughter," Emma said, choked-up. "And Mom was . . . as tough as nails. She was always brave and nonstop during a commotion, and that's what I needed to survive."

Dillon revealed in a gentle tone, "Last night, in my dream, Mrs. Leary wanted me to tell you that she loves you, and for you to always 'stay strong.'"

"How in the world . . . how can that be?" she asked, flabbergasted, and totally dumbfounded. "A month before Mom died, we had a private talk, and she made me promise her that I would always 'stay strong,'" Emma admitted with a crackle in her voice while tears streamed down her face.

Taken by surprise, Dillon lifted my left hand closer to the phone.

Inching closer to her smartphone, Emma's eyes almost popped out of her head. Puzzled, all bug-eyed, she asked, "How can that be? How did you get Mom's ring? I thought it was lost forever."

Dillon replied, "Mrs. Leary has been vividly visiting me in my dreams. She had me memorize the ring, and I had a jeweler make it."

I had so many additional questions for Dillon about his dreams, but I knew not to stop the flow.

"I still don't understand," Emma said, confused, moving her head slowly from side to side in total disbelief.

Very softly, Dillon asked, "Emma, last night did you have a dream about Maureen?"

Emma replied, "Yes."

Dillon asked, "Besides her, were there other people in your dream?"

"Yes."

Dillon, the alpha dog, was in full control. Softly, he asked, "Was it a pleasant dream?"

"Yes, it was a very happy dream," Emma said as Dillon perfectly boarded her on the 'yes' train.

Dillon asked, "Was Patrick sitting next to Maureen in the front row . . . she was wearing her roller skates?"

"Yes!" Emma said, startled. "But how do you know—"

Softly interrupting, Dillon asked, "Can you please tell us, Emma, what you were doing in your dream?"

Rising from her chair, Emma started to softly sob. Walking over to the counter, she retrieved a paper towel to wipe her tears. For once, the queen of carefully chosen words was humbling speechless.

"It's okay, Emma," Dillon said with finesse, "you can tell us."

98

"**I WAS FACILITATING,** you," Emma said choked-up. After taking a sip from her water bottle, she admitted, "And Zoey, getting married on the beach."

"Thank you, Emma," Dillon replied.

Reaching behind his back, Dillon handed me the beautifully wrapped gift. "Please, open it, hun."

When I finally unwrapped it, Emma thunderstruck said, "Now, I've seen it all!"

Quickly, I turned around the *present*—a magnificent watercolor painting. Oh, my God! How did Dillon know?

Framed in luxurious mahogany wood, I witnessed with my own two eyes, the most amazing piece of art ever! Dillon painted—manifested the exact scene that Emma just described in her dream. In the background, two dolphins were cresting the breathtaking, calm turquoise ocean. Everyone was wearing relaxing island attire. Mom and Dad were sitting in the front row. Mom sported her new skates, and Dad contentedly had his arm around her shoulder. They looked peaceful—spectacular! With our hands connected, Dillon and I were smiling, gazing into each other's eyes as Emma was facilitating our wedding ceremony.

I lunged at Dillon for a brief kiss. "Thank you, I love you!" I said stoked in total amazement. "I have so many questions!"

Proudly, Dillon had his arm wrapped around my waist while we were looking into his smartphone. With enthusiasm, Dillon asked, "Emma, we love you. Will you marry us?"

"I love you guys, too. And yes, I will marry you, anytime, anyplace. And Dillon, I'm deeply sorry for calling you out like that. And Zoes, I just need a word with you in private, please."

"I'll call you back in a couple of minutes, Ems."

Dillon, my future husband, a great out of the box thinker, my king, my everything, pulled off the greatest miracle I'd ever personally witnessed, and saved our lifetime friendship!

"Dillon, this is the happiest day of my life!" I proclaimed in his arms. "Thank you! I love you!"

"It's the happiest day in my life, too!" Dillon concurred. "I love you more!"

99

WE SPOKE FOR about twenty minutes. Emma wholeheartedly apologized, and lightheartedly congratulated us. She mentioned that Mom was her hero growing up. Also, with Mom and Dad's involvement in Emma's childhood development, it made a positive everlasting impression of how a normal family life should resemble.

Unbeknownst to me, a month before Mom died, she had a lengthy, personal conversation with Emma because they shared—suffered traumatic upbringings. Unfortunately, Emma was subjected to life's hardships, unfairness, and cruelty throughout her entire childhood compared to me. She was forced to grow up quicker, whereas, my parents by design, sheltered my upbringing up until their deaths. During their talk, Mom mentioned to Emma despite the fact that we were only six days apart by birth, it was more like the equivalent of six years.

Also, from their private conversation, Emma revealed that Mom and Dad altered their Christmas budget they spent on each other for many years to provide a young Emma with clothes and toys. As a young, innocent child who was raised by two devoted and loving parents, I just thought it was normal for Santa to drop off Emma's gifts at our house. Mom and Dad's unselfish sacrifices made our childhood memories awesome and everlasting.

Mom's main message to Emma was: Tough times—the storm you're currently weathering will eventually pass, and every challenging experience will only make you tougher and mentally stronger. Mom also shared with Emma to never lose faith, laugh often, forgive quickly, and above all else, no matter how bad you think it is—it's really no big fucking deal. And whatever happens to you, whether you liked it or not, life *will* go on, you just gotta stay strong. That one memorable and powerful talk with a young, teenage girl gave Emma the inner confidence to cope with her current hardships, and forge a positive future.

The loving influence my parents had in Emma's life, and in Dillon's dreams, profoundly impacted and sculpted my kismet. So, to all the naysayers that predicted the rebellious young lovers—Misfit Lovebirds wouldn't amount to much, and their future was bleak, can kiss my ass. Over the years, their eros love blossomed into holistic love which continues to soar. The nostalgic memories and spiritual presence of my parents are still alive—thriving with unlimited power.

Of course, Emma was dying to know about the sex. I gave her the short version, and I'm not quite sure if it was in the correct order: Mind! Fucking! Blowing! I confessed to her that I was obsessed with Dillon for weeks, and came one hundred percent clean about everything, including my ulterior motive during our dinner.

Emma alluded that Dillon was having mysterious insights to the other side. I didn't divulge anything to her about Dillon's suicide situation. My hunch said that Dillon crossed over, and was experiencing vivid spiritual visions. And when the time was right, I was dying to know more, especially when Mom and Dad were involved. My newest, darkest secret burning inside was, if and when, I should reveal to Dillon that he actually (for a period of time) died. Could he emotionally handle it?

Dillon admired how I went out on a limb first—that's true. I took a chance, a leap of faith if you will, and became extremely uncomfortable. Something inside of me was so compelling, that I had no choice but to risk embarrassment, ridicule, humiliation, failure, and a lifetime friendship to discover my destiny.

And once again, Dillon placed a huge smile on my face when I received my very first text from him: "Hope your call is going well. Please text me when you're done and STAY in the bedroom. Love you more!"

In less than twenty-four hours, Dillon accomplished more wonderful goodness in my lifetime than any other person. He just needed to hear, see, and feel my spark of hope which I strategically placed into the universe. Furthermore, I'm forever grateful that Dillon cultivated my scintilla of sunshine into our new, flourishing destiny.

The way Dillon looks at me, touches my heart, expresses his devotion with loving words, and convincingly with special acts of kindness, I truly feel blessed. Truth be told, the way Dillon touches my body—makes love is the greatest feeling ever—true bliss. And outside the bedroom, Dillon miraculously tops that, which makes me desire him all the time. Unequivocally, Dillon is my hero. Not only did he save me, he set me and my parents free.

Coming Soon

Virgin Clueless, Part Two: Sexual Soulmates
Candace, unexpectedly pregnant, returns, and Isosceles gives Dillon a harsh ultimatum. Norah lays a bombshell on Zoey. Emma's hall pass comes to fruition. Will Zoey's love for Dillon prevail when three strong-willed women collide?

Virgin Clueless: Unleashed
Before Zoey, Dillon's dad educates and persuades him to sow his oats. Dillon's erotic trysts include: Candace, his calculus teacher, Mafalda, Norah's former sparring partner, and Emma.

ABOUT THE AUTHOR

Scott Becker lives with his wife, Lori, and their two rescue dogs, Rex and Gator in Rhode Island aka the Ocean State. They thoroughly enjoy each New England season, especially the summertime when they visit the many beautiful state beaches.

For all books purchased, Scott donates a portion of his proceeds to various food banks and animal shelters.

The release dates for *Virgin Clueless: Unleashed* and *Virgin Clueless, Part Two: Sexual Soulmates* will be announced on www.VirginClueless.com

www.ingramcontent.com/pod-product-compliance
Lightning Source LLC
Chambersburg PA
CBHW020149310726
48970CB00006B/2066